A DARK FAIRYTALE...

When Deanna's missing friend Hyde turns up at his father's funeral to claim his corporate empire and inheritance, she is swept into his glittering world of paparazzi and wealth.

But Deanna has a secret – and somebody knows. Someone who is out to get Hyde. And if she doesn't play along, and help the enemy take Hyde down... she will be sold to the highest bidder in the black market for human swans.

Now Deanna is struggling to break free from the gilded cage that would trap her forever...

SARAH RAUGHLEY

Feather Bound

STRANGE CHEMISTRY
An Angry Robot imprint
and a member of the Osprey Group

Lace Market House,	Angry Robot/Osprey Publishing,
54-56 High Pavement,	PO Box 3985,
Nottingham,	New York,
NG1 1HW,	NY 10185-3985,
UK	USA

www.strangechemistrybooks.com
Strange Chemistry #31

A Strange Chemistry paperback original 2014

Cover design by Jessica Drossin (Trevillion Images)
Set in Sabon and La Figura by Argh! Oxford.

Distributed in the United States by Random House, Inc., New York.

ISBN 978 1 90884 490 3
Ebook ISBN 978 1 90884 491 0

Printed in the United States of America.

9 8 7 6 5 4 3 2 1

To my mom and dad

1
Funeral

At precisely seven in the morning, my oldest sister, Ericka, arrived at our Brooklyn shack and was horrified to find our dad sprawled out on the couch, basting in a sea of beer cans. Half an hour later, he was waxing poetic about his freshly dead college chum, too drunk to put his pants on the right way, while Ericka tried to shove a tie around his neck. She looked like she'd rather strangle him with it.

"Deanna! Right sleeve!"

"What?"

I could barely hear Ericka over the music blaring and her baby's screeching. The poor kid had been shoved in a baby car seat and abandoned in the corner of the room, probably hungry and definitely mad as hell.

"Right. *Sleeve!*"

"OK, OK! *Goddamn.*"

I pulled both spaghetti straps back up on my shoulders and went to work. My job was my dad's jacket, which was ten years too small for him. But then, I didn't even have *my* clothes fully on yet, what with my black dress half-zipped and the right leg of my sheer pantyhose dragging on the floor. My other sister Adrianna, on the other hand, straightened her hair calmly in the bathroom opposite Dad's room. I could see her shaking her head through the bathroom mirror across the hall, probably secretly wishing she could record this mess and put it up online.

Must be nice to be the sister who doesn't give a damn, I thought. I would have yelled it, but Dad's armpits were in my face. Needless to say, it was imperative that my mouth stayed closed.

"Ade!" Ericka shot her a withering glance from behind Dad. "Can you at least turn the music off?" Since it was coming from *her* laptop. "And Dad, for God's sake, pull yourself together!"

"I'm sorry." My dad slurred his words because drinking in the wee hours of the morning never failed to test one's alcohol tolerance level.

I wiped my brow before a droplet of sweat could drip into my eyes. In a house that was already intensely stuffy, being under Dad's pits did not help. "Oh God, look, let's just forget the whole thing," I said, dropping his arm half-sheathed and straightening up. "Dad, you haven't even talked to Hedley in years."

I already knew what he'd say before he said it. "No, we're going. After everything he did for us. All the opportunities, all the chances..."

Ericka mangled his collar until it was respectably flat over his tie. "Deanna has a point, Dad. My mother-in-law was friends with Hedley's wife so *I* have to go, but you don't have to come with me." With a desperate smile, she added, "Why don't you just stay home and let me represent the family, hmm?"

But Dad just shook his head. Ericka's smile dropped from her face. Couldn't blame her for trying. Dad was a fiasco waiting to happen and a girl could only repress so much.

"I just can't believe it. *Cancer.* I didn't even know he was sick." Dad sighed. The sudden onslaught of booze, halitosis and stale nachos nearly made me faint.

"*And?*" Ade put on her eyeliner. "Dad, you told us yourself, the guy didn't even talk to you after you got fired. Then he kicked it. So I mean, what's the issue? No point in getting all broken up over it. At the end of the day, he's just some dead rich guy."

"Adrianna!" Ericka hissed, fighting with Dad's collar.

She shrugged. "What? Am I wrong?"

Technically no, but Ade was never really one for details. Dad and Ralph Hedley were actually really good friends in college. Dad had been an ace student in high school and managed to land a full ride to Yale where he met Hedley, the son of a billionaire who owned an entire magazine company – boringly named Hedley Publications. I still couldn't really fathom how the two of them managed to strike up such a strong friendship. Not exactly two of a kind.

To Hedley's credit, he managed to score Dad a job as an accountant for one of his magazines.

"Whoops, down he goes," said Ade when Dad tipped over, though Ericka kept him steady.

Yep, accountant – before the binge drinking finally landed him on the unemployment list. Only so much a friend can do after you throw up on one of your co-workers.

So, there we were, the Davis family, cramped in one of the many yellow boxes lining the street while the "head of the household" packaged beverages in a warehouse, because after a string of firings and a ruined reputation he couldn't get a job anywhere else.

I guess in a way, going to Ralph Hedley's funeral was a nice gesture on Dad's part. Paying his last respects, seeing an old friend off to the afterlife or whatever the hell. But if there was anything worth weeping over, it was living in a house with light fixtures that were rusting off the walls and faucets that periodically leaked in floods.

Ade finally breezed into Dad's room, crisp, clean and cloaked in mournful black – which made the breathy, gossipy lilt to her voice all the more jarring: "Oh, by the way, have you guys actually heard the rumours about Hedley?" The way my dad's shoulders tensed told me he had. "Pretty messed up, right? And if they're true–"

Dad's bottom lip curled. "They're not." He said it with the sort of hard edge that would have been an intimidating conversation ender if Dad weren't wobbling ridiculously on his feet.

"Ah, the rumour," I said. The one about Hedley and his wife.

"Yup! I mean, if it's true, then that'd pretty much be proof *right there* that Hedley was a complete monster when he was alive. And now he's dead. See? No great loss after all!" But Ade stopped there, flashing Dad an innocent grin when he glared at her.

It *was* just a rumour... but honestly, it was part of the reason I couldn't understand why Dad would drink himself half to death over this. Ade was right: whatever memories he was holding on to had long since ceased to be relevant.

Actually, if there was anyone here who had a reason to get lost in nostalgia this morning, it wasn't Dad. It was me.

Dad wasn't the only one with a dead Hedley to mourn.

A crash. Ericka's screaming baby started shrieking as if he were determined to shatter the mirrors with his mighty baby lungs. Dad finally collapsed onto the bed, exhausted and half-dressed. Ericka stayed Ericka, which generally involved copious amounts of freaking out.

Leaning against the wall with the right leg of my pantyhose pooled on the carpet floor, I stared up at the cracked light fixture hanging from the ceiling and shook my head. "Just kill me," I breathed.

Ade slinked up to me and patted me on the shoulder. "OK. I'll go turn off the music."

They kept the casket closed throughout the church service. Thank God. Seeing dead bodies always made me nauseous, even when the bodies were on TV and the death was painted on with brushes. The last time I'd seen a body in real life was nine years ago, when I was eight. It was my mom. The blood had been sucked out of her veins, replaced with a mixture of chemicals that gave her skin a waxy coat. She'd looked as if she'd been wrapped in plastic: glossy and dried up until she wasn't even my mother anymore.

Hers had been a winter funeral; her casket lowered under metric tons of snow. Today was way nicer. A bright, hot, sunny June day: much better weather for burying a rotting carcass.

Oh God. *What the hell is wrong with me?* I pried my hands away from each other because I'd just realized that I'd been wringing them too tightly. A pool of red flooded my palms. They were shaking. Mom's bracelet jingled as it dangled off my wrist.

I understood, just then, why Dad had been drinking last night. Burying Mr Hedley meant digging up the past. The days of Mom.

A hand touched my shoulder – Adrianna's. "You OK, Dee?"

Standing next to me, she looked almost as pretty as Mom always had during Sunday mass at church. Ade's hair, whenever she straightened it, cascaded down her back like a charcoal waterfall, but it never looked as good as the natural curls all three Davis sisters had. Mom's hair.

I gripped her hand, squeezing it appreciatively. Ade was nineteen – two years older than me – and yet in that moment, with that one maternal gesture, she was able to feign the kind of maturity I knew she didn't actually have.

"Yeah, I'm OK." I'm thinking about our decomposing mother, I didn't say. "I'm just hot."

A half-lie. I *was* hot. Maybe my mind was playing tricks on me, but I could have sworn the heat was actually searing the hair off my arms. I could feel the sweat beading underneath my clothes. I took off my cropped jacket and slung it over my shoulder.

The bearers had already lowered the casket into the hole in the ground that would be Ralph Hedley's final resting place.

"They say you can always tell how a man lived his life by the gathering at his funeral. And from what I can tell by looking at you all, Ralph Hedley was a man well-loved."

I wondered about that. It was hard to judge from the sea of emotionless and distracted faces surrounding the gravesite.

Adrianna stood next to me with her long, willowy limbs crossed. While her eyes were on the casket, they looked almost glazed; it was hard to tell whether it was a pensive, introspective sort of glazed, or if she was really just bored.

Dad wasn't doing anything humiliating, but he did look as if he was going to puke, though I didn't know whether that was because of his emotional turmoil or the hangover.

Ericka held her baby tightly in her arms. Beanpole – er, her husband – wasn't anywhere in sight. Odd, considering his rich mother was the reason why she'd come in the first place. She pursed her lips, undoubtedly annoyed.

And then there were the guests. Elite types, naturally. All of them in thousand-dollar suits and funeral-appropriate black couture. Good of them to take the time to show up, except not one of them could even muster enough energy to act as if being at a friend's funeral was a *sad thing*.

Holy hell, these people. Coldest funeral *ever*. The poorly concealed photogs sneaking around – cameras in hand – made it all the more awkward.

"Whoa," Ade nudged me in the ribs and flicked her head their way. "The pap. How's my hair?" she added rather tackily.

There were two of them – no, three. I saw one hiding behind a tree, clicking as fast as his finger would allow. At a funeral. Well, at the very least they had brass balls to go along with their utter lack of human morals.

Except the guy sitting on the bench a few yards away by a stone cross. I couldn't see a camera on him. He was just sitting there in a black vest and gray beanie, his arm slung over the back of the bench. He barely even flinched when a reporter in a long beige trench coat skulked passed him. He was too busy watching us. Intently. Huh. Probably memorizing the details for his inevitable blog post.

The priest, with his back to them, didn't seem to notice. "Despite the joy he brought to many of us, Ralph had his share of loss in life, some might say more than many men. As per his request, we bury him here today next to his wife, Clarice Hedley, and his adopted son–"

"Hyde Hedley." I'd whispered out the name with a tremor of breath. At the sound of it, the muscles in my arms twitched and my stomach churned. I bit my lip as if the pain would help me shove the image of a ten year-old's chubby face back into the recesses of my memories. It didn't. Like I said, Dad wasn't the only one with a dead Hedley to remember.

"Nine years have passed since his wife and son returned to God. Let us pray now that Ralph finds peace with the people he'd loved with his whole heart."

"Except he didn't."

The trench-coated reporter stood just a few feet away, her shaggy hair as fiery as the righteous indignation in her eyes.

The priest's white moustache crinkled with his frown. "I beg your pardon, young lady?"

Shutters flew at the speed of light. Her pap friends must have put her up to it because they were sure getting a kick out of it now. And yet the more I looked at Trench-Coat Girl, the less I was sure she was a Page Six employee.

"Mr Hedley loved his family with his whole entire heart, huh?" Her bare ankles peaked out from under the beige cotton of the coat, a flush of pink between that and her worn out Hello Kitty sneakers. With her arms folded over her chest, she stared down the congregation with an almost war-like readiness. In all honesty, I couldn't even figure out if I was supposed to take her seriously. "So he was a family man," she went on. "On a scale of what, Stalin to Hitler?"

"Who the hell are you?" said a woman who hid her turnip face behind a net of black. "Who do you think you–?"

Trench-Coat Girl took off her trench coat.

"Oh. My..." Ade couldn't even finish. The sound of an entire funeral congregation gasping all at once would have drowned her out anyway. The paparazzi didn't even bother hiding anymore.

Apparently, neither did Trench-Coat Girl.

Her feet were the only parts of her bare pasty-white body I couldn't see. That alone was shocking enough. But then she turned, just slightly, and there they were – feathers draping her back. They flitted in the breeze, some fluttering to the freshly cut grass in a shower of white down.

No one could talk.

"You really want to know how much Mr Hedley loved his wife?" continued the girl, whose trench coat had now been thoroughly discarded. "Come on, I'm sure you've all heard the rumours. For those of you who haven't, you'll hear it here first."

And then Trench-Coat Girl spread her arms wide, her feathers flying up as if blown by a sudden gust. "Ralph Hedley's wife," she announced so the paparazzi wouldn't miss a word, "was a swan."

Silence. Silence and pictures.

"You all know this. She was a swan, like me. Like some of you, I bet. And Mr Hedley 'won' her love by stealing her feathers. Slavery: a love story for the ages, am I right?"

My dad stumbled back. Ericka grabbed his arm with her free hand. For a second I thought he was going to have a heart attack.

"I'm sorry to disrespect someone on the day of his funeral, I honestly am." She didn't look it. "But it's time to stop turning a blind eye to the suffering of others! It's time to stand up and do what's right! End Swan Slavery! Freedom for feathers now!"

I barely had time to process what I was watching before she took off down the street, her feathers leaving a trail of white strokes behind her.

A Tale

Somewhere, just outside a tiny village, is a lake. Eight heavenly maidens bathe there. They sit by the shore, oblivious to the world. Water shimmers in their cupped hands, trickles through their fingers, runs down their legs. Moonlight coats their white feathers.

The young man sees them from behind the trees. Their beauty enchants him.

Quietly, he comes back and sends his dog to steal the feather robe of the youngest. The seven sisters cry out and fly off into the sky. But the youngest cannot.

Now she is his.

Once of the heavens, she is now bound to the earth. Bound to the young man.

He builds a house and they marry. Their children sing every day.

Behind every myth is a truth that inspired it. Everyone knows about swans. But I learned the fairytale first. When I was a child I thought it was romantic. But then I began to wonder. The young man – when did he learn the poor girl's name?

2

Ghost

"Oh my God, it's like I can't text fast enough."

Ade certainly tried. The funeral was in chaos. Since the protester had left, about half the congregation were on their phones. Scandalized whispers blanketed the graveyard. I didn't know why any of them were pretending to be shocked, though. Ralph Hedley's wife was a swan. The news had broken almost as soon as Hedley had died, plastered everywhere from the blogosphere to CNN.

I wasn't quite sure how people even found out, to be honest. There was no way a prominent New York socialite like Clarice Hedley would have told anyone she was a swan. The shame alone would have killed her.

I personally tried not to let myself get carried away with unproven rumours. But I was almost a hundred percent certain that half of the millionaires and socialites currently feigning shock right now had already gossiped about this at length behind closed doors.

Soon the limos started to arrive. People were fleeing. I was sure they'd turn up to the reception to gossip some more. Ericka blocked her baby's face from the paparazzi and turned to the rest of us. "We'll have to wait at the church until our ride gets here. Come on." A little too eagerly, she yanked me by the wrist, so hard I almost dropped the jacket still slung over my shoulders.

"Relax, Ericka," I said, pulling my arm out of her grasp. After one last look at the feathers on the ground where Trench-Coat Girl had stood, I followed her.

"Ugh. Are we seriously still going to the reception? After all that?" Ade leaned over the back of my pew, her head cushioned by her arms. "When a naked swan shows up at a funeral and accuses the dead guy of enslaving his wife, isn't it time to call off the after party?"

"Ralph Hedley, a feather stealer. But it's just a rumor, right? I mean, how could she really know for sure?" I swiveled around to face Ade properly, one leg on the pew, the other balancing Ericka's sleeping baby. "I mean, just because a man has a swan for a wife, that doesn't necessarily mean he stole her feathers to…" How did Trench-Coat Girl put it? *To win her love.* It was just so creepy. I rested my head against my hand. "Who was that girl, anyway?"

"Way ahead of you."

When I looked up again, Ade's cell phone was in my face. On the screen was a picture of Trench-Coat Girl, minus the nudity, being dragged away by an officer while a mass of young adults yelled things at a line of police officers in riot gear. The headline above it read:

Activists Arrested at G8 Summit. Chaos in the streets.

"Her name is Shannon Dalhousie and apparently she's a domestic terrorist. Or an activist. One of those."

I took the phone out of her hands and inspected the picture again, scrolling down. "Oh, there's a statement from her: 'I know a lot of people in this country don't want to face reality, but the truth is forced labor is a real problem in this country. People turn a blind eye while companies in Arkansas, California, Florida, Georgia, New York and so many others smuggle in so called "guest workers" to till the fields that make our bread. They use that term because it's so much easier than calling them what they are: swans – swans promised a better life and then forced to work for no pay without any social securities. How can the leaders of the world meet in their ivory towers to discuss the world's economy without addressing the vast social, economic and political inequalities that keep money in the hands of the few, while–?'"

"Damn, we get it. You're a defender of *truth* and *justice* and whatnot. Shit." Ade rolled her eyes and slipped her phone into her purse. "You know, what I don't really get about this whole Hedley thing is, if he really did steal his wife's feathers, why didn't she just say something? Like call the police or something? At the very least Shannon Dalhousie wouldn't have had to flash her tits in front of a congregation of mourning millionaires. At least not so early in the morning."

"I don't think Hedley's wife could have told anyone even if she wanted to…"

And that was the part that always freaked me out the most about feather-stealing. They say that once a swan's feathers are stolen, so is his or her free will. After that, a swan'll have no choice *but* to stay silent. If Shannon was right and the rumors were true… then Ralph Hedley really was a monster.

Dad never really talked about him much when we were growing up, even though for a short period of time I was friends with his son, Hyde. Well, "friends" may have been a strong term for it. The two of us had met at a Hedley Publications benefit my dad and the other accountants had been invited to. After that, Hyde just sort of followed me around, crossing the Brooklyn Bridge for "play dates" he'd scheduled on his own. The boy was definitely a little needy. But I came to like him anyway. I'd always wondered what Ralph had thought about Hyde and me hanging out, or if he even cared. Maybe he was just too busy enslaving his wife to notice what their adopted son was up to.

Ericka approached, phone in hand, her heels clicking on the tiled floor. "Charles *finally* sent a car to pick us up." Charles, aka Beanpole, aka Ericka's rich husband. Her face looked wiry and old, the way it always did when she was flustered.

"What's wrong?" I asked. "Something happen?"

Ericka blinked. "What? Oh, no. Nothing."

Ade and I exchanged a glance. Fight. Beanpole wasn't exactly Prince Charming. Case in point: you'd think having a wealthy brother-in-law would mean that we, at the very least, would be able to afford a new sink faucet.

"*Ericka, we've been over this: handouts will just make your father even more lazy than he already is.*" That was what he'd said the last time I saw him – more than a full year ago. Did I mention he lives in *Manhattan*?

"Well, Charles is a bit busy right now. Now that Ralph Hedley is dead, there are a lot of legal matters that the company's lawyers have to sort out – like who'll head the company, where his assets will go, and so on and so forth. It's a lot of work, so he's a bit..." She fell silent. As usual. "Anyway, I'll take François. Thank you."

"Yeah, no problem."

Ericka lifted her baby out of my arms and, after a little while, we left the church, walking down the stone steps together. A sleek black car waited for us on the other side of the graveyard with a black-hatted driver standing to attention by the door. I tried not to think of the bones beneath my heels as we zigzagged past the headstones. We stayed well away from Hedley's grave, just in case there were still photogs milling about, except, from what I could see, they'd pretty much cleared out.

The only one left at Hedley's gravesite was a guy – just one random guy.

No, he had been at the funeral too. I realized it once I got a better look. He was the guy on the bench. In his black vest, short-sleeved shirt and gray beanie, he stood directly in front of Hedley's grave. The stone angel towered over him, silent tears carved into its face.

The driver opened the door for us. In front of me, Ade shot a bemused glance my way. Fancy cars and drivers with hats. Since Charles controlled all of his money, we really didn't get opportunities like this, despite being Ericka's little sisters. I put my hand on the door.

"Oh damn!" My hand flew to my right arm instead. Bare. "Where's my jacket?"

Ade peered at me from inside the car. "Didn't you take it with you?"

"Maybe you left it in the church," Ericka said, lifting her baby higher in her arms.

"Shit. I'll go look." I slipped passed her. "Don't go anywhere without me!"

"Hurry up, Dee!"

Well yeah, that was the plan. I took a shortcut; a straighter path that took me past Hedley's grave. I wouldn't have looked twice at the stone angel, or at the young man keeping silent vigil in front of it, at any of it – but suddenly, I heard a muted, dull sound, like water on soil.

Hold up.

Oh God.

It wasn't water.

The guy in front of Hedley's grave kept his back turned, but that didn't stop me from noting the steady stream of liquid pouring onto the ground.

From between his legs.

"Oh for Christ's sake! What is *wrong with you people*?" Because really, what the hell? Feathered flashers, paparazzi and now public urination? "What, is this Desecrate a Grave Day?"

He turned, just a little. The first thing I noticed was his smile – tilted at a sly angle, not quite a smirk, but decidedly crooked. He was amused. At me. As if I were the freakshow here.

Then he turned all the way around. That's when I saw the open beer bottle in his hand – and his still zipped pants. Oh. "Whoops."

I could tell he was holding back a snort. "Yep."

"I uh… may have over-reacted a bit."

"You think?" His smile lingered. "So I take it you've never heard of pouring a little alcohol on a grave to pay your respects?" He cocked his head to the side and waited for my answer.

Why would I? "Nope," I said instead.

"Really? People do it all over the world." He shook the half-empty bottle in his hands. "In the Gold Coast, the Akan peoples spill it on the graves of their friends to help them transition into the spiritual world."

"Huh." Nutcase.

He looked about Ade's age, or barely a day over twenty, at the very *most*. Hard to believe Ralph Hedley qualified as a "friend" to someone of this guy's age. And a peculiar guy at that. Well, this situation was already way too weird. Besides that jacket had cost fifty bucks.

"OK," I said, eyes narrowed. "Well, bye."

"Hey, wait."

I didn't even bother pretending I wasn't exasperated. "What?"

"You want to try it?"

"Huh?"

He held out the bottle, eyes sparkling with mischief. My face scrunched. "Sorry, I'm busy."

"Suit yourself." Just as he began turning from me, he stopped suddenly. It was as if some startling epiphany had just seized him by the neck. He started staring at me. Furrowed eyebrows, bright brown eyes under an unruly fringe of dark hair. Weirdly intense. Or maybe just weird.

"What did you say your name was?" His voice was nearly a breath when he asked me. He searched my eyes.

I frowned. "I didn't." And I wasn't going to. "Like I said, I'm busy so–"

But I could only take about three steps before he grabbed my wrist. It was like a fire alarm went off in my head. The fight or flight in me started gathering up air for a scream as I shook. Strangest thing was, he looked earnest. Eager, but earnest. But then they always did before the stabbing started.

"W-wait," he said, but I didn't let him finish.

"Let me go!" I finally screamed and, after yanking my hand away, I punched him with it. It was a weak punch, but he stumbled back against the gravestone, shocked as he hit the ground. I half-expected he'd come at me again, but he just sat there. His cheeks were flushed, but not in anger. There was no bloodlust in his eyes, no hacksaw crazy. Just a timid sort of shame.

Shame. Maybe that was why I wasn't running yet.

"Sorry," he whispered, lying against the gravestone. "I really didn't mean to scare you. I just… " He glanced up at me again, fast and fleeting, before gathering himself and focusing instead on the fresh grave dirt beneath him. He patted it twice and stood, slowly. A solemn mask grayed his face, aging him suddenly. "See you around, Old Man," he told the headstone.

Old Man?

With one graceful movement, he swept past me, taking a modest swig of whatever was left in his bottle. Ericka's driver started to make liberal use of the car horn, but I could only stare – at the young man and his bottle of booze.

"Oh, and Deanna? You are Deanna, right?"

The young man stopped before he'd gotten too far. My heart had almost given out when he'd said my name, because it was right at that moment I'd finally realized who he was. Except it was impossible.

No way. That can't...

He smiled at me. "See you at the reception," he said, and walked off.

I crumpled Mom's bracelet beneath my fingers. "Hyde?"

3

Inheritance

Hyde Hedley.

"Not Hedley," he would always say, back when we were kids. He'd had another name before being adopted by the Hedley family at age six. Thompson, maybe. Johnson? The fanfare that came with the Hedley name made it hard to remember. But he always corrected me as if he were afraid that he'd forget himself one day.

The Hedleys, see, were as philanthropic as the next billionaire couple. With all of Manhattan's elite busy donating infinitesimally small fractions of their endless wealth in order to distract everyone from the fact that they lived three streets away from starving families, how exactly could one stand out amidst all the white noise? Especially a mogul whose struggling fashion magazine was, at the time, desperate to secure a major advertising deal with a family-oriented department store chain?

And Ralph Hedley, at the end of the day, was a businessman.

"He's a chess piece, the poor boy," I heard Mom tell Dad one day, after Hyde's first visit to our Brooklyn flat – where we used to live. "Come on, honey, you know it's true. As horrific as it sounds, I wouldn't put it past Ralph. You know how he is. Don't know why you keep defending him."

Chess piece. It didn't occur to me what Mom had meant until after Hedley died. I mean, it'd be pretty tough to win the good will of a family-oriented store while your marriage was failing and your childless wife was trying to kill herself, which is what the rumor mills had been churning out back then. Why give cash to poor, socio-economically disadvantaged kids when you can just adopt one from an East Brooklyn orphanage? The latter had more headline potential.

Hedley spent quite a lot of time boasting about his son to the press – incredibly intelligent for his age, fast-adapting, motivated, athletic, bright future ahead of him at the company, etcetera, etcetera. And not once during the two years I knew Hyde did I see the two of them smiling together, except for when they were having their pictures taken.

He was a good kid, though, Hyde. He'd have a driver take him across the bridge to Brooklyn every weekend to play with me and Ade. He came to my birthday parties with extravagant gifts that I'd eventually have to send back because either I didn't know what they were, or they wouldn't fit through my front door. He was mischievous and brash, but tender and sweet all at once. He was my friend.

Then he died.

"So, you think that your childhood boyfriend arose from the dead and will at any second crash his father's funeral reception?" Adrianna had a way with words.

I glared at her while she lifted her glass of non-alcoholic wine off the table and sipped it calmly. She preferred the real deal, but figured fake IDs were tacky at a funeral.

"As usual, your tact astounds," I said before scanning the reception. It'd been an hour already. Drunken socialites, mingling, mingling, busboys serving those little sandwiches, and yet more mingling. But no Hyde. He hadn't shown up yet.

Because he won't, because he's dead. Dead and buried and fully decayed. It was impossible for Hyde Hedley to be breathing when Ralph Hedley himself had confirmed him dead to the press all those years ago. They buried his body in the very cemetery I'd just left. It was ridiculous. The guy was clearly a jackass trying to stir shit. Asshole.

And yet he knew my name.

"But no, seriously, Dee." Ade shifted in her seat so her judge-y glare could get a better angle. "You honestly think that the guy you met at the cemetery is someone who's been dead for years? And you're thinking this while being fully sober?"

"I know. It sounds stupid." I'd been trying to convince myself of that for the past hour.

"No, it sounds like old wounds tearing open." She tapped my chest with a finger. "Hyde Hedley." She laughed. "You liked that kid a lot. I know. We all knew. You were all 'ooh' in love or whatever."

My face flushed. "What? Ew, no!"

"Yep. Totally imprinted on him." Ade snorted. "That one Christmas break I caught you planning your wedding. You had *lists*."

I slumped in my seat. "I recall no lists."

"Look, just drop it, Dee. It's only natural that you'd think about him at his dad's funeral, but your zombie boyfriend fantasies just aren't healthy. It's been years. You need to let shit go."

She was right.

"Wanna play 'Spot the Celeb'?" Ade smoothed her long hair over her shoulders and flicked her head past me. "Look. It's totally that judge on *Sew or Die*!"

"Holy crap, *really*?"

"Yep. Two o'clock. See her?"

I had to stand to see over the sea of heads, but I found her: a woman with a white-blonde bob and some pretty insane earrings on top of that. Seriously. They dangled from her ears like thin streaks of pure gold. They probably were.

"Beatrice-Rey Hoffen? Hoffer? Hoffer-Rey?" I shook my head.

Neither of us were that into fashion really, but watching designers spiral into major depressive episodes on an almost periodical basis while being given increasingly ludicrous challenges day after day made for fun Thursday nights. Beatrice Hoffer-Rey was on *Sew or Die* because she was the editor in chief of *Bella Magazine*: published, of course, by Hedley Publications.

And, you know, I was the daughter of a guy who packaged drinks at a warehouse, so obviously I didn't feel out of place here in the slightest.

"Hey, Dee, remember that one episode when she pushed *Vogue*'s creative director into a fountain because of some perceived slight?"

"Yeah?"

"I *loved* that episode. Oh!" She'd yelped because of the young man who'd snuck up behind her and slid his hand up her shoulder. A sharply dressed young man. One of plenty in the vicinity, of course, but this one had a name I actually remembered. Why wouldn't I? His stepmom had pushed *Vogue*'s creative director into a fountain on reality TV.

"Hey," he said.

"Anton?" Ade strategically let a girly little flutter into her voice. She always said that some guys just needed the ego boost.

Anton Rey. Beatrice Hoffer-Rey's stepson. Ade had pointed him out to me as soon as we'd arrived at the reception. I only recognized his perfectly styled blonde coif because it somehow always ended up tangled in some model's willowy fingers if his countless Page Six appearances were any indication. And yet, while I could barely muster the courage to step within fifty feet of him, the moment we'd signed the guest book Ade had just walked up to him. Fifteen minutes of charm later...

"So, you're coming Saturday, right?"

There was this oily, slick to his smile that immediately put me off, but Ade returned it with a coy shrug. "Oh, right. Your birthday. I'd love to. But like I said, I'll have to see if I'm free."

He straightened up, folding his arms over his Lacrosse-chiselled chest. Probably Lacrosse. He certainly *looked* preppy enough to play Lacrosse. "That's cute. See you then."

Ade laughed. "You're not even a little curious, are you? As to whether or not I'll actually show?"

His eyes brimmed with the arrogance of an asshole rich boy who could mail order hookers from Budapest if he wanted to get laid. "Anton Rey just invited you to a party. Trust me. You're free."

My mouth stayed open even after he'd left. "Did he just refer to himself in the third person?"

"Would seem so." Ade shook her head with an amused little grin.

"Utterly amazing. So, are you–" I stopped. "Are you actually gonna go?"

"You kidding? Hell, yeah."

"Really?" I sat back in my chair, just staring at her. "You do know this is going to be a party filled to the brim with rich kids, right? Like, wealthy, *wealthy* kids."

"Exactly," she said. "Partying in Manhattan with dead-eyed socialites? When's the next time I'll get the chance? It'll be like a Greek Odyssey. Plus it's a Saturday – there's never anything good on TV."

Half an hour of canoodling in the corner with a guy whose mother told Hollywood celebrities what to wear.

Half an hour was all it took for gorgeous Adrianna Davis to be invited to a party that would undoubtedly be filled with everyone under twenty-five who mattered in Manhattan's social scene. And the best part was I didn't need to see the lazy tilt of her head to know that it all literally meant nothing to her.

There was never anything good on TV Saturdays. It was that simple.

"It really is good to be the sister who doesn't give a shit," I muttered under my breath.

Ade shrugged. "You can totally come too, if you want."

Rolling my eyes, I twisted around. Anton walked by a giant ice sculpture in front of which Beatrice Hoffer-Rey chatted with a few men in suits, wineglass in hand. As he passed, she touched his arm lightly with her free hand, flashing him a demure grin. He stared at her for about a second before jerking his arm away and stomping off. Huh. Stepmother and stepson were certainly "close".

Ade saw me staring and pointed out the man next to Beatrice: a tall guy just teetering on the edge of overweight even though he filled out his pinstripe suit well. His slicked back dirty blonde hair matched Anton's perfectly.

"Anton's father," Ade explained. "Edmund Rey."

An executive at Hedley Publications. With Ralph Hedley gone, Anton's dad was poised to control the majority share of the company, as I'd learned from eavesdropping on drunken conversations.

The majority share. That was probably why Edmund and Beatrice looked so jovial, chatting and laughing during what was supposed to be a day of sorrow and mourning. Ralph Hedley clearly had made the best of friends.

"Oh hey, look," Ade flicked her head towards the door, "it's Beanpole."

Ericka's scrawny lawyer husband came in through the door with two of what I was assuming were his colleagues. With pale and panicked faces, they approached Edmund and Beatrice, who excused themselves from the crowd. The more they all whispered conspiratorially, the deeper Edmund scowled. He scoped the reception hall and then hissed at the lawyers. Just like that the four started to leave.

The door flew open before they could reach it.

"Hyde," I whispered.

Ade blinked. "Um, qué?"

I could only point as the guy who'd poured cheap booze on Hedley's fresh grave breezed into the hall with a brigade of suits. He passed by Beatrice, Edmund, and the three lawyers with little more than a wink and a wave.

"Hyde!" I pointed again before I lost him in the crowd.

Ade let out an impatient sigh. "Again with the Hyde nonsense." She flicked my ear with her finger, but I was far too focused on scanning the crowd to notice.

He reappeared at the foot of the stage and, with a swish of his hand, plucked a wineglass out of a woman's hands, tipping it to show his thanks. People were starting to notice – eyes looking up, conversations stalling. Not that any of them suspected that the young man climbing the stage at the front of Ralph Hedley's funeral reception was his dead son.

No way. I shook my head. *It's not him.*

Grabbing a pen out of his jeans he tapped the glass. "Hello? Can I get everyone's attention please? Hello!" Whether annoyed, confused, or intrigued, the gathering finally quietened down.

He waited. I could feel every jagged beat thudding against my ribcage. The silence only made the pounding seem louder.

God, this was absurd. It wasn't him. It wasn't Hyde Hedley. It wasn't Ralph Hedley's son.

"Hey, everyone," he said. "I'm Hyde Hedley, Ralph Hedley's son."

Confused whispers. Ade simply narrowed her eyes, suspicious.

"Hyde." Someone had hissed his name from below the stage. A man. I couldn't see him, but he sounded exactly like I did whenever Dad was embarrassing himself in public. Didn't seem to do any good, though.

"Yes, yes, I know," the young man went on. "None of you believe me. And how can you? I've been dead for nine years." He shrugged. "I wouldn't believe me either."

He looked as if he were fighting back a giggle. Was he drunk? He was obviously drunk. A drunk, confused boy who'd tragically stumbled into the wrong social gathering.

One of the suits who'd flanked him as he entered the hall finally stepped onto the stage. He was a much older man with a full head of gray hair and a beer belly that made his suit stick out at an odd angle. He leaned over and whispered something to "Hyde", who laughed in response before pulling the man firmly to his side.

"Everyone, my father's former legal counsel, John Roan – well, I'm sure you're well aware already. He was quite active in the company, as I remember, before Edmund Rey fired him. He thinks I should take things slow and I agree. I just figured that since it *is* my father's funeral and all, I should pay my respects. I also thought it might be a good time to let you all know that I'll be taking over his company from this day forward."

Pandemonium. Shock. Whispers. I saw a few people pulling out cell phones – to do what? Take YouTube footage? Ade looked from me to Hyde and then back again, her lips parted. I gripped my chair so tightly the metal was pinching off my veins.

"What the hell are you talking about?" yelled Edmund, his face blood-red and bloated. "Who is this kid? Someone get him out of here."

If I weren't so dumbfounded, I might have wondered why Hyde was staring at Edmund – and only at Edmund – with a glint in his eye and a knife in his grin.

"And John! What the hell do you think you're doing?" Anton's dad raged on.

The man Hyde had called John Roan spared Edmund a quick, particularly contemptuous glance, but didn't answer. Instead, he whispered something else to Hyde, his face far more stern this time around.

"All right, all right, he's right, I'm sorry. Didn't mean to make a scene." His smile was devilish – too devilish for that to be true, and far too devilish for it not to be Hyde Hedley's. "I'll leave. Oh, but one last thing, to those of you who work for Hedley Publications: don't worry about anything. I promise I'll treat my workers right."

And with a wink he swooped back out of the hall. Edmund, Beatrice and even Anton stared wide-eyed as he passed, each of them stunned dumb. I clutched the tablecloth with a trembling hand.

"My God, was that really Hyde?" Ade tucked her hair behind her ear, shaking her head in awe. "He got hot."

4

Confirmed

Nine years ago was a different time. Mom was alive, for one. And with Mom alive, Dad had tried that much harder to stay on the wagon, which meant our family had stayed together. Different times.

Every once in a while, Mom would take me, Ade and Hyde out to Prospect Park (not Ericka – by the time she hit puberty, she couldn't stand to be around us half the time). Hyde, the poor kid, was almost embarrassingly eager – with his medically prescribed orthopaedic footwear – to join our outings. He'd have his driver drop him off at our place and then he'd spend the whole day with us. Sometimes I'd catch him staring at us. Just staring. With that gaze of his – a warm acrylic brown – and that broad brush of a smile, he'd paint us stroke by stroke onto a big white canvas and call his art, "The Davises".

I wouldn't have thought our lives were so idyllic, but then maybe they were. Neither Mom nor Dad needed the presence of cameras to spare a smile for their children.

I remember once, while she was hanging upside down from the monkey bars at a neighbourhood park, Ade asked Hyde if he had any friends besides us – and when he went deathly quiet, she did too. She hadn't meant for it to be a rhetorical question.

"Ugh."

One in the afternoon. Monday. I dragged myself into the house and practically collapsed against the wall, feebly sweeping the front door shut with my foot. An hour of sleep last night, and then work in the morning. As far as summer jobs went, being a grocery store clerk wasn't so bad, except today I was sleep-deprived, my back was sore and, oh yeah, I'd spent a good five minutes trying not to cry when an incredibly large man in a sweaty purple tank top yelled at me for crushing his loaves of bread underneath a case of canned tomatoes.

Ade was sprawled on the couch, her bed's comforter twisted around her. With her mouth half-open, she watched infomercials in a half-glazed stupor, the remote control dangling weakly in her grip. An open bag of potato chips rested on her stomach.

"Glad to see you've been keeping yourself busy." I walked past the filthy kitchen to the stairs.

"Hey, I work on weekends."

Telemarketing. Six months after dropping out of college after her first semester, Ade had been flitting between that and watching TV while on her self-proclaimed search for her "true calling". I honestly wouldn't have minded; if she would just stop leaving her dirty underwear in the bathroom and eating half of everything in the house, considering she never helped pay for any of the stuff she shovelled into her stomach.

The muscles behind my shoulder twitched while I took off my awful red and acid-yellow uniform and changed into sweatpants and a tank. A sore back usually meant it was that time of the month. "*Ugh*."

"Has Casper called you yet?" Ade asked once I'd come back down, a bottle of acetaminophen in my hands.

"If you're referring to Hyde, then no," I answered coolly and popped three in my mouth. "And stop it. You know it's not him. The guy at the reception was probably just some drunk asshole playing a prank."

"He had Hedley's old lawyer with him."

"OK, so they're both sober assholes trying to get their hands on Hedley's assets or something. Use your imagination."

"Right. Then again, you did say he knew your name."

True. I frowned. "So?" Folding my arms, I shifted uncomfortably on my feet. "Whose side are you on anyway?"

"Logic." Ade whipped off the comforter and it was infinitely annoying to find her still in her pyjamas. "Let's be completely real here. Why would he waltz into a funeral reception and demand Dead Guy's cash knowing that he'd have to take a DNA test to prove he is who he says he is, if he *isn't* who he says he is?"

Also true. Crap. I sat down and pulled my legs up on the couch, staring at my knees.

"Honestly, I don't know why this is bothering you, Dee. If my dead childhood boyfriend randomly showed up one day and he looked like *that*, I'd put that in the win column." Ade shook her head. "And he could possibly end up being a millionaire? Or billionaire? Damn. Only *you* could turn that into a reason for angst."

I snatched Ade's bag of chips and started clogging my throat in the hope that it would make all the confusing things in my head go away. Ade flipped through channels with one hand and sporadically dipped her hand into the bag with the other until–

"Ooh! It's your zombie boyfriend!" Ade clapped excitedly.

I sat up straight and, without thinking, snatched back the remote and turned up the volume. It really was him. Hyde; his dark hair perfectly trimmed and his jeans and beanie traded in for an impeccably tailored suit. He had his lawyer, John Roan, next to him with a flock of other suits trailing behind. Reporters swarmed him with microphones and cameras.

One reporter, during the one second I could concentrate on her babble, told me that they were outside the Hedley Publications building. But I couldn't focus on anything other than the caption at the bottom of the screen.

Breaking: Funeral Crasher Confirmed to be Ralph Hedley's Adopted Son.

"Wow. So I was right and you were wrong. Or, I guess you were right and I was wrong first?" Ade stuffed her face with chips.

Both. My fingers loosened around the plastic. Ade grabbed the bag before it could topple onto the already dirty rug.

"Up until now, Ralph Hedley's son was believed to have died nine years ago, drowned off the coast of Brazil while on vacation," the reporter said. My head thickened, squeezing everything inside until all I could hear was myself, crying at his funeral. It was another closed-casket like his dad's – a tragically tiny box, ironwood, with square-cornered edges and golden rims. Except this time, the casket had been closed because they didn't have a body to show. Ralph Hedley's son was believed to have died. Everyone had believed it. I'd believed it. I'd cried about it. I'd had nightmares about it.

"Dee, you all right?" I looked up to find Ade with her lips slick with grease, studying me, watching for any sign that the thin shoestrings usually keeping me together day by day were starting to unravel.

I couldn't pretend I didn't feel them tugging by the knots, so I focused on Hyde instead. He looked content enough. He couldn't even hide it – the little devil grin turning his face wicked even as he dutifully waved off the reporters with an annoyed flick of his hand. His lawyers stashed him in a long black limousine and moments later they were off.

"Funeral Crasher." Ade repeated that part of the caption with a snort. "Poor Swangirl. Resurrected billionaire babies take precedence over feathers and boobs, I guess."

"Shut up," I whispered in a tone so silently spiteful it shocked even me. Without another word, Ade curled up in her corner of the couch and changed the channel.

I spent the whole afternoon in my room flipping through old pictures of me and Hyde. In the one I held between my fingers, Hyde gripped me in a bear hug. It was my eighth birthday, the last we'd shared together.

But why? All these years he wasn't dead. So where was he? Living it up somewhere while the rest of us – me – cried ourselves to sleep for months? Why would his dad lie about something like that? What could any of them have possibly gotten out of it? None of it made any sense. It was *senseless*.

"Whatever." I suddenly felt incredibly annoyed. I shoved the picture back into my drawer.

Ten o'clock. Dad called and said he'd be out late. Poker, probably. My cell phone rang just as the smell of Ade's burnt rice started seeping into my room. Lying down on my bed, I picked it up. "Hello?"

"Hey, Deanna."

My fingers twitched. I sat up, my throat tight. "Is… Is this…?"

"Oh, yeah. Yeah. It's… me. You know. Hyde." He sounded almost awkwardly boyish. Or maybe boyishly awkward. I could practically hear the nervous energy in his voice. It was a far cry from the Hyde who'd smarmed his way through an army of the press.

"Hyde," I whispered, the word heavy with dread, because it really was him after all.

He'd obviously picked up on my tone because his changed as well. "Should I not have called?"

"How did you even get my number?"

"Your sister," he chuckled.

"What? *Ericka*?"

"Yeah. I called her and asked."

That was the thing with Hyde. There was no way of telling whether or not he was shitting me, and if so, how thoroughly.

"After the shock wore off," he continued, "she figured it'd be a good idea for us to..." He paused. "You know. Talk."

"Talk? *Talk*?" I shook my head. "What are you...? Why did you...?" I had to force myself to breathe. "What the hell is going on?"

There was a slight hesitation in his voice. "Is that any way to treat a friend you haven't seen in years?" Maybe it was my imagination, but he sounded almost hurt. Maybe. He covered it up well. "Aren't you just a little bit excited? Happy? Relieved? Intrigued?"

For some reason the more I heard him talk, the more I wanted to smash something. "You're just having a shitload of fun with this, aren't you? You know, I'm starting to think you faked your own death for the drama of it."

"Well, I admit, the drama is part of the fun."

"Go to hell."

"Wait!" he cried, just as I lowered the phone from my face. Hesitantly, I raised it back up to my ear. "Look, I'm sorry. I'm just nervous. I haven't... I mean, it's been

years. Trust me; this is incredibly awkward for me too."
His laugh this time was barely a breath. "I feel like I've
been asleep, you know? For years. And I–" He stopped.

Shifting onto my knees, I tugged on a loose thread on
my comforter, waiting for him to say something else,
anything else. He didn't.

I made sure my sigh was loud enough for him to hear.
"So where have you been, Hyde?"

"You looked so beautiful at Dad's funeral, you know."

I dropped the thread. "What?"

"Thanks for going, by the way. My father was an
asshole, but he was still my father. I suppose. And I'm
sorry for scaring you that day. I just… I couldn't believe
it was you."

My grip tightened around the phone. "Hyde, *where
have you been?*"

"Come see me tonight."

"What?"

"How about we meet by that ice cream shop at the
corner of Sterling and Underhill? Nine o'clock?"

"I'm hanging up."

"I'll tell you everything." He rushed the words out
as if he were running out of time. "Just… meet me.
OK? Let's do something together." He sounded half-
desperate. It was almost painful to hear. Embarrassing.

I mulled it over, chewing the insides of my cheek,
curling and uncurling my toes on the bed sheets. Finally,
squeezing my free hand into a fist, I gritted my teeth
and nodded. "Fine. But I can't stay out too late. I have a
curfew." Of course, Dad being out this late meant he'd

stumble back home sometime around midnight too drunk and tired to care where his daughters had been all day. But Hyde didn't know that.

"Good, that's fine. I won't keep you too long, promise."

"And just to let you know, it's not an ice cream shop anymore."

"What?"

"The place on the corner of Sterling and Underhill. It's a thrift store now."

"Oh." Hyde's weak chuckles limped out of the receiver. "OK. I didn't know."

"Things change." I let a bit of my frustration slip into every syllable. I wanted him to feel it. "Guess you slept too long."

I hung up.

5

Reminiscence

I'd planned to get to the thrift store at least fifteen minutes late, but who was I kidding? I checked my watch. Nine o'clock on the dot.

The night's chill sent a violent shiver down my back, still sore despite all the aloe I'd been rubbing on it. I bet it was my damn mattress' fault.

I glanced up and down the modestly busy streets, absently tugging on my sweatshirt. No Hyde. Not yet. There was a guy scratching his privates at the hotdog stand, though. Very classy. The vendor grimaced too.

Even after wrapping my arms around my chest, which usually gave me a false but comforting sense of security, I felt oddly exposed. I still wasn't entirely sure that this was a good idea, so I decided to stay out of the thrift store's light, which beamed out of overlarge display windows. Instead, I kept to the shadow of the alley next to it. At least that way I'd be able to see Hyde coming before he saw me. If I got cold feet I could sneak off without him noticing me. And of course, if he didn't show up, at least I wouldn't look like a jackass standing around in the cold.

I shuffled over to the alley, but the second I rounded the corner, I rounded back just as quickly. I pressed my back against the thrift store's dirty bricks.

There were two boys at the other end of the alley, behind a dumpster. Obscured, but not nearly obscured enough. By the sound of their voices they were fairly young – probably my age. But then there's only so much you can garner from moaning alone. It sounded heavy too.

Damn it, Hyde, this is on you. I hated PDA with a fiery passion, if only because it reminded me of my own pathetic, non-existent love life.

"Stop!" one boy suddenly cried out, sharply enough for me to hear him.

"Come on, you said you'd show me." From the sound of it, the older boy was not only older, but sly enough to pretend he was also wiser. I turned the corner again, making sure to keep hidden. He was taller too, broad and lean. He perfectly filled out the black jeans hugging his hips, though without more light, I couldn't tell much more.

Taking the younger boy's hand, he began to pull him away from the dumpster into the alley. For a second I could see the younger boy's hair, black bangs matted against his forehead, and his thin frame – deathly thin, clad in a beat up shirt that pooled around his waist. For a second, the younger boy seemed mesmerized, unable to resist the siren song calling to him. But at the last moment, he pulled back.

"No. I changed my mind, Jack. It'll hurt too much."

Even from here I could see the older boy's body go rigid. "So what, Devon? Don't you trust me?" I wouldn't. The hard edge in Jack's voice didn't exactly inspire confidence.

What am I doing? This wasn't any of my business. I boosted off the brick wall.

And heard a crash. It was the dumpster – or more precisely, a body smashing into it. I looked around. Some people walking by had obviously heard but decided it wasn't any of their business either. Or maybe they thought it was a cat. I swiveled back around the wall. Both boys had disappeared from sight, behind the dumpster, but every once in a while I could see the bodies thrashing. And I could hear muffled yells – muffled by a hand.

"Just let me see them," Jack whispered. "Come on, you promised."

First one feather. Then two. They fluttered to the ground.

"You said I can have you."

Even with his voice muffled I could tell Devon was whimpering.

What do I do? Every bone in my body told me to rush in and knock the other guy out, as if I could – but I had to at least try.

A surprise attack. I could sneak in and hit him in the back of the head or kick him in the nads. Something, anything.

It's what Ade would do. But my body froze. I could hear Devon scraping against brick, but my feet wouldn't move.

I should have moved. Why wouldn't I move?

I felt it. Something deep and primal that grew heavier with each of Devon's feathers that fell to the ground. Something pulling at me from the pit of my stomach. Self-preservation. Fear. The instinct to protect myself. Against what? What was I afraid of?

My fingers pressed against the brick. I considered calling for help, but then that would mean exposing Devon. How could I know who was walking by and how they'd react when face to face with a young, vulnerable swan? The person who saved him could just as easily pick up where Jack left off.

"You can have mine too." Jack's voice thickened with a kind of lust that shriveled me up from the inside. "Just like we promised."

I was thinking too much. I needed to act.

I shut my eyes.

"Don't worry, Dee," Hyde whispered beside me. He gave my shoulder a delicate squeeze, his fingers smooth against the crook of my neck. With a sharp breath, I jerked back, but before I could even see him properly, he walked into the alleyway.

"Hey," Hyde said, and paused as if thinking of what to say next. "Stop that."

The struggling indeed stopped. Jack practically leapt away from Devon, standing in the middle of the alley like a spooked stray cat, his hair bristling, his eyes wide, his body poised to attack. "Who the fuck are you?"

"Hyde," Hyde answered.

Really, Hyde?

But somehow, his almost cartoonish confidence made it easier for me to follow suit. Not with the confidence thing, of course, that wasn't going to happen. But at the very least I made my presence known.

"So what the hell is this? What are you guys, the fucking police?" Jack puffed out his chest, his false bravado clearly meant to sell his alpha-male façade.

Hyde didn't take the bait. "Do you happen to see any uniforms?"

"Well, douche bag, we were having a private conversation, so how about you screw off before I really get pissed." As if heeding a wordless commandment, Devon slinked up to his side, or started to, but each step dragged. He never quite got within Jack's reach. But at least now I could see him clearly: fresh faced and ashamed.

Hyde moved ever closer to the pair with a sinister kind of sway. "First: private conversations work better in private places," he said. He stopped right in front of Jack, who took a step back despite his not-too menacing glare. "Second–"

Hyde punched him – one hard hit to the jaw that launched Jack to the asphalt.

"Hyde!" I ran up to him while Devon rushed out of the way. "What are you–?" I stopped. One look at the quiet, stifling fury seething in Hyde's eyes and I stopped.

"Now, I just got here, so maybe I'm jumping to conclusions, but for a second there it looked as though you were about to do something people generally should never do. *Ever*." Hyde loomed over the boy who rubbed his face and squirmed beneath him. Then, kneeling down, he grabbed Jack by his collar and pulled his face close. "I might punch you again," Hyde said. "I'm mulling it over."

"Don't!" It was Devon this time. Another feather slipped from underneath his shirt and got stuck in his shoe. His face flushed as he squeezed his hands into fists. "Did I ask for your help? God, j-just..." He pulled his shirt, scrunching the fabric in his hand so that it pressed against his back – maybe to keep more feathers from falling out. He stared at Jack, his lips trembling, struggling to find the words. "Just forget it!"

And he ran off. As soon as Hyde released Jack from his grip, the boy stumbled to his feet and fled too, though in the opposite direction. That was comforting at least.

Hyde stood up and dusted himself off. "Huh. Well, he'll thank me one day."

I stared down the alleyway, my hand at my mouth. I'd never seen... I mean, people generally didn't do that sort of thing out in the open, if at all. I mean, it may have started out as consensual, but... tearing out someone's feathers in an alleyway... I mean wasn't that against the law or something? I was sure it was.

Hyde faced me. "Dee. You OK?"

Dee. He'd said it so casually. Like the last nine years, nine *seconds* hadn't happened. I couldn't even answer.

Any anger I'd seen etched in his face had already

vanished as quickly as a whisper. His smile was soft, shy. He gazed at me as if studying every pore on my face – and there were many. Then, as if suddenly noticing that I could see him too, he turned, shifting on his feet. "Sorry I'm a little late. I had to go visit someone at the…" He cleared his throat. "Well anyway, I'm glad you came. Honestly, I wasn't sure you would."

"Honestly, I'm not sure I should have." Understatement. "I'm still not sure."

"I understand. No, I completely understand. Man you've gotten taller. How old are you now? What, eighteen?"

"Seven… Wait, what? Just like that, you expect me to–"

But his eager smile was just too sincere. Everything about him was. The fidgeting; the avoiding eye-contact. It was the joy and excitement and nervousness of seeing an old friend again.

Maybe he really did just want to see me. Maybe not. I stayed silent.

"Let's go for a walk," he suggested, straightening out the sleeves on his jacket. "We… we can catch up. Right?"

"And you can tell me all about the wacky adventures you've been having while me and everyone else who cared about you thought you were dead."

He flinched. Oh, so he felt the sting? Good. Being alive meant feeling pain. It was his choice to rise from the dead. It was high time he got reacquainted with it again.

Hyde recovered quickly. Walking up to me, he offered me his arm. I didn't take it. "All right then." He smoothed his hair instead. "But about the whole 'everyone *else* who cared about me' thing? If I remember correctly, I'm pretty sure it was just you, Dee."

I kept my eyes on the street.

Once the silence between us had become so unbearable I considered making a run for it down the intersection, Hyde decided to tell me why he wanted us to meet at Underhill. As if I didn't already know: Prospect Park. I guess the place still had meaning for him. I guess he remembered the times when we'd gone there, me with my bushy brows, him with his orthopedic shoes and that offensively lame bow tie he loved to wear because he thought it made him look cool. Ade and I would always mock him mercilessly on sight.

"Something funny? You're smiling."

When I looked up at him, he flashed me a toothy grin, perfect white, just adorable enough for me to stop silently resenting him for about a second.

Seconds passed.

"Nope."

"Really? Not even a little? Or maybe you smile at random intervals to confuse and thus emotionally manipulate your dates?"

Dates? I gave him an incredulous look. "I guess I just have zero control over the motor muscles in the lower half of my face," I said flatly. "Which is one thing we apparently have in common. Or is there another reason why you'd call whatever the hell this is a date?"

At least he had the decency to look sheepish. "OK, I'll give you that." And yet, while we'd been weaving through people at a comfortable distance apart, he seemed to take our exchange as a cue to slide closer to me.

Oh God. I shoved my hands into my sweatshirt pocket and stared at the traffic. "So, Hyde, are you actually going to tell me where you've been all these years or are we just going to exchange witty banter for a while and then call it a night? Curfew, remember?"

"France."

I stopped. An angry-looking guy in a newsboy cap knocked into my left shoulder as he brushed by, but I barely noticed. "What?"

"Well, Paris, technically, though I did spend some time in Monaco every so often since it's close enough a drive–"

"You were in *Europe*?"

"Well…" He paused. "Kinda, yeah."

My fingers twitched inside my sweatshirt. Funny. I didn't exactly know what I'd expected, and yet now all I could picture was him drinking champagne in some obnoxiously trendy nightclub surrounded by a troupe of gorgeous, scrawny French models hanging on his every word as he fed them olives and laughed it up. All while I was alone and depressed at home, trying valiantly to get over my dead best friend.

"Are you shitting me?" I'd yelled it loud enough to spook some poor child as she climbed into a parked car by the side of the road. The mother shot me a withering glare. I lowered my voice a little. "Don't give me that crap, Hyde. Your dad *said* you were dead. It was in the papers. Why would he say you were dead if you were living it up in France?"

"Paris," he corrected, though the way his face pinched and cheeks flushed made it clear that he knew how stupidly unnecessary that was. "Look, can we sit down somewhere? Hey, Grand Army Plaza's right over there." He let out a nervous half-chuckle. "Man, Army Plaza. Remember how we used to–"

I crossed the street and stopped, directly in front of Bailey fountain, and turned to face him, folding my arms. "Well?"

Hyde gazed at the water shooting up from the ridges, showering the stone bodies in an endless stream. Wearily, he sat down on a nearby bench. "Ralph Hedley." He let the name linger for a moment, waited for all the breath to drift out of him and rise into the air as a quiet offering to the dead. "He was a lot of things. 'Truthful' wasn't one of them."

"Well I guess one shouldn't expect honesty from a man who could enslave his wife and still show his face at many a social event."

"I guess not," Hyde said.

I blinked, shocked at Hyde's honesty for a moment. "Why would he lie? What would make Ralph Hedley tell the world his one and only adopted son was dead?"

Hyde traced his finger along the bench. "I don't know. That's a good question. Maybe he was ashamed

of me? I did like to go to girls' birthday parties after all."
Grinning at me, he added, "Or maybe he just got tired
of me. It happened after Mom died, and he'd already
gotten his deal. Maybe he just didn't need me anymore."
He leaned over, his arms on his knees. "Then again, his
company was going through a bit of financial trouble
at the time. Maybe he just needed to cut back on his
expenses? Really, Deanna, who knows…"

"Stop it."

He was lying. He had to be. Hyde had that way about
him. He'd told me he'd dined with a prince of England
once and waited to see if I bought it. He'd offer me lies
wrapped in pretty ribbons and laugh when I swallowed
them whole. A trickster. A jack ass, now. It was fun, he'd
told me once, only because I always fell for it. But that
was nine years ago.

"Hyde? Tell me the truth; this doesn't make any
sense."

"What's there to tell? Sometimes life gets dicey and
your dad fakes your death."

True or not true. I couldn't tell. I thought I could
scrutinize his every movement, break him down to his
micro-expressions and figure it out. Nothing.

"Your dad *faked your death* because… life got 'dicey'?"

"Yes. Death threats, ransoms and all."

Death threats? Why would anyone threaten Hyde?
To get to Ralph?

"And you, what, lived as a meagre shepherd boy these
past nine years until you could reclaim your rightful
place on the throne?"

"Or some variation of that. But with fewer musical numbers."

"Are you telling me the truth or aren't you?" Even to my own ears, I sounded desperate. It was embarrassing. Just a minute ago I was sure I'd figured him out.

Hyde was still looking at me when he answered. "Maybe. There's nothing I can tell you that you'd believe anyway. None of it makes sense because none of it is supposed to. But I'm here. I'm alive. That's the truth. Isn't that enough?"

Anger crashed down on me. "I'll tell you everything," he'd said. He'd promised me he'd tell me everything, but it was just a ruse to get me here, wasn't it? I could have laughed. He was a coward. No amount of faux-existentialist drivel would change that.

Hyde looked up at me, almost broken; his arms stretched over his knees at odd angles, his body folded, his eyes empty. If there were something he wasn't telling me, there was a reason. At least that much I could see.

He could keep it. I didn't care anymore.

As the fountain rippled behind me, filling the silence, I finally let the last few days settle like dust. Once they did, I could see Hyde clearly. No longer the chubby little boy who'd followed me around Brooklyn. He was older, leaner. A better liar and a worse liar all at the same time. He was arrogant. And he was tired. I could see that too, as clear as day. Worn down as if laden with battle scars. He couldn't hide it, as hard as he tried.

"You've changed, Hyde," was all I said.

"Oh?" He crossed his legs and gazed up at me. "But isn't that my line?"

"What do you mean by that?"

He examined me, not seductively, but clinically, like he was taking stock of the inventory and comparing it against past data. "I've been thinking about it since the funeral. But you do look a little... worn."

"*Excuse* me?"

He stood up and approached me with calm, even steps. I stepped back. "I don't know. The last time I saw you, when we were kids I mean, you were much brighter. It was like you were bursting with life. What happened?"

He looked a little sad. A *little*, but a little was enough to nearly send me into a rage. How dare he? How dare this asshole, who lied and lied about everything, make me feel like a child being scolded by her parents because she didn't run fast enough to win the sprint?

"I don't know what you're talking about, and clearly, neither do you."

I thought of the sheen on my mother's coffin when the light from the stained glass windows hit it at just the right angle. I thought of my dad, that same night, passed out on the couch. I thought of myself, picking up the bottles and staring at the peeling paint on walls I could have sworn were closing in.

"You used to tell me that you were going to write the next *Sound of Music*. You wrote little stories about us all the time." Hyde gave me a sidelong glance. "Did that change too?"

"Everything changes."

He looked as if he wanted to reach out to me so I turned, quickly, and checked my watch. "It's almost half-past ten. I need to get home."

"I'll call a car," Hyde said, reaching into his pocket, probably for his phone.

"Don't bother. I'll take the bus."

Before I could snatch it away, he took my hand in his. It didn't feel awful, but then, it didn't feel good either. "I'm sorry, Dee," he said, and looked like he meant it. I hated him for it. "I'm sorry. I didn't mean to hurt you. I don't want to hurt you, believe me. I wish I could be more open, but I... This is all just really..." He searched for the perfect word and found the worst imaginable. "Complicated."

"Oh. Well, problem solved." I ripped my hand from his grip. "You hurt me. You're still lying to me. Why should I ever trust you again?"

He let out an exasperated sigh. "You know what? It's OK," he said finally. "It's not like I was expecting a tearful reunion or anything." The twinge of disappointment in his voice told me otherwise. "But I'm back now. I really hope we can see each other more often." He must have noticed my doubtful look because his next words rushed out in a nervous stream. "Can't we? I mean I've still got this whole thing with taking over the company and stuff, but aside from that we can hang right?"

Oh, so he was back to humor.

"Dee?"

"Have a nice life, Hyde."

I left him alone by the prattling fountain. And I didn't look back.

6

Swan

My back was still aching. It got worse in the middle of the night. I fluffed my pillows, slept in awkward positions, took as much aspirin as I could without killing myself. Nothing.

"Probably that time of the month," Ade said, with a mouth full of pop tart Saturday morning. Dad was still sleeping, otherwise he'd be chugging coffee and telling us dumb jokes in an effort to alleviate his guilt over staying out late last night, yet again. "Oh hey, I was thinking of wearing leather to the party tonight. Do you think Anton would mind?"

I spread jam on my toast as steadily as I could. "Somehow, I think he'd be into it." I joked because I didn't want Ade to notice the way the knife quivered slightly in my hands.

I still couldn't believe I'd let Ade talk me into going to Anton's party. Anton was the wealthy son of a wealthy businessman whose wealthy wife terrorized people on television once a week. His party would undoubtedly be attended by yet more wealthy people, and me? I was Deanna Davis, daughter of that guy who worked in that warehouse with the boxes. Hedley's funeral had been uncomfortable enough, even before Hyde crashed it. I didn't think I'd be dropped down the rabbit hole again so soon.

"So? What are you gonna wear, Dee?"

"I dunno." I plopped into the rickety chair, terrified for a second, because sometimes it wobbled just enough to make us think it'd collapse on impact. "I haven't even thought about it."

"Of course you haven't." Ade sighed. "OK, OK, I'll check out what I've got and see what I can do."

I had to hand it to her: she was doing a very good impression of someone who did this sort of thing all the time. The girl had her fake ID ready like a gun in a holster. But I knew she was nervous. She had to be. Otherwise, why hound me into going with her?

She knew as well as I did: this wasn't our world.

True to her word, by 8 o'clock that night, as soon as she'd dressed herself, she took it upon herself to dress me. She made me squeeze myself into four of her own dresses because apparently none of my clothes looked chic enough. I finally convinced her to let me wear my loose Catalina tank, if only for the sake of my spinal cord. She still managed to force me into the chiffon skirt she'd bought cheap because it had a hole in it.

Makeup. Hair. This was far too much effort to go through for someone who wasn't dead. We did the requisite "assuring Dad that we'd be home before midnight" thing (as if he'd be home himself) and left around nine.

I rubbed my back against the seat throughout the entire cab ride over the Brooklyn Bridge because it was now not only burning, but itchy. It was probably the tank.

"Well, it always feels fine whenever I wear it," Ade said. She wouldn't switch with me.

Soon we were at Anton's Penthouse on Fifth. A stream of beautifully dressed twenty-somethings were already getting out of limos and walking through the door – a door held open by a bloated man stuffed in a suit and wearing white gloves and a ridiculous hat. He looked both underpaid and wholly dissatisfied with his life.

"This is certainly new," I said, but quietly because I'd suddenly become extraordinarily aware of myself; my unprofessionally teased hair and the black leather bag I'd bought online last summer, the one that had *PLADA* written on it in very plain gold letters. Ade held hers with pride. Normally I wouldn't care, but the blonde haired girl who'd just stepped out of a limo behind us grimaced at me as if she just knew.

I shook my head. "I thought this was a casual event?"

"Can't you tell?" Ade winked. She looked way better than me, as usual, in a plum beaded halter dress she'd spent her last pay check on – instead of something we needed, like say, food.

Into the lobby and up the elevator. The second the doors parted, we were hit by a wave of electro dance punk. The lights were just a little dimmed. Socialites mingled by the open kitchen turned bar, vodka cranberries in hand. Photographers – actual *photographers* – were making their rounds through the loft, gathering groups of gorgeous girls for pictures that would no doubt find their way onto Page Six. Someone gave Ade an approving once-over before floating past us for more mingling – was he an actual designer? I shook my head. How Ade had managed to worm her way into social Asgard was just beyond me.

"This is... kind of amazing," I said, but quietly, because I was surrounded by socialites, and I was sure they'd take my awe as proof that I was some kind of flop from one of the "lesser" boroughs, which I was. I tried to grin instead, but my back still felt like someone was squeezing it from the inside.

Ade disappeared almost immediately. I figured she was headed to where Anton was, except moments later I spotted the birthday boy sitting on a sofa swallowed by girls. Huh. I doubted Ade would have cared even if she could see him. He'd already given her the invite, which meant he was now about as relevant as a used phone card. She was already chatting it up with a group of other gorgeous people by the open bar.

I could see Anton through the crowd, except while most of his girls were clearly vying for his attention, Anton didn't so much as look at them. He was glaring at something straight ahead of him. He was saying something too, but I couldn't hear him over the techno.

That is until he stood up and bellowed, "What did you just say to me?"

The laughter died. The mingling stopped. I saw Ade by the bar, a drink frozen between her lips. All eyes were on Anton. Anton noticed.

"What the hell are you staring at?" He barked, rubbing his neck as if it'd suddenly become too hot. Hesitantly the crowd continued their hobnobbing, most definitely with a new topic of discussion.

I was almost to the bar myself before I heard someone call my name.

"Dee?"

I turned. Oh God. "Hyde?"

"Oh good, you showed!" Hyde's eyes lit up. He sat on the sofa opposite Anton's, which itself was on the other side of a long, expensive-looking crystal coffee table. When he waved me over, I briefly glanced in the direction of the elevator only to find my escape route blocked. Ade wouldn't mind if I made a run for it, would she? But people were looking. At me, at him.

"Damn it," I hissed under my breath and walked over. Hyde smiled as I approached. For one weak moment, I let my eyes slide down his black unbuttoned shirt and open blazer to the white pants sheathing his slender, crossed legs. But then the moment was over. With great effort, I focused on Anton.

"Happy birthday," I said awkwardly to this guy I didn't know. He didn't even respond.

"You look gorgeous, Deanna," said Hyde. His breath hitched when he added, "Absolutely stunning. Ladies can you give me a little room?" Hyde stretched his arm out to me with an eager, boyish smile. I sat on the arm of the sofa instead.

Anton threw his arm around one of the girls as if she were the perfect accessory with which to assert his alpha male aggressiveness.

"Anton, ladies, this is Deanna, my old friend." Hyde gestured to me, too busy being high on life – or drunk on wine – to notice Anton's malice. Wine and high class parties. Ah the privileges of the rich.

"Oh," said one girl with a bored look and, after exchanging glances with two of her friends, they stood up and walked off.

"Did I interrupt something?" I said half-amused, pretending that hadn't stung.

"What? Not at all! My cousin Anton and I were just discussing a few things."

Cousin? Oh right. Anton's father was Hyde's uncle, from his mother's side. I wondered how he felt about his nephew blowing up his major deal to take over the company. It certainly explained Anton's sunny disposition.

"Not really." Anton never took his eyes off Hyde. "Hedley's just been trying his hand at some stand-up comedy." Hyde smirked. "Definitely not a talent you should be banking on."

"Which is why I'm trying my hand at business." Hyde sipped his glass of "water". "And like I said, my first act as head of Hedley Publications will be firing your father. How's that for a punch line?"

My jaw dropped. The few remaining girls on the sofa were already texting. I kept waiting for Hyde to give Anton the "'just kidding, bro!" wink and finger-gun, but he was deathly serious. It was written all over his face, despite the innocent grin.

Anton didn't move, except his hands, which curled into fists so tight his knuckles went pale. "Like I said: stand-up really isn't your thing." The tremor in his hands betrayed his cool tone.

"Look, it's nothing personal." Hyde shrugged. "Over the past few days, I've heard that Edmund Rey was involved in more than a few dirty dealings, to say the least, during Ralph Hedley's time as CEO. Doesn't it make sense that I'd want to clean up my company before moving forward?"

"Hyde!" I started, shocked, but the dull pain started drumming again, this time against the small of my back before moving up my spine.

Anton looked murderous. "What gives you the fucking right–?"

"My dad's will." Hyde's smile was as sharp as a blood-soaked blade. He returned Anton's glare with the same intensity, and more. It was personal. Completely personal. And out of everyone in the room, Hyde was the only one who knew why.

Anton's fists shook. "You fucking–"

"Ah!" As the pain shot through my spine, I sprang to my feet.

"Deanna?" Hyde put away his claws just long enough to worry about me. "Are you OK?" The armor slid off his body piece by piece. He didn't give a second glance to Anton, despite the fact that the birthday boy was more than likely planning his murder. Sliding to the end of the couch, Hyde tried to take my hand, but I pulled it out of his reach.

"Yeah." I shifted my shoulder blades, turning my head slightly so he wouldn't see my uncomfortable grimace. "No, don't worry about me. I, um... In fact I should probably be going."

"Deanna, are you sure nothing's wrong?"

Rather than answer Hyde, I stared out at the terrace behind him, at the bright lights of New York flickering into the loft.

"I'm–" I winced. "I-I'm fine," I said with a shrug, turning away, but even that one shrug hurt – so much that I tripped over someone standing next to me and fell onto the glass table with a horrible crash. It shattered. To say it hurt like hell would have been an understatement. My body ached. My muscles seared. My arms and face bled.

That was the trigger.

From bad to worse in one explosive second. The pain in my back scraped my spine all the way up to the neck, branching out every which way as my veins were leaking acid.

Hyde jumped up and helped me to my feet, but I doubled over. "Deanna! Somebody call 911!"

"No, no! I'm fine! I'm OK. They're just scratches. I'm OK."

Hyde cupped my face. "Deanna, what's going on? Did you drink too much?"

Did I? No, I don't even drink. Not even a sip. So then what was happening? What'd *been* happening? My back had been hurting since Monday. Why? It didn't make any sense.

I shook my head. "No, I'm fine," I said more to myself than to anyone else. "Anton, where's the bathroom?" But Anton just stared. "I'll find it myself."

"Deanna!" called Hyde behind me, but I was already making my way through the crowd. Shannon Dalhousie suddenly flashed in my thoughts, baring it all furiously at Hedley's funeral, her feathers spraying the wind as she fled.

"No, no," I muttered under my breath just before asking someone for bathroom directions. Down the hall to the left. I saw Ade rushing at me from the corner, so I had to move fast. Digging my nails into my palms, I searched for the bathroom, half-blinded by the pain.

Regular back pain. I chanted it under my breath.

But this happens all the time doesn't it? said an annoyingly innocent voice in my head. You've heard the stories. A girl about to sing a solo in front of her entire school. A guy smack in the middle of writing an exam – and then it happens...

"Stop it," I told myself in a harsh whisper.

Always unexpected. Always excruciating. And it all starts with the backaches...

"Hey!" cried one short blonde when I pushed her out of the way to get into the bathroom. A scrawny girl with jewelry that probably cost three times as much as the combined net worth of everything my family owned stopped making out with her boyfriend to glare at me the second I walked in.

"Um, occupied," she said bitchily, folding her arms while her boyfriend just kind of stood there awkwardly.

I grunted and doubled over. With my arms wrapped around my stomach, I leaned against the sink's counter for support. "Get out."

"What?"

"I said get out! *Out!*" It came out louder than I'd expected; the last word scraped my throat raw, but it did the trick. After shooting me a poisonous look, she grabbed her boyfriend's arm and dragged him out the door. I locked it after her.

Check. I had to check.

My stomach pressed against the sink counter. I held the tap so tightly I could feel my blood pumping against the silver. A twisted face in the mirror gaped back at me, alien, bloody, terrified. Beads of sweat slipped down her cheeks and her rounded chin into the sink.

I lifted the tap. Water flowed out. I had to check. I wouldn't find anything anyway so who really cared?

"I'm Deanna Davis." I said it with the resolution of a dying man and lifted up my tank. The fabric slid like sandpaper against my skin. My back burned in the open air. I turned it towards the mirror–

And stifled a scream.

Veins. Dozens, hundreds, millions of them interlocked just beneath the skin. I could count each one. They smoldered when I touched them; streaks of agony shooting straight up into my brain with each ill-placed prod. I laughed. Sharp, desperate, chuckles. How could I not? There were rivulets of blood mapping cities in my back.

This isn't… this can't be…

A strangled whimper caught me by surprise before I realized it'd passed through my lips. "This can't happen." I shut my eyes and repeated it. "This can't happen."

As the pain ripped through my back, my teeth clamped down on my tongue. I dropped my tank as blood filled my mouth. Run. I had to run. I had to get out of here. I stumbled towards the door, but stopped short a step, staring at the knob. Best case scenario, I'd stagger out this door looking wounded, drunk, high or all of the above, and drawing attention to myself was the last thing I needed right now.

Worst case scenario…

I bit my lip. Worst case scenario, it'd happen for everyone to see. Dozens of witnesses, dozens of cell phones snapping pictures and capturing videos, each file internet bound, travelling across cyberspace until everyone who cared and everyone who didn't care knew what I was.

And you know what happens to freaks like you, right? hissed a voice nastier than I thought I'd ever hear in my own head.

"Freaks like *them*!" Freaks in a constant state of silent panic, their fear cowering behind every smile, their eyes flaring at every touch because of who might be touching them and why.

"Oh God!" I covered my mouth to mute the scream as I stumbled back towards the sink. The pain was devastating, like hot pokers burning through my flesh from the inside, tearing out of my skin, trying to grasp the open air. I could feel my shoulder blades shifting and something hard poking through.

"I'm–" An involuntary gasp shuddered through me. I shook my head. "I'm Deanna Dav–" My side hit the counter. I grabbed hold of the tap to keep myself steady and looked up.

A feather. Just one. It lay daintily on the counter, covered in my blood. With a shaky hand, I reached out to touch it – and I managed to, just before my back cracked open like an egg.

They came out all at once, the feathers. It wasn't loud and dramatic, like in those movies where an angel's wings unfurl gloriously out of his back. It was messy, slow – and these sure as hell weren't wings. Blood and feathers slopped down my back like a cape, some draping from my shoulder blades, some sticking out from the rips in my back. I could see my flesh tearing in the mirror.

I staggered forward blindly, choking on the bile in my mouth, and fell over by the base of the toilet. My elbow hit the seat hard. Some of my hair dipped into the water, my body balanced somehow between the seat and the toilet-paper dispenser. I tried to move, but it took every inch of my will power just to keep from shrieking for help and every bone in my body sizzled.

Gradually, achingly, I reached back and touched them. The feathers. They covered the entire surface of my back. For a second I thought I smelled something burning. Flesh. Mine. It probably was.

"Deanna?" It was Ade. I'm sure Hyde was out there too. *I'm fine! I'm just cleaning myself up.* I tried to say it, but my voice shriveled. I sat on the tiled floor, broken, with my hair in the toilet and a cape of feathers pooling on the ground. And even then I still didn't want to believe it. Still tried to stop the truth from sinking in.

"I'm Deanna Davis," I whispered.

I was also a swan.

A Tale

The witch plots to kill the king's children. The witch plots to kill them all.

Cut out their little throats, my lady, and let their necks grin red.

Pluck out their little eyes, my lady, and hear them plead for light before the end.

Rip out their little tongues, my lady, and watch them feast on their own blood.

No, death is too kind, she says, secret whispers seething with hate. Death is too kind. What shall I do?

She transforms them instead – the children. Their backs turn to feathers. Their noses to beaks. Their castle becomes a lake.

They curse the night-star and wait for death.

7

Escape

My tears dripped onto Anton's toilet seat; I didn't even have the will to lift my cheek off it. "Please." I bit my lip. My body ached. "I don't want this. Please, somebody... take this away..."

"Hey! Dee, you in there?" Ade again.

This time I answered, "I'm fine! I'm just cleaning myself up," like I'd meant to before. "These sure are some awful bruises I got myself here," I added, and almost immediately grimaced. I was aiming for "Banged up but Still Cheerful and Thus OK," but somehow gave her "Little House on the Goddamn Prairie" instead.

"You sure you're OK?" Ade asked before someone slammed into the door. It was the shock I needed to snap out of my stupor. My heart leapt into my throat. I could hear the gasps of the scandalized rich from here.

"You think you can do whatever you fucking want?" Anton. "Huh? Like you can take everything, like none it of fucking matters?"

My guess was that Hyde's body was the one currently twitching in pain against the door. One more hit like that and it would bust open.

And then they'd find me.

Quickly but silently, I boosted myself off the toilet and tucked my cape of feathers into my underwear. They tickled my skin.

"Anton stop!" someone cried. I heard yelling, swearing, grunts of pain. Anton and Hyde were really fighting. I had to get out of there soon.

The feathers made my skirt bulge in the back. If I walked out of here right now, would they notice? Would feathers fall out? Would they see them? Take them? And then would they own me?

My stomach clenched. I could be owned.

I placed a hand against my chest to stop it from heaving, tried to shut the tears in and scoured the floor for feathers, scooping up every one I found and flushing them down the toilet.

My phone! I rushed to my purse on the sink counter and rummaged through it for my cell phone. If the world were fair, I'd be able to sneak out of the bathroom while everyone was distracted and get away cleanly. But the world wasn't fair. I needed an escape route, and out of everyone in Anton's penthouse there was only one person I could trust.

I started hitting the keypad.

I Need U!! PlZ get me long jacket. Dusnt Matter Whose. Tell me when u have it! Plz!

I sent the text to Ade and prayed. Two minutes later, my phone vibrated.

Have It. What now?

I'll open the dor. Come in quick.

Hyde and Anton's fight had moved further down the hallway. Their voices sounded more distant, and the door wasn't rattling anymore. Sucking in a breath, I opened the door just a crack. Ade came in fast and locked the door after her. A feather fluttered out from my skirt. The look on her face said it all, but I just didn't have time for words. I grabbed the feminine, asymmetrical trench coat from her hands.

"I need to get out of here," I said, my eyes bulging and wet. "Please, let's get out of here!"

Ade didn't ask any questions. Picking up the feather, she shoved it into the jacket's inner pocket after I threw it on. I clamped my arms around myself.

"Ready?" she whispered. It was the most solemn I'd ever seen her since Mom's death.

"Yeah."

She opened the door and we barged out. I made sure to pull on the hem so that the jacket pressed against my thighs, just in case any feathers leaked out. Hyde was nowhere to be found. Whether he'd been drawn and quartered, or just escorted out, I really couldn't care right now. We headed to the elevator–

"Hey!"

I'd made a wrong turn around a fashion photographer

and bumped into Anton, his face bruised and cut courtesy of Hyde. My fingers lost their grip around the fabric, and I felt something slide down my thigh, but I couldn't think about it. I just had to go.

"Oh, it's you. Hyde's bitch, right?" My blood ran cold as Anton slithered next to me. Every muscle in my body tensed. "You find assholes hot, huh? Then how about–"

Ade kicked him in the shins with her two inch heel. He stumbled back. "Your party sucked ass," she said and shoved me into the elevator. Once the doors closed, I clung to my trench coat, closed my eyes and buried my face in Ade's shoulder.

We were silent the entire ride back to Brooklyn. Ade looked as if she was expending the last of her willpower trying to keep herself from breaking. I, on the other hand, was already in pieces on the dirty cab floor.

We stopped in front of our dilapidated, narrow yellow house, a couple of narrow yellow houses down from a Chinese restaurant. I scooped up the pieces of myself and trudged out the door, waiting while Ade paid the driver.

I could see her out of the corner of my eyes. Her gaze travelled from my bloody face, down my water-logged hair to the stolen trench she knew hid the feathers pressed against my back. I looked like a mess and felt like one too.

"Dee," she started, her voice shaking.

I shut the door behind me. "Just don't."

"But–"

"Seriously, don't say anything. Please." Tightening the jacket around myself, I forced my drying throat to swallow.

Dad was sleeping on the couch. An empty bottle rested on the floor beside him while his hand dangled over the armrest. I could have laughed.

"Deanna, what are you doing?" Ade followed me into the kitchen.

"I'll take care of it," I muttered. Scissors could do it. Or a knife – that big one I always used to slice through chicken bone.

She watched me, wide-eyed, as I rummaged through the drawers for a sharp enough blade. As soon as I grabbed a butcher knife Ade's hand wrapped around my wrist. "What the hell are you thinking?"

I shoved her off. "I said I'll take care of it!"

When she wrestled it out of my grip, all the heat rushed to my head and I lunged at her. She threw the knife in the sink and held me back.

"Stop it!" I struggled against her, my eyes burning. "Please, Ade! Please! *I have to get rid of them*!"

It was the first time in a long time I'd seen my sister cry. It was wrong, unnatural. She pulled me into a desperate hug, gripping me as though I'd dissolve into nothing if she didn't. I did anyway.

"Please," I coughed out, because I was choking on my own tears. "I need a knife. I need to get rid of them." I longed for the kiss of a sharp edge, needing it so desperately that I knew I'd die without it. But who was I kidding? My life was already over.

"They go back in." Ade's breath brushed against my neck. "I heard they go back in on their own. Just... just..." She shook her head. Then, pulling away from me, she gave me a smile that nearly made me forget she was hurting almost as much as I was. "It'll be OK. First we'll get you cleaned up. There are bandages and Band-Aids in the pantry. After that, just go to bed. You'll feel better in the morning. OK?" It was like she was trying to convince herself. But all I wanted was to cut the awfulness away.

"But I need a knife... just give me..."

Ade hugged me again and I fell silent. They go back in on their own. I had to believe it. I had to. I pressed my lips into a thin line, forcing myself to stay on my feet.

"You'd better be right," I whispered. "Please be right."

8

Self-Help

I need a knife.

I woke up thinking it. I was on my stomach, and I opened my eyes to find myself lying on a pile of my feathers. It was itchy, like sleeping on a pile of hay. I pushed myself to my knees, staring at each one, crushed and matted together from my sweat and heat. Instinctively I touched my back. Nothing. I lifted my shirt and checked my back in the mirror. The feathers were all gone from my back? They'd fallen off. Just like that.

So Ade was right. Sort of. But that didn't change anything.

It was like there was an open hole in my chest that nothing could fill. I trudged back to my bed, as limp as a corpse, and scooped all the feathers into my garbage bin, shuddering a bit at each touch. After flushing them down the toilet, it was back to bed.

Sunday passed in a blur, though probably because I spent the majority of it staring at my bedroom's awful blue wallpaper. Ade kept coming in and asking if I was OK. Then Dad came in the afternoon. He hadn't a clue what was going on, but he'd overcome his hangover just long enough to notice that he'd seen only one daughter all day. I said maybe two words to him.

Early Monday morning, I refused to go to work. Called in sick. Ade vouched. She went out for a while after that, and about an hour later dumped a pile of pamphlets on my bed.

"Don't worry. Dad didn't see me with these."

"*So You're a Swan,*" I read, pushing one with my finger. "*Learning to Love Your Feathers?*" I looked up at Ade, unamused. Her already self-conscious smile faltered just a bit.

"I went to the free clinic early today and got them." Her eyes avoided mine.

Must have been really early. No way Ade would want someone thinking she was getting them for herself. I slid the second pamphlet closer. "You picked these up for me?"

"I just thought, you know." She paused. "I mean, it might help. With all the…" When she paused again, I lay back down, throwing my bed sheets over my head. "Come on, Deanna!" Ade shook my arm. "You can't just check out of life. Come on, Dad's worried! Even Ericka's worried."

My sheets flew off me in a second. I sat up and grabbed Ade's wrist. "You didn't tell her, did you?"

"Wha–? No, no, not about what happened!" It was odd seeing Ade panic, though her impression of a startled deer was quite good. "Dad called her and told her you weren't feeling well. So, I mean, of course she's worried."

I rolled my eyes. "Right. Like nouveau riche Ericka Davis gives a shit about any of us anymore."

Ade became very quiet. "Well, you know I give a shit, if that's worth anything."

I remembered how tightly she'd hugged me last night; the tears streaming down her face as she cried almost as loudly as I had. Letting go of her, I stared at the mess of pamphlets on my bed and sighed. "I know. Thanks." With a shaky hand, I took the pamphlet nearest me, flipping it open. "Oh hey, did you know that 'almost three percent of the world's population are or will become swans during their lifetimes'? Huh. Maybe it's time I start picking lottery numbers for Dad." I tried to let some sun slip into my voice for Ade's sake.

She nodded. "Yeah I read that part. Kinda surprising."

"Why?"

She sat on the bed and shrugged. "Three percent. That's still, like, millions. Just never really seems like there are a lot of…"

Again with the pause. I cleared my throat. "You know, I'm somehow doubtful that swans are itching to reveal themselves to the general public. What with the whole 'possibly losing your autonomy forever' part of their genetic make-up."

You mean "our", hissed that bitchy voice in my head.

"Actually, there are totally some celebs and other random famous people coming out as swans now. Like you know that one girl who was in *The Last Happening*? That shitty hipster actress who smirks a lot?"

"Mmm, Julia Something. Wait!" I gasped. "No way."

"Uh-huh. And trust me, there are others. OK, granted, most of those are rumors. Still, I mean, at the very least that proves that the whole swan thing..." Pause. "I mean it's not really something to be ashamed of..." Yet another pause. "Not that I thought that *you* thought of it as something to be ashamed of. And I'm certainly not suggesting that it's normally something that people would think of as something to be ashamed of. Or that it *should* be – I'm totally not assuming or insinuating that by any stretch of the imagination..."

Well, at least she made me laugh. The sound of it seemed to loosen Ade's shoulders. "You're confusing," I told her. "Also, just to note, this is starting to sound like that ridiculous conversation Winnie had with Kayla last month when she caught her making out with Shelly."

"You gonna tell any of them? Your friends, I mean."

What kind of a question was that? I liked my friends just fine, but this was not the kind of information you shared. Period. "No. Never. Dad and Ericka too. They can never know about this."

Neither could Hyde. He'd sent me several hundred texts over the past twenty-four hours. In fact, Hyde was the reason why my phone lay in my dresser drawer, turned off. He could never know about this either. He already had too much on his plate what with the war he'd apparently decided to wage on the Reys. I didn't want him to have to worry about this too...

Worry? I caught myself. No. He could never know because this wasn't any of his business.

Ade nodded. "It's between us then." I noted the hint of pride in her voice while she picked up the *So You're a Swan* pamphlet and started reading. "What are Swan Feathers? How do you get them? How can you tell if you have them?"

"And now I feel like I'm learning about venereal diseases."

"Hey, at least you don't have one of those, right? Bright side."

She gave me a thumbs up. A beat of silence. Then we both cracked up. Ade spent the rest of the morning in my room. We went through all the pamphlets semi-seriously, and while I found them at least partially helpful, deep down I knew there was something I needed to know, something the pamphlets weren't telling me because they were so deadly concerned with sanitizing the blood and guts out of being a swan.

At my request, Ade brought in her half-busted laptop: an old hand-me-down from Ericka that always overheated in a matter of minutes. While Dad was watching TV, we took the opportunity to do some of our own research. There was no greater abyss of random knowledge than the internet, after all.

I clicked and clicked. "Man, I had no idea how many support forums there are dedicated to this stuff: 'The Swan Lake.' 'Be Down with Your Down.'"

Ade grimaced. "This shit is cheesier than the pamphlet."

"'Manifestation can happen at any time, though it typically doesn't appear for the first time in people under the age of ten or over the age of eighteen'," I read and glared, bitterly, when Ade couldn't hide her relieved little sigh. "Manifestation…" I frowned. So there was a name for what happened to me last night. "Freak show" worked just as well.

"'But after that,'" Ade continued reading, "'whether or not your feathers emerge is up to you!'"

"What?" I whispered. "'Intense physical distress and often emotional distress.' Those are the triggers?"

"Hey, that's great! So basically if you just stay calm forever and never get hurt you'll never have to see those things again!" With a big smile, Ade shook me by the shoulder.

Right. Easy enough to do.

Pages and pages of anonymous, personal anecdotes ranging from benign tales to inappropriate tell-alls corroborated the theory. A mother at the funeral of her husband and only child. And this charming little story, as told by *princesssugarbitch2000,* whose boyfriend apparently blew his feathers before he could "blow his load". Classy.

I think I get the idea. We went back to surfing, hoping we'd chance upon another useful forum with maybe less of the load-blowing.

How to Catch a Swan.

My hands froze over the keyboard.

"Don't," warned Ade. She started to take the laptop away, but I pulled it back. I don't know why I clicked the link. Or why I didn't take the first line, "first you need to get them scared," as my cue to get the hell out of there. Pictures of cattle prods and Tasers. I felt every muscle in my face as it contorted in horror. Naked men and women twisted in piles, feathers strewn about as if torn from a pillow.

"Then you rip them out."

"That's enough, Dee." Ade reached for the laptop but I blocked her hand.

"No wait." There was a link. Of course there was. My gag reflexes were already on alert. But I needed to know. Ade must have known it too, because she didn't stop me.

It routed to an uploaded video of a couple of kids standing around in what looked like some pre-teen's bedroom.

The two kids certainly looked around that age. And there was a third; clearly someone had to be holding the camera since it wobbled every few seconds. Sunlight gave the girl's dark hair an almost violet hue before she skipped up to the window and shut the drapes. Her friend flicked the light on before taking his shirt off.

Ade gagged. "Jesus, is this kiddie porn?" I would have laughed at the face she was making except I was making the same one.

I braced myself with my finger on the mouse pad, the cursor poised over the X at the top right of the screen. *Please let this be relevant.*

The girl's friend grinned at the screen and said something in a language I didn't recognize. German, maybe? It sounded German-ish. He turned to show his back, his friend pointing to it unhelpfully with a ridiculous, mugging grin on her face. Next they showed the knife: a tiny, pocket switchblade that popped out of its holster with one clean slice. The boy sat. The girl smiled.

And shoved it into the boy's right thigh.

My hand had clamped the yell before I even realized I'd done it. Blood oozed out of the wound, dribbling down his leg and staining the pink sheets red as he writhed around on the bed. When the girl stuck her finger into the wound, my trigger-finger twitched, but I couldn't close the window. I skipped ahead in the video instead, stopping when I suddenly noticed the sheet of white draping him. I let the video play.

The girl was already wrapping a bandage around the boy's lacerated leg. The good that would do; the white turned red in a matter of seconds. But it was the feathers the girl was after – she eyed them almost hungrily as the boy dragged himself onto his feet.

The camera zoomed in on his back, panning slowly down its length. The feathers were thinner than mine were; long and almost oval with a faint black line stretching up the vein. They came out of his shoulder blades, just like mine had, draping down half his back, but I could see more of them peeking out of the skin itself, all the way down to his underwear. They were matted to his back in one continuous unit.

The girl chattered throughout the close-up in a frighteningly upbeat, tour guide-esque tone as if this were some sort of educational video appropriate for middle schools and bondage rooms everywhere.

It was like pulling a carrot out of the ground from the stalk. She yanked the feathers from the main stems and they all came out together. With a hand, she smoothed the cape over her forearm as it dangled there, limp, luscious and pristine. All the while her friend gazed up at her. The light was gone from his eyes.

"Turn it off," Ade said in a voice so small I figured it was the last time she'd have the energy to tell me. I did.

9

Capture

"Deanna? You OK?" My dad hesitantly opened my bedroom door Tuesday evening and came in with a bouquet of flowers.

"This is a first." I turned over in bed and sat up. "Usually when you feel guilty about something you buy us donuts."

Dad hunched his shoulders and scratched his head, clearly avoiding my eyes. "Well, uh." He cleared his throat. "It's not from me."

"It isn't?"

When Dad tossed the bouquet onto my bed, a white envelope slid out from between two posies. It was from Hyde. Dad stood there awkwardly as I let out an ugly sigh. Hyde had been calling nonstop since Anton's party. So he's moved on to flowers, huh?

It wasn't that I didn't appreciate the concern, but I just wasn't in the mood and there was something particularly vile about a guy who refused to take a hint.

"Thanks Dad," I said and threw the bouquet in the trash. But that was just Tuesday.

"Hey, Dee, someone's stalking you." It was Ade this time, because it was Wednesday morning and Dad was at work. I looked up from the couch and had to throw out my arms quickly when Ade tossed the bouquet of flowers at me.

"Another one?" I flipped over the card. "Ugh."

Ade shrugged. "Well, he's persistent," she said before scouring the cabinets for another bag of chips.

Hyde certainly was: he sent three more bouquets throughout the day and upped the ante with chocolates Thursday morning.

"Wait!" Ade said as I began clicking on my phone. "Don't call him!"

I frowned. "Why? He can't keep doing this."

"Are you mad?" She waved the now empty heart-shaped box of Belgian truffles in my face. "Chocolate! Let's just… wait and see where this thing goes."

We did. The next day brought Adrianna much joy: chocolate boxes, this time carts of them. Giant teddy bears, enough to fill a small storage room. All this capped off with DVDs of all the most popular movies of the past year. Of course, Hyde couldn't have known what I was into so he was probably just covering all the bases.

"Nice to see he's making good use of his dead adoptive father's money." I lay back on the couch while Ade debated which comic book movie to put into our brand new DVD player.

"That kid did always have a soft spot for you, Dee," Dad said once he came back from work and saw our new treasures.

Sure, except his soft spot had the tendency towards creepy obsession.

Friday followed along the same track: cupcakes from that shop on Utica Avenue I used to love as a kid and more flowers – a garden of them. I didn't think he could top himself after the DVDs. That was before the bell rang that evening. Wearily, I crept up to the door while Ade bounced on her feet behind me.

The Mariachi band started playing as soon as I opened the door: "*Deanna, please forgive me! Whatever I've done to offend youuuu!*"

"Has he... *has he lost his goddamn mind*?" After slamming the door, I collapsed against the frame while Ade laughed so hard, she tumbled over the arm of the couch. I could hear the band members shuffling down the front steps, muttering their complaints on the other side. This had gone too far.

I strode to the kitchen and plucked my phone off the table.

"What are you doing?" Ade started, but I put up a hand to silence her before dialing Hyde.

"Deanna! You called! Are you OK?" Incoherent chatting and techno music bleated in the background on the other end of the receiver. And yet I could still hear the elation in his voice.

"You're a psychopath."

"What? I can't hear you," he shouted. "What did you say?"

"*You're a freaking psychopath!*"

"Bad at math?" OK, now he was just shitting me for the fun of it. The little laugh proved it. "Deanna, you *are* OK, right?"

Yes: the "OK" that people usually are after a soul-sucking, traumatizing event. "Yeah," I lied. "But–"

"Good... in that case I'm going to have to call you back. Sorry, it's just that this is a really bad time."

"Excuse me? You've been calling me for days and now suddenly 'Oh sorry, totes busy, ttyl?'"

"I'm at the cover party for *Bella Magazine*."

"Oh, well, *lah-dee-friggin-dah*."

My hand was shaking. I didn't think it was possible for one human being to piss me off so... so *completely*. As if the feathers weren't enough to deal with.

"Deanna," Hyde said, his voice suddenly clearer. The music was harder to hear. Probably found a quieter spot. "I know I don't have the right to say this but... I want you to be careful from now on."

I sat on the arm of my couch and scowled, sorry he couldn't see it. "What the hell do you mean by that?"

He paused. "Anton. He's here too, with his stepmother. And he's being unusually friendly."

Anton. The mere memory of the venom in his drunken snarl as he'd tried to grab me raised the hair on my arms.

"Friendly? After you fired his dad and beat him up and humiliated him at his birthday party?"

"Exactly. And he asked about you."

I swallowed. "So?" I tried for nonchalant and would have gotten there too if it weren't for the tremors in my voice. "Why wouldn't he? The way you were all over me at his party, it's no wonder he's curious."

"I don't like it. I don't know what it means, but, please, just take care of yourself."

I considered his words, considered the quiet panic lacing them. I thought of him standing there in his crisp suit, hobnobbing with the very people he was apparently out to destroy. "My life has nothing to do with yours," I said finally, more for myself, as if it were a promise. "Not anymore. Remember that, because this is the last time I'm going to say it."

"But Dee–"

"And the next time I find a Mariachi Band ready to belt out *your* apology I will castrate them all without hesitation. Then *you*. Got it?"

That was pretty much a conversation-ender.

Live footage of Beatrice Hoffer-Rey and Hyde striding into some Manhattan "it" club told me where Hyde was. This time Beatrice's white-blonde hair was long, draping down the back of her fur coat. Of course, if one had to ask why a human being would wear a fur coat at the end of June in New York, then one was very clearly an unenlightened plebian who had no right to look upon the transcendent radiance that stained the ground after every step Beatrice Hoffer-Rey made on the undeserving asphalt with her snip-toe pumps. Or something like that. I was only half-listening to the reporter's yammering. This was Fashion TV after all.

Said reporter narrated her dramatic entrance while standing a few feet away from the pandemonium. Every time the door opened to let more people in, the music seeped out, shaking the streets. According to the reporter's excitable prattle, Hyde was looking "dapper." Nice to see he was staying busy.

"But one can only guess at the kind of reception the new head of Hedley Publications is currently getting at the cover party, especially from Beatrice, third wife of former executive Edmund Rey, who was fired just this morning."

So Hyde was off to a good start firing Anton's dad and making enemies. But maybe that was a part of his plan. It was his father's company after all. His legacy. His by right the second his dad had bought him for aid space.

There was something more to it, though. The way that Hyde had stared at Anton – and at Edmund, too – at the reception: a gleeful sort of malice. There was something I wasn't getting.

Shaking my head, I turned off the TV. It was not my problem. If Hyde wanted to play out some revenge kamikaze drama, then that was his prerogative.

"Hey, Deanna, I'm going to *Flex* tonight with the girls." Ade put her hair up in a ponytail while coming down the hall. "It'll be fun... you in?"

"No, I'd rather watch people have fun on TV, to be honest."

Ade's shoulders drooped as she sighed. Running her finger down the two foot pile of DVDs on our table, she stopped at one and slipped it out without toppling the rest. "Here, watch this, then. It's about a seventeen year-old drama queen who opts out of life and consequently spends the rest of her days old, sad and alone."

"Is it in 3D?"

Ade threw the DVD at me and left. It was a children's movie – and it *was* in 3D. Or at least it was now. Certainly it wasn't when Hyde and I had first watched it in that busted old movie theatre over on Coney Island Avenue. Afterwards, he'd taken me to one of the best bakeries in New York where I'd had my pick of everything and anything I wanted. Even sixteen year-old Ericka, who hadn't come because she wouldn't be caught dead running around New York with a bunch of kids, had been crazy jealous when I came back home in a sleek, white limo. Hyde had always been a little over the top.

I lay down on the couch, running my finger down the plastic casing of the DVD. Why had he latched on to me so strongly back then? Because he was lonely? He'd told me he didn't have any other friends. He didn't have any parents either, not really. Taken from your home to live with a strange new family you know deep down doesn't really care about you. Caged in a hollow home. Alone.

He was still alone, even now.

But it didn't matter. There was nothing I could do at this point. This was Hyde's battle. And my life had nothing to do with his anymore.

I put in the DVD. Just a few minutes before the penultimate animal sing-along at the end, my phone rang. Ade's number?

"Hello? Ade?"

"Hello, is this... Deanna Davis?"

It was a voice I didn't recognize. Male and adult, though young enough to make me think he was college-aged.

"Who's asking?"

"My name's Paul. I'm the bartender at Stylo."

"OK. Why do you have this phone?" Wasn't Ade at that other club? Plus, it wasn't like her to leave her phone somewhere. The last time she did, she nearly freaked out and we had to walk all the way back to the movie theatre where she'd left it.

"There's a girl here who definitely looks like she needs someone to come get her. Brunette, tall, skinny, pretty." Paltry descriptions, but each one made my heart thud that much louder. "She's barely conscious–"

My hands shook against my lap. I had to make sure. "The phone you're using – does it have a pink leather strap hanging from it?"

"Yeah. She's got your number on speed dial, so I called it."

My heart pounded against my ribcage. Ade, what the hell? This wasn't like her. Ade took pleasure in skirting the law when it came to alcohol, and she usually got away with it. But she was never careless. Passed out in a bar? No. That wasn't Ade.

"Look, if you're her friend or something, you definitely need to come pick her up. She looks sick. I'd call her a cab, but I don't know where she lives and, to be honest, she's so wasted right now I doubt she can remember her own name, let alone an address."

My fingers tightened around my phone. I could feel the metal digging into the joints. "Aren't you supposed to keep that from happening? What the hell kind of bartender are you?"

"I—"

"Forget it. I'm coming. Just don't let anyone near her."

I couldn't tell Dad about Ade, though a part of me wanted to. He was blissfully ignorant of Ade's nightlife, a feat that she worked diligently to achieve. He wasn't the best father, but if he knew Ade was passing out at clubs, he'd find a way to keep us padlocked indoors for good. I had to keep this to myself. I owed that to her. He was out anyway, at his friend's for another poker night.

I checked my watch. Eleven, almost on the dot. Dad usually came home drunk at midnight. That didn't leave me much time. Hopefully, I'd be back with Ade before he stumbled in.

On the way, I thought of a million different scenarios that might have explained how she ended up drunk in some random bar at night alone, when she was supposed to be (less) drunk in another random bar at night surrounded by her horde of friends. What the hell had happened? Regardless, I wasn't about to let Ade get manhandled by some assholes.

A subway trip and a short taxi drive took me close to Chrystie Street on the Lower East Side. Ade was definitely going to have to pay me back for the fare. I walked the rest of the way to Stylo. It definitely looked shoddy from the outside – certainly not as fancy as the pretentious French name would suggest. There were no windows in the red brick, just the building's number, 297, in big letters shaded under a shabby red awning. The door was old and decaying, the paint rusting off its surface in sheets of moldy brown. I couldn't see anything through its tiny window; just the crinkled, gaudy curtain draped over the glass from the inside, off-white and dirty as if it'd been used to clean a rusted bathtub decades ago.

Sucking in a breath, I went inside. There wasn't even anyone checking IDs. I'd never actually been inside a bar before. Unlike Ade, I actually feared the long arm of the law when it came to the legal drinking age. I could barely tolerate the taste of beer anyway, which, of course, made me the designated loser in my already lower-rung social circle at school.

I looked around. The place had a kind of musty smell with a sharp coat of alcohol layering the mix, a shot to the senses. It was almost as dark inside as it was outside, but the dim lights were certainly bright enough to light up the burlesque dancers writhing on stage.

Wait, what?

"Ade, what the hell?" I whispered, gaping. Ade in a burlesque house? Was this some new fetish of hers? Except, I'd never seen her express an iota of interest in the corseted arts. But more importantly, I couldn't find her anywhere.

"Excuse me?" I said once I'd walked up to the bar.

The bartender barely spared me half a glance as he dried off glasses. "ID."

"What?"

"ID."

Crap. I clutched the cinched tote bag Ericka had gotten me for my last birthday. "Uh... I'm actually... under-age. Kinda." Long arm of the law.

"Oh," he said. "Get out."

"Wait, you're the guy who called me a little while ago, right? About my sister? I've only come to pick her up, that's it! Once I get her, I'm gone, I swear."

That got his attention. He stared at me, the cloth in his hand motionless against the wineglass he'd been wiping. Then, with a quick cough to clear his throat, he set it down and picked up another one.

"Oh?" He slid right back into the whole "talking to me without looking at me" thing, and though it wasn't any less annoying than before, this time was different. The way his eyes seemed less focused, his hands more jittery... Something was off here.

"Hey, where is she?" I tried to force his gaze to me. "She didn't leave with anyone, did she? What the hell! Didn't I tell you not to let anyone near her?"

"Relax." He scratched the modestly-sized silver bead embedded in his left brow. "She's upstairs in the back. She kept falling off the stool so I let her sleep in one of the empty VIP rooms on the second floor. No one else is in there."

VIP rooms. I could see them from down here, behind the railings. The bartender tossed a silver key onto the table. "Here, take it. It's the first room on the right hand side, just around the corner."

After one more judgmental glare, I silently took the key and headed upstairs. To be so wasted she needed her own private room to detox? It just wasn't like Ade.

My fingers twitched – so violently, I nearly dropped the key. I stopped half way up the stairs, peering at the rooms, not sure why I suddenly felt flushed. Something was wrong.

Almost instinctively, I whipped around, but there was no one behind me. So then why was my heart pounding? What was this? The hairs on my arms rose off the gooseflesh and I half-expected someone to jump out at me. But I was on a staircase – where would they possibly come from? The ceiling?

Stop being stupid. Go find Ade.

Shaking it off, I rushed over to the VIP room, first room on the right-hand side, just around the corner, and opened the door.

The girl lying half-conscious on the velvet couch next to the giant metal cage in the wall was not Adrianna. It wasn't the blonde hair that gave her away. It was the feathers.

"What–?"

An arm wrapped around my waist at the same time the cloth smothered my nose and mouth. I was out in seconds.

10

Caged

Sounds of laughter. Men were laughing. I struggled to pry apart my eyelids. Soft fiber brushed my fingers, smothered my face. I slid my legs across it, slow and sluggish, and though it burned my skin, I still couldn't figure out what it was or where I was. My muscles ached.

"What? You're not having fun?"

Were they talking to me?

Somewhere there was a frail whimper. Female. Young. Scared.

Open your eyes, I commanded myself, to no avail. My lashes were practically glued shut.

"What about her, guys?"

I felt a hand running up my legs, tugging at the hem of my shorts. If I could have died just then to escape the slick of that sweaty, grimy hand, I would have. I wanted to run instead, but it wasn't an option. My muscles weren't responding fast enough.

"No, not yet." Youthful voices: college-going, polo-playing, upstanding-young-man-chatting-with-you-at-a-bus-stop voices. The kind you didn't think twice about.

Somehow, I managed to slowly drag myself across the floor far enough to free myself from his grip, though he probably just let go on his own accord. That was all I could manage. I lay flat against the ground with my heart pounding in my ears.

What happened? What happened? Think, think, think Deanna! Each breath nicked my chest from the inside.

That cloth... the fabric against my lips, the sweet scent, a lung full of it.

They'd drugged me.

What did they give me? Why were they doing this to me?

What were they *going* to do to me?

The girl screamed. That was the shot I needed to finally pry my eyes apart. I saw the red nylon first. It was a rug. It was too dark. A wooden leg of a table. A set of car keys on the floor. A single leather pump.

Rasping for air, I flopped onto my back. I could see them now, all three men. Young, like their voices. Well-built. Well-dressed too: a trio of spoiled bastards. One of them winked at me.

"All right, Joe, it's my turn. Get back."

Two of them crowded around a girl who sat on a velvet couch as black as her underwear. Black panda eyes upturned to the ceiling, she blew strands of blonde hair off her face, wet from her saliva, with each scrape of breath she exhaled. Pale, thick fingers tangled themselves in the feathers draping her back.

"No, stop." I'd slurred the words so badly, they came out nonsense. "Leave her alone." Too weak, this time. They didn't hear me. Or maybe they didn't care.

The girl was crying as she boosted herself onto her knees. She had lacerations all up her arms, shallow cuts, fresh wounds. And yet she still looked healthy enough to stand up, maybe even run. Why wasn't she? Why did she simply sit there, haggard, bloody, but obedient?

The tallest of the men, a redhead, sidled up to her and lifted her chin with a finger. The look she returned was not loving, not even civil. Just hollow. Ready. My stomach heaved.

Oh God. Tears trickled down the side of my face and down my ears, sinking between the carpet fibers. Ade... Dad... Ericka...

He draped her feather robe across his shoulder. She didn't complain when he started kissing her, but I could see it on her face: a suffocating hollowness. It was etched into her body, her movements. The way she put a hand almost dutifully on his arm, the way her back arched almost as if it knew it should. It was a perfect mimicry of a girl kissing her lover, except the details were all wrong. Everything was wrong. She didn't have a choice.

I wouldn't have a choice either.

I turned away when his hands started to move down her stomach, but I needn't have. One of the boys blocked them from my view. He knelt next to me.

"Don't worry, baby." His dark, slicked-back hair was almost as greasy as the smile he gave me as he knelt. "She isn't doing anything we haven't paid her to do." If only the sound of my heart thudding against my brain was loud enough to shut out the moaning. Slick Hair turned to the others. "I don't get it though. Why her? She looks harmless enough." He paused. "Payback?"

"Dude, who cares? When a piece of ass falls into your lap, you don't whine about it, bro," said one I couldn't see. He was behind me. "Just do what *you* were paid to do."

Oh God. I raised my right arm, but it wasn't mine anymore, not really. The drug was starting to wear off, but not fast enough. A sloppy, random swing drove my hand into the side of the table. Slick Hair grabbed it, crushing it as if it weren't already searing in pain. He yanked me onto my stomach.

"No, no…" My tongue tasted the nylon carpet as I coughed out the words. I clenched everything, pressing my forehead against the floor, hoping the pain would dull everything. But I still felt my shirt sliding up my back, still screamed when the blade slid across it. It was a sharp, shallow cut, and apparently, for me, that was all it took. Feathers shifted just beneath the skin, unfolding and unraveling, before breaking through, slipping down from my shoulder blades, cascading down my back. They grew like weeds; thin, prickly. I didn't smell blood this time, but it was no less excruciating. My feathers were out. The young man stroked them. I shuddered. I wriggled and writhed to get his fingers off me and failed.

It was going to happen to me. That awful thing they only talked about in hushed voices. It was going to happen to me. His hand pressed against the small of my back and I prayed he'd simply kill me instead.

Somebody...

The door opened. Silence.

"Hey," said Slick Hair, but he was cut off.

"Get out."

It was Anton. *Anton?*

"I said, get out. This is my room now." There was a cool chill in Anton's voice as he strode inside clad in the three-button charcoal suit and black tie he'd probably worn to the cover party. "You're done," he said. "Leave the keys on the table."

The three muttering boys packed out of the room, one of them tossing a pair of keys onto the table next to me before slamming the door behind him. It clattered against the glass surface.

Anton stepped around my feet over to the couch and gave the blonde girl her feathers. It was incredible. The second she touched her feather robe again, the second she held it against her chest it fell apart. Feathers burst into a pile on the ground, a stream of down. And then the light returned to her eyes. She was herself again.

"Anton?" I coughed.

"She's fine," Anton said. "Once you get your feathers back, you're your own boss again. They won't go back in. But swans'll always grow more." He turned to the girl. "You can go now."

She grabbed her lost shoe and left. She was her own boss, but she obeyed him anyway. It didn't make sense. She was here because she'd been paid. But this was a burlesque club.

Unless it wasn't.

"Swan... parlor?" I whispered, tucking my hands under me, hoping I had enough energy to boost myself up.

"Yeah, that's right," replied Anton, as the swan closed the door behind her. "Stylo's one of a few in New York."

He was too calm. How did he know I was here? Where was Ade? As soon as I started my struggle to sit up, Anton knelt beside me and helped me the rest of the way.

"What's going on?" I gazed at him sideways, but that was mostly because my head was still throbbing. "Those guys–"

"Drugged you," answered Anton, simply.

My blood ran cold.

"Go on," he whispered, his breath hot against my ear. "Ask me why."

My fingers grasped for the table. I was almost on my knees when Anton picked me up by the stomach and flopped me onto his shoulders. I screamed, screamed so loud it could have torn my larynx to shreds. No one came. I knew no one would. Anton slipped Ade's phone out of his jacket pocket with one hand and waved it in my face. The men. The bartender too. Anton had paid them all.

Slipping the phone back into his pocket, he swiped the keys off the table and strode over to the cage in the wall. My prison. He tossed me inside and shut the metal door in my face.

"What are you doing?" I clung to the iron bars, shaking and shrieking. "What are you doing? Let me out!"

Anton took a seat over by the couch and, with his foot, brushed aside the pile of feathers left behind by the swan. "I will." He crossed his legs. "But not yet."

I swallowed tears with each gasp. "Why? What are you going to do to me? How did you even get my sister's phone?"

"It's easy enough to have someone followed." My fingers curled as Anton took out Ade's phone and turned it around in his hand, considering it like a work of art. "You know, I couldn't believe it when I saw you leave my loft. That feather you left behind."

Blood drained from my face. So he'd noticed.

"It was yours. Who else's could it have been? The look on your face pretty much said it all."

He dropped the phone back into his pocket. The iron bars slid against my sweaty palms.

"Swans." He laughed, shaking his head. "To some people they're irresistible. Ralph Hedley caught one. New York has cages of them working in the shadows, just like every other city in the world. From the brothels to the streets. Been that way for as long as swans have existed." Anton turned to the wall opposite me. It was carved into dark, interweaving boxes, dimly lit by little candles enclosed in amber glass. He was too busy admiring the flickering flames to acknowledge my screaming. "Do you have any idea why?"

I rattled the cage. "Please let me out! *Let me out!*"

Anton sighed. "Regular girls'll give you what you need, whether it's your garden variety sex, or something darker."

That's when he finally looked at me, his blue eyes sanding my skin.

"But swans are different. It's the helplessness, the fact that once you have their feathers, you are in complete control of them." When he licked his bottom lip, I knew he was speaking from experience. "It's not a Simon Says type of deal, of course. 'Stand up, sit down,' no, it's not as if they'll obey my *every* command. But that's not what I want from them. It's the loyalty. Pure and absolute. It's not just that you own them, but that they understand themselves *only* as being owned by you. Once you take a swan's feathers, they belong to you completely and they know it. After that there's nothing the swan can do except give you all of them. Power, Deanna. Swan parlors, brothels and everything in between. Power is what they sell."

"So if it's power you want, why not come over here and get it, you asshole."

Not the smartest taunt, I know. My brain might have been completely fried by now, but I knew that I couldn't let him keep me in this cage.

Wait till he opens it. I repeated the words like a mantra, my grip like a vice on the bars. Once he opened the door, I could knock him out and take off. My body was still sluggish, but I didn't need to be on top form. Just one blind swing – or I could scratch his face. Put out an eye, blind him, then tackle him. Anything, anything. Just open the cage...

"Come on, Deanna, don't be ridiculous. I don't want your feathers." Once again, Anton laughed. "I already own you."

"W-what?"

He got off the couch and sat on the table, facing me. "Most swans will do whatever it takes to keep their identities hidden. They know the cost of a leaked secret. I take it you're the same. I know you're a swan. I can do a lot with that information."

My throat closed up as he leaned over.

"There are plenty of brothels that would love a pretty girl like you. Lovely skin. Hair that curls around your fingers. I'd earn a shitload of cash selling you to traffickers."

Somehow I was on my feet. My muscles were working overtime, but they kept me upright. My back pressed against the brick wall behind me as I struggled to keep my balance.

"Hey, human trafficking is a worldwide multi-billion dollar business, you know. But when they find swans like you... boy, it's like winning the jackpot, isn't it?"

Tears blurred my vision, but I could tell he was walking towards me. I pressed my back harder against the wall, and one insane part of me actually believed that if I tried hard enough, I could go through it and fly away.

"Do you know what they'll do to you, Deanna?" His fingers curled around the bars, his eyes gray with an almost gleeful malice. "They'll drug you. Rape you. They'll pass your feathers around, force you to have sex with fifty men a day, maybe more. They'll put you in cages smaller than this and take turns."

"Stop it!" I huddled in a corner, my stomach clenched, my arms tight around my knees. This wasn't happening. It couldn't be happening. It couldn't be. "Stop it! Please, please just shut up! Let me go, oh God let me go! Please!"

"Did you like how it felt? When those guys drugged you? When they had their hands on you? Did you like the feel of it, Deanna? The way they touched your back, your feathers?"

"Please..." I shook my head. "My dad...my sister... they'll be worried about me...please, please..."

"Oh, right. You want to go back home?" Anton leaned against the cage. "You don't want that kind of life, do you? No, you're too sweet for that. Right?"

Biting my lip, I forced myself to look at him, to look him square in the eyes. I hated every molecule of him. "What do you want from me?"

"Simple. I want you to destroy Hyde Hedley."

An awful, sour taste slopped down my throat as I swallowed hard. "What?"

"Today, the new head of Hedley Publications fired my father. But that's not all." He gritted his teeth. "That asshole has something on my dad. Something that could ruin him. He hinted as much at my party.

He hasn't told anyone yet. Maybe he's still working on getting the proof, but I can't guarantee he'll keep his mouth shut once he does. I'm not old money, Deanna. If my dad loses his job, we could lose everything." As if by instinct, he clutched his suit like a security blanket. "I don't know what the hell he has against my father, or what he's trying to get, but I don't have the luxury to care. And you: you're an old friend of his, aren't you? He said it himself at my party. He cares about you."

The flowers, the Mariachi Band. The thousands of messages he left on my cell phone needing to know that I was OK. "No, that was…that was years ago. I don't even know him, now. Hyde isn't my… I'm just… I'm just–"

"Close enough to Hyde to sabotage him." Anton smiled. "Ralph Hedley may have given his son the reins of his company, but the board still has the option to replace him with his legal guardian, which if I'm not mistaken is presently his uncle – my father. They're already a little insecure about Hedley giving his legacy to a nineteen year-old. But it's in his will. Not to mention they're all well aware of how smart that bastard is." For a moment, Anton looked a little jealous. He shook it off. "But the one thing the board doesn't need right now is a scandal. Not while they're desperately trying to keep the Colemans from bolting."

"C-Colemans?"

"The Coleman family. Come on, you know, Colemans? 'Family starts at the home' Colemans?"

I recognized the slogan, but only because it came at the end of countless tacky commercials with smiling white nuclear families hanging out on their new patio sets or watching a movie on their new entertainment system – all courtesy of Colemans Department Store.

"The Coleman image is all about family values and wholesomeness and all that other bullshit they peddle to fatties in the Heartland. Ralph Hedley almost lost them once, what with all the rumors about his wife, but he managed to keep them on board by pretending he had a family of his own."

Hyde.

"But Hedley's funeral brought those rumors back to the fore, thanks to that swan. The Colemans might ditch after all. That's a lot of money gone poof."

I swallowed carefully, my throat dry from screaming. "So?"

"Hyde doesn't trust me enough to let me manipulate him, but you? He'll let his guard down around you. All you need to do is set him up for the mother of all falls. Something publically humiliating. Something that'll give the Colemans the incentive to finally leave for good. Then the board'll see just what a waste of skin he is; what a goddamned liability he is."

Me? Sabotage Hyde? I could feel the feathers crushed between my back and the wall and for a moment I wondered what it would feel like to have countless hands ripping them off me. I just wanted to go home. I wanted to be back in my bed again, to have a normal life. Hyde didn't need some stupid company. What did it matter if he lost control of it or not? Me or Hyde. When I really thought about it, there was no contest.

So then why did my chest ache at the thought of it?

Whenever we were kids, Hyde's eyes would light up at the sight of me. They still did.

"When I asked him at the party, he told me you wanted nothing to do with him anymore. He also told me he was more than happy to oblige, but I think we both know that isn't true." Anton flashed a devil grin. "Get close to him. Real close. Then ruin him. Simple as that."

"We don't need to do this." I heard myself say the words I couldn't quite believe were mine. "If you just talk to Hyde... make him see reason – I could help you do it. Maybe he'll give your dad his job back."

Anton went deathly silent. "Oh. Oh. Just make him see reason. Right! That'll solve everything! You think so? You fucking think so?" Anton pushed off the cage and started pacing before kicking it with his leather shoe. "God, you know what? Maybe I should sell you right now. Right this fucking second. Would you like that? Huh?"

"No." I shuddered violently.

"When they're done with you they'll throw your broken goddamn body in a gutter like trash. Do you want that? Huh?"

"No, please, no!" *He's crazy. He's a psychopath*! But he was right. He didn't need my feathers. He already owned me.

"Hyde hates me. He hates my dad, and he'd love nothing more than to see us all on the fucking streets tap-dancing for a Denny's coupon. No. You do what I say. Do what I say and don't you dare tell anyone about this or I will have you on the first boat to Russia. And maybe I'll destroy your family too. If I'm bored." He swiped the keys off the table. "Do you hear me? *Do you?*"

Crying openly now, I nodded, burying my head in my knees until the sound of jangling keys made me lift it again. Anton was dangling them in front of me, teasing me with the promise of freedom. I let a few short breaths rake my throat before lunging for them, but the moment I did, he threw them back on the table.

"Anyway, even if you were to tell someone, it's not like anyone would take you seriously. And if they did? There are benefits to wealth, Deanna. You'd be surprised how fast lips close at the thought of an inflated bank account. As head of Hedley Publications, Hyde will be invited to hundreds of events in Manhattan. Plenty of opportunities for public disgrace. Find a way to make it happen and fast. I don't need to tell you what'll happen to you if you don't."

Straightening his suit and tie, he strode up to the door, calm and business-like, because in his world that's all this was: business.

"Wait!" I scrambled to my knees. "Wait, let me out!"

"Don't worry. One of the girls will. In an hour or so." He turned, leaning against the door frame with his Armani-sheathed shoulder. "Think of this as an opportunity to mull over what I've said." He grinned again. "I'll be seeing you, Deanna."

Then the door shut behind him and I was alone.

11

Desperate

The house was empty when I got home. I immediately headed for the shower. Water washed off the sweat and oil. Beads of it trickled down my hair, neck and back – a back bruised and sore, but bare: my feathers lay scattered in the custom-made steel cage built into Stylo's VIP room. My thoughts were there too, just as scattered, fragments of touches and words and sights bubbling up and dissipating with the steam.

I turned the shower nozzle to make it hotter. The water couldn't wash away the feel of hands, the thought of hands, the threat of hands. I made it hotter and hotter so that it would. It burned. I yelped and stepped out of the line of fire, twisting the nozzle, turning the shower cold. From one extreme to another. Neither helped. Crouching in the corner of the tub, I cried.

I thought of crying myself to sleep, but I realized I'd have to stop crying once my family came home. I couldn't tell anyone. But for now I cried and cried, and tried to wash it all away.

My family still hadn't come home by the time I went to sleep. That night I had a series of dreams that were more terrible than the ones I'd had after my mother died. I dreamt of faceless men tearing me apart from the outside in and the inside out. I dreamt of my feathers drenched in blood and sweat. I dreamt of living a life of hollow eyes and vacant smiles that should have been screams.

"Deanna?" Ade shook me so hard my head nearly came off my neck. For a second, I didn't know who she was. "Are you OK?"

My dad was in the doorway, face ashen, eyes sunken and booze-binge-red. I checked my alarm clock. Three in the morning. That must have been some world class horror movie-style screaming if it'd been enough to spook him awake.

"I'm OK," I rasped and turned on my side. "I'm fine, sorry. Just a bad dream." Pulling the covers over my head was my way of telling them to go away. Not that I wanted them to. More than anything I wanted that comfort, that familiarity. I wanted Dad to rub my forehead, or Ade to climb into bed with me like when we were small and I would cry because I was afraid of the dark. The warmth of an embrace that made me feel safe – that was the kind of touch I wanted.

But if I let my guard down, would I spill everything? Ade and Dad would not stand by and let Anton get away scot-free. They'd confront him. They'd do whatever they could: hire whatever shitty lawyer they could afford to try in vain to take the Reys down, or maybe pull a Shannon Dalhousie and protest naked at the next cover party. If I told them what happened, they'd do something to let Anton know that they knew – and *I* knew what would happen next.

Anton's words haunted me. *You'd be surprised how fast lips close at the thought of an inflated bank account.*

He'd find me. He'd find me, and he'd ruin my family. And me.

"This is ridiculous," I whispered to myself after Ade and Dad had piled out of my room and shut the door behind them. There had to be some loophole, some way to nail Anton to the wall and leave him there bleeding and pleading for forgiveness.

I could go to the police. But with what evidence? If Anton had thought far enough to pay the employees of Stylo to help him set the stage for his twisted power play, then he certainly would have thought far enough to pay for their silence. Plus there was no telling just how many upstanding members of New York's law enforcement were open to bribes from the filthy rich. He'd said as much himself. I couldn't take that chance.

But what if I went to Hyde? He had next to unlimited money and resources, and I knew he'd destroy Anton before he let him destroy me. Really, how much would it even cost to have Anton shipped off to the coal mines in Serbia anyway? He'd be doing his country a favor.

Anton had warned about me telling anyone, but how would he possibly know? Or did the idle rich have "eyes everywhere"?

Under any other circumstances I would have laughed at the Skull and Bones foolishness of it all, but right now, as I huddled under my bed sheets in the dark, the thought of being under constant surveillance seemed a little too plausible. Maybe he did have eyes everywhere. How would I know otherwise?

And did I want to risk finding out?

If I told Hyde what happened, how long would it take for him to get rid of Anton? How long would it take for Anton to find out what Hyde was planning?

How long would it take to drug me up and throw me in a Russian brothel?

This whole thing was fucked up. All of it. *All of it.*

I shoved my arms underneath my pillow and clutched it to my face. I tried to muffle each pathetic whimper with the cheap fabric, but it was a struggle. *Somebody please... please help me.*

No one could.

The words repeated in my head, again and again, refusing to let me go back to sleep. I didn't think I could anyway. I stood up and looked at myself. Eyes more sunken than my father's, dry sickly skin and cracked lips. I checked my back. It was instinct now. Nothing. I thought I'd grow more because of the nightmares. What, did they not qualify as a – what was the term they used in the brochure – psychic and/or physical stressor? Stressant?

I opened my drawer, found the brochures and scoured all of them. Stressor or stressant? Physical or physiological? Might as well know. Why not learn about myself? They were all talking about me, after all. Swans. All these sheets of paper with lines of ink intended to tell me what it meant to be a swan. To educate me.

With all of them in my hands, I collapsed onto the ground. Do you know that almost three percent of the world's population are or will become swans during their lifetimes? Now I did. Do you know how it feels at the precise moment your languid body crashes onto the surface of a hard stone floor after you've been thrown into a cage made especially for not-quite-human things like you? Yes, that too. But none of the brochures would tell me anything about it.

I was shaking. I tore each brochure to pieces, even the scraps, and left them scattered in a pile in front of me. I could still feel their hands – Slick Hair and Anton. I couldn't forget their eyes on me. I couldn't forget that blonde guy, or what he did to the swan, or her tiny smile of pleasure that somehow matched her dead eyes perfectly. Would I look like that too? If I delivered Hyde to Anton on a silver platter would he still sell me? Or would he take me for himself?

My head throbbed. Strange, wheezing noises slipped in and out of my lips.

Mom. What would she think if she could see me, if she knew what was happening to me? She'd have probably already murdered Anton. A single shot to the chest followed by a life sentence carried out with no regrets. If only I had half her strength.

But there was something I could do. Something I needed to do – and now.

I called Hyde.

He was obviously sleeping. I got the answering machine twice. I called for a third time, and on the second ring–

"Hello?"

I hung up. I knew it was stupid. But I couldn't take the sound of his voice, not yet. I texted him instead.

Meet me at my place in 1 hour. Please. I need you. – Dee.

I waited on my doorstep, because I didn't want Hyde to knock on the door and wake up my family. It was late. Way late. Too late to be sitting around outside. If Dad somehow managed to wake up, and if he found me out here with some guy, he'd freak out so bad he'd probably ground me out of spite.

It was stupid, and I wasn't in my right mind, but I needed to see him. I needed to.

Immediately, I did a periphery sweep of the area from where I sat – the seventh time since sitting down. There was still no one around – just me and some sparse traffic.

My nerves were shot nonetheless.

Every shadow movement made my muscles seize up. I kept expecting him to slither out from behind a lamppost – Anton. Him, or Slick Hair, or any other thug who had pockets to line.

Stop. Don't let Anton get to you. That was what I'd told myself a thousand times while sitting here. And yet here I was, waiting alone outside in the middle of the night, completely vulnerable.

I laughed as I thought of the torn brochures I'd left on the floor. I couldn't let Anton get to me. But then, obviously he already had. I was barely sane. Being here was proof enough.

I held my head in my hands for a long time.

"Deanna?"

I almost shrieked, but snapped my lips shut before the sound could leak out. Don't wake Dad and Ade. Still, the bastard had come out of nowhere. There wasn't even a car in sight. I pressed a hand against my heart and attempted, feebly, to act natural, but he must have noticed I was spooked.

"You OK?" Hyde asked in a soft voice as he walked up the steps, calmly. He bent over me, extending a hand that for one second looked frighteningly large and alien.

Stop being stupid. It's just Hyde. I still flinched when he touched my shoulder. He must have noticed because he backed off immediately.

When I didn't respond, Hyde sighed. "Deanna, are you OK?" he repeated. Kindly. Gently. It just made everything unnecessarily harder.

I shrugged. "Everyone keeps asking me that."

He sat down next to me and lifted his hand again, this time tentatively, as if asking permission. When I did nothing, he made a move anyway, to brush my hair over my shoulder. I blocked his hand with mine.

"Dee, not everyone's lucky enough to have people in their lives who genuinely care about them," he said quietly, lowering his hand.

"I suppose." I stared at the narrow yellow houses on the other side of the street, shrouded in darkness, waiting for a light to flick on, a door to creak. For Anton to step out.

God, what am I doing out here? Hyde was no doubt wondering the same thing, and yet he simply waited, watching me patiently, keeping his distance though he was still close enough to touch. So I did. I touched him. My hands ran over his pullover at his waist. It was soft, probably cashmere: the benefits of inheriting your father's business. And pissing off the sons of his employees to the point where they would be willing to threaten and terrorize innocent people who have nothing at all to do with any of this mess? That was probably just for the thrill of it. Too bad he couldn't be bothered to consider the consequences, but then nobody ever cares about the collateral damage, do they?

"Deanna?"

I blinked and realized that my fingers were clutching the fabric. Hard. I was actually surprised my nails hadn't torn through it.

Hyde detangled my fingers from his shirt and looked me up and down, once, from head to toe. Not like the guys at Stylo. No, there was nothing disgusting about his gaze, nothing licentious. He was noting everything – my bloodshot eyes, maybe, or the stone-hardness of my face. He must have figured out by now that something had happened.

Hesitantly, nervously, he touched my cheek. It was soft. Pleasant, so much more pleasant than what I'd felt hours ago. "What's going on with you?" he said, this time with more urgency. "Why did you ask me to meet you here?"

"Why did you come?"

"What?"

I'd asked it before I could stop myself. But I couldn't get Anton's words out of my head. "I texted you at half-past three in the morning, asking you randomly to meet me at my place and you came running." I held his hand to my face and watched him stare at me. "Why?"

Hyde lowered his head. "Deanna…"

"DVDs, cupcakes, bands, flowers, teddy bears. Same as when we were kids. Ever since you came back I keep remembering that time you climbed up a tree to get my scarf. You nearly killed yourself. Why?"

Hyde shrugged, but as if he couldn't help himself, he let a harmless touch of mischief into his expression, his lips curving just a little. I felt something stir in the pit of my stomach when he answered, "I guess I like you."

He always reminded me of a fox when he looked at me like that. It was his eyes just as much as the smile. Now, more than ever, now that we weren't kids anymore, it did something to me.

Of course, I knew about half of it was bravado. It was a little sad, really, that part of his fox grin was so clearly meant to distract me from the earlier, sheepish downturn of his eyes.

And yet the something in the pit of my stomach stirred nonetheless.

"You like me. That much?" I said carefully, my heart beating rapidly because I could hear Anton laughing at me. "Why? Why that much? What is it about me... Actually, you know what?" I flung his hand off my face. "No, it doesn't make sense. At all. We were kids the last time you saw me, Hyde. How the hell are you going to come back a decade later and be all sending me gifts and whatever the hell? It's ridiculous. Hyde, it doesn't make any *sense*."

"Why not? I like you." He'd said it so simply that I wanted to punch him.

"But *why*?"

I had to know. It was why I came, after all. It was why I needed to see him. What was it about me – and about him – that made him care enough to make me a target?

Hyde was quiet for a long time, long enough to make me nervous. Then he sighed. "All those years when I was away. When I was..." He left the next words hanging from his tongue, waiting for that last breath to push them over the edge. He swallowed it instead. When he pressed together his lips, it was like he was struggling with something within himself. "When I was away," he repeated finally, rubbing the skin beneath his shirt collar absently, "all I could think about were the old days. You probably think that sounds insane, but it's true. I thought about you all the time."

I looked away. "Why me?"

"You just kept popping up in my head. Smiling. Thinking about you reminded me of the way things used to be. Happy, I guess. Peaceful. It helped me get through it. Yeah." He lowered his gaze. "I like to think that it was you keeping me alive all those years."

I shook my head, trying to understand. "Keep you alive… But why would you…?"

He looked at me. For a moment, it seemed as though he wanted to tell me millions of things at once. I could see the stories in his eyes. Too many to count. But with a blink they were gone. His lips spread into an easy smile. "What can I say? Paris was hell. Don't let their delectable wines fool you."

He was lying again, and so plainly. In that one moment I wondered if he'd ever even set foot in France.

He touched my chin with a finger. It felt nice. Too nice.

"What does it matter why I like you, Dee? I do. I…" He stopped and suddenly both his hands were pressed against the sides of my face. "When I came here, I knew it was my chance to finally see you again. But I was scared. I didn't know whether you'd want to see *me*… or whether you'd even remember me. I was terrified."

Warm. His hands were warm. Not hot and vile like Anton's. Warm and sweet.

"Mom is gone. Dad is gone. I have no one but lawyers and enemies and memories. I'm not asking anything from you, Deanna. I just… I wanted to think that we could be friends again."

Warm and sweet. The difference was almost staggering. Overwhelming.

I was starting to forget what their touches had felt like. And Hyde... Hyde was looking at me so earnestly. And when the lights flickered across his face, when his lips curved into that honest smile, he looked more beautiful than he ever had before.

"I know at this point you probably see me as more of a stalker than friend-material and... I'm sorry, Dee. I really am. If you want me gone for good, then I'll–"

I kissed him. I didn't care. I let my lips part his, let my body sink into him. I let myself forget the memories crawling over my skin – no. Soon I wouldn't even feel them anymore. The more I kissed him, the more they faded to a faint whisper.

He was shocked, but only for a few seconds; then his arms enveloped me. I needed more. The memories were starting to fade. I pulled him up onto his feet, not caring who was watching. I pushed him against the handrail, grabbed the back of his neck, lifted his head to mine and sank deeper into the kiss, his breath heating the roof of my mouth. What could he be thinking right now? Maybe he wasn't thinking at all.

That was the point.

As if something came over him, he twisted me around and pinned me against the banister, the twisted metal biting my skin. I arched and twisted my body until I could feel the contours of his through my clothes. Chest, stomach, hips and legs. I wanted to feel all of him, as much of him as I could get out here in the dead of night, enough to smother the rest of the memories into nothing. Hyde crushed me to him as if he were doing the same. Maybe he was.

Anton was right. Hyde did want me. But Hyde also had no one. I was probably the only person left in the world who could betray him.

"Hyde," I whispered into his ear after forcing us apart. "Owning the company. Is it that important to you?" I tried hard not to let any of my desperation slip into my voice. The question was strange enough as it was. I didn't want to give myself away.

"What?"

"I just need to know because I don't understand." I let my finger play over the wetness of his lips. His eyes lost focus. "Why is the company that important to you? All those people hating you, waiting for you to screw up. Why put yourself through it?"

Hyde's hands slipped all the way down to the small of my back. I almost flinched. Why didn't I? His hands should have terrified me. Actually, they did a little, but my body just didn't react the way I thought it would. I'd authorized his touch, after all. Me. I'd sanctioned it. That alone loosened the knots in my chest.

"If the company isn't mine, then it's his."

"Your uncle?"

"I can't let that happen."

"Why?" I let my hands rest on his shoulders, feeling the muscles tense beneath my fingers. "What does it matter if he's in control or not?"

"He wants it. I won't let him have it. I won't let him have anything."

Hyde said nothing else. I knew he wouldn't. His face had hardened with resolve. He was serious. He'd never give the company over to Anton's dad. Not if I asked him to. But maybe he didn't have to.

Just tell him, I told myself. Tell him what happened. Telling him would solve everything.

I opened my mouth. My hands shook against his shoulders.

It's not like anyone was watching us. It's not like Anton had eyes everywhere. He wasn't a god. He wasn't Big Brother or whatever the hell.

"Hyde," I said, and stopped, because I remembered the way Anton's lips had twitched as he casually threatened my life.

Do what I say and don't you dare tell anyone about this or I will have you on the first boat to Russia. And maybe I'll destroy your family too. If I'm bored.

The whole thing was a scare tactic. I couldn't let myself fall for it. I had to be brave. Anton couldn't do anything to me. Nothing.

Hyde was staring at me. "Deanna? Are you shaking?"

No. I couldn't be scared. I couldn't let some jackass waltz into my life and scare me into doing whatever he wanted. Then when would it end? Anton couldn't do anything to me.

But what if he could?

No. Telling Hyde would solve everything.

But what if it didn't?

What was I willing to risk to find out?

I'd never been the bravest of girls. My mom had three daughters, and among the three, I was the one most likely to chafe at the thought of taking a risk. But I wasn't a coward. I could stand up for myself, if I needed to. It was what my mom had taught me. I didn't want to let her down.

I didn't *want* to.

And yet, when I closed my eyes, flocks of swangirls smiled vacantly back at me.

"Deanna?"

"It's OK," I whispered. "It's OK." And I kissed him again.

He buried his secrets as if it was a learned skill, but Ralph Hedley's son couldn't quite hide how desperate he was for love. And maybe he mattered to me. But my life mattered more. So I decided: I would give Hyde exactly what he needed. I'd take his heart and then everything else until he had nothing left. I'd give him love. And then I'd ruin him with it.

There was no other way out.

A Tale

I am to be your bride, she says, the beautiful woman with hair that shines like the moon.

He is an honest boy, a son of the countryside. He tills in the paddy field day and night, hands calloused with the scars of his labor. And when she takes his broken hands in hers, how can he know, the young man, that he'd glimpsed her beauty once before? That where there is a girl at nightfall was once a crane he'd saved at midday?

He sees her skin, fresh with youth, and her eyes, large and gray. He sees the cloth she drapes over his arms, weaved in secret in the silence of the night. He sees the sum it gives him. A high sum, for a son of the countryside.

He didn't see the feathers. He didn't see her pluck them from her back, one by one, and weave them into the garment. He didn't see the flesh in his arms when he traded it for gold at the marketplace.

He never heard her cries.

12

Mark

Before Ralph Hedley's funeral, Hyde was my dead childhood friend. Before Stylo, Hyde was my dead childhood friend who was actually quite alive enough to annoy me.

Now he was my mark.

I'd resolved to take him down. Anton's brilliant idea depended on the media's insatiable appetite for public humiliation – and of course, you can't suffer public humiliation unless you're in the public eye. So the next day, I called Hyde and asked him out.

"A date?" he'd said with an eagerness that was almost heartbreakingly cute.

Yes, a date. I had a job to do after all. If I was going to get out of this mess, I'd have to do it right.

Coney Island in the summertime was packed. Lots of witnesses. Plenty of opportunities for a scandal. Except I still couldn't figure out how to hurt him. And the more

Hyde tried to dazzle me with his proficiency at super lame carnival games, the less I wanted to.

"Wow, thanks," I said when Hyde dumped a giant panda in my arms. "I'm in awe of your skill, but now I can't help but feel slightly inadequate. I need to get in on this – oh, how about that?"

I slinked up behind a pair of tweens trying to bludgeon the Whack-a-Mole booth, chuckling giddily because the kid playing sucked, and was clearly starting to lose the last vestiges of his sanity as clowns, cartoon cavemen, and I think a former president ducked out of harm's way, always at the very last second.

It took a good clean look at the "moles", though, for the grin to fall off my face. My hand almost snatched the mallet out of the kid's hand about a second after he hit a beaked girl on the head. But Hyde was right next to me. I couldn't give myself away. Not to him.

"Actually, let's just keep moving," I muttered.

I remember learning about it in school last term: in Early Modern Europe, a woman with a beak was a literary and visual emblem of swans – but it was more than that. It was a metaphor. As far as they were concerned, the swan, with her feathers, stood in that liminal space between human and animal.

I learned a lot that term. I learned that feathers made good dowries. I learned that in pre-colonial Upstate New York, swans were respected as counsels and mothers of generations. I learned that up until the eighteenth century, English families would rather smother their sons than admit that they were the parents of a boy with feathers. Half a year of historical facts that never seemed to matter, never seemed to have anything to do with my life...

Hyde took the abandoned mallet and swung it around. "You sure you wanna go?"

"Yeah," I said softly.

"All right..." I could have applauded him for keeping that smile plastered on his face. Couldn't have been easy. "Let's try the rides instead. The Cyclone looks pretty bad ass."

We were keeping secrets from each other, Hyde and I. It didn't stop him from trying to get close to me. Buying me funnel cake, telling me bad jokes to subtly distract me from his hand brushing mine. But when he finally grabbed my hand, my breath hitched nonetheless.

It's 3 o'clock. I should probably get around to ruining his life.

The thought was sobering.

We walked to the aquarium. As we stood on the crowded walkway cocooned by a glass dome separating us from coral reefs and homeless fish, I watched Hyde. He was silent for a long time, the movements of jelly fish casting shadows over his face. Silent. Eerily so. What was he searching for, I wondered, behind the glass?

"It's kind of terrifying, isn't it?" I sat down on the bench next to a little girl with a dripping ice cream cone. "That glass is the one thing keeping us from being crushed under metric tons of water and sting rays."

"Must be more terrifying for them." I could see Hyde's eyes following a jelly fish until it disappeared behind a forest of reefs. "Trapped like animals up there."

"They *are* animals."

That made Hyde smile. "Guess so. Still sucks, I bet."

I remembered Stylo's cage, remembered Anton's threat, remembered why I was sitting here beneath a ceiling of sea, and nodded in agreement. Then, I buried my face in the fat, fluffy neck of my giant panda.

"Come on. You said you wanted to see the whales, right?" Hyde extended a hand to me with an inviting smile, wordlessly enticing, waiting for mine, itching for touch. I finally had to admit to myself that this had long stopped being an "operation". It was a date. A regular date. A nice one.

I took his hand and wondered what it would cost me.

That evening, after Hyde had dropped me off, I resolved to do better. I resolved to do whatever it took. But Sunday passed. Then Monday.

Hyde didn't have a lot of free time, but when he did, he tried to spend it with me. Movie on Friday. Karaoke on Saturday. He was partial to Sinatra. He had a real taste for jazz. He had Charlie Parker albums on his iPod, and the purest of hatred for sea food.

I started to notice things about him; things I hadn't before. I was getting to know him. I was dating him.

I was screwing up.

Tuesday evening, Hyde took me out. I'd left my house while Ade and Dad were watching some gross-out comedy on TV, Chinese take-out strewn about the coffee table. He'd come right after the dinner he'd had with one of his lawyers – John Roan, the man who'd been with him at Hedley's funeral reception – so he was still in a suit when he met me at Grand Army Plaza.

My heart was pounding as we walked into the woods, but not because of Hyde – though admittedly he did look quite good in a three-piece suit. Anton hadn't contacted me at all since that night at Stylo, but I was sure that he was keeping tabs on me. The thought alone was enough to give me what I hoped wasn't a permanent twitch.

But getting close to Hyde was part of the plan, wasn't it? I was still on track. I had to believe it.

"Tell me what happened to you, Deanna," Hyde asked.

I knew what he wanted: the life I'd lived during the years he'd been away.

It wasn't something I liked to open up about. Or maybe I just never really had an opportunity to. I looked up at Hyde, at his gentle gaze. I couldn't help it. "Dad fell off the wagon hard after Mom died. Ericka was too busy dreaming of freedom and Ade too busy avoiding responsibility, so I was the one stuck trying to keep everything from falling apart."

Hyde listened intently.

"I kept writing for a while," I told him. "You know, like those little stories I used to let you read when we were kids. But eventually I just... stopped. It didn't seem like it really mattered anymore, you know? But I dealt with everything anyway. By myself. It's just what I do."

His eyes lost focus, dimmed. It was as if he were seeing something other than me, as if the reality around him ceased to exist, abandoning him to a different place and time entirely. He didn't even realize when I'd stopped talking until I nudged him – almost half a minute later.

"Sorry," he said in a tone so quiet and pained it stilled my pulse. It wasn't the kind of apology one gave when spacing out was the only crime committed. "I'm really sorry. If only I'd…"

"If only you'd what?"

Silence. "If only I'd been there." He left it at that.

"Hey," I said, as I stepped out of his limo in front of his townhouse – a century old neoclassical beauty on 74th.

"Yeah?"

"Are you OK?"

"What?" Narrowing his eyes, he shrugged. "No less than usual. Why do you ask?"

My feet were killing me. I should have known not to take out my old, barely-cushioned sneakers for a walk through a public park. Since we started "dating", I'd resolved not to accept any more gifts from Hyde, which meant rejecting the several pairs of three hundred dollar shoes he'd offered.

Smoothing my skirt against my legs from behind, I sat down on the steps. "I just noticed tonight you were a bit…" I thought of a good word to use, but the only one I could think of was "off", which sounded both vague and insulting at the same time.

"Sorry," he said, sitting next to me. "If I seemed off at all tonight, it definitely has nothing to do with you." I nodded. "A lot on my mind is all."

"Company stuff, right?" I rubbed my ankles. "How does that work, anyway? I mean what exactly do you do all day?"

My heart skipped a beat when Hyde swiveled me to him. For a second, I thought he'd kiss me. Instead he bent down, lifted my feet and put them on his knees. "Lots of boring stuff, really." He slipped off my shoes, the first and then the second. "I'm still young, so it's not like I control the show or whatever the case may be. There are other executives. But Dad's will gave me the majority share of the company and authority as a senior executive. That means I show up to a lot of meetings."

Of course he started to rub my feet. Of course he did. My base instinct told me to yank them out of his hands before he could get a whiff of something less than pleasant because, you know, old sneakers and all. But once those thumbs started working their magic, it was all I could do to stay upright. As a compromise, I kept my feet where they were but squeezed my eyes shut out of embarrassment. A flush of heat positively burned my face from the inside.

"And n-none of it fazes you?" I stuttered out the question with my eyelids still pinned shut. "I mean you're what, twenty? How can you handle all of it?"

"Nineteen," Hyde corrected and the little laugh that shook the word from his lips told me he could probably see me not seeing him. "I've always had something of an affinity for this kind of thing. When I was away, I studied. That's practically all I did for a while. I'm also pretty smart, or don't you remember?"

"Yeah, yeah."

He could help, a voice kept hissing in the back of my mind. He's smart, right? He could help you. Just tell him about Anton. I tried. Every time I saw Hyde, the urge to spill everything would kick in so strongly, it was as if I could feel the words forming on my tongue. But every time, I'd think back to the cage. I'd picture Anton leering at me. Then I'd just clamp my mouth shut and hope my lips weren't trembling as I smiled instead.

Hyde was smart, yes, and he was obviously cool-headed when he needed to be. But how could I forget how frantic he was after I'd hurt myself at Anton's birthday party? He was the kind of guy who'd call fifty times a day when he was worried about someone, send Mariachi Bands to cheer them up, run out in the middle of the night to meet them when they asked. If I told him what Anton had done to me, what he was doing to me, how could I be perfectly sure that he wouldn't freak out and try to beat him ragged? And then what would happen to me? To my family? Could I count on Hyde to fix this? Could I trust him?

I shivered and slipped my feet out of his grip. "Still, I assume it takes more than that to head a company."

"Technically a person just needs to be the biggest asshole possible. There's no faster path to success."

"Asshole, huh?" Putting my shoes back on, I stared at the pavement. "Like firing someone's dad?" When Hyde didn't answer, I shoved his knees. "Honestly, Hyde, I know Edmund Rey obviously wanted the majority share of the company. But you have it now. Doesn't that solve the problem? Did you really need to fire him?"

It was a tough card to play; how could I forget that night on my front steps – the way Hyde's eyes had frozen solid the moment I'd brought it up?

I waited for Hyde's answer regardless, watched his expression, only half-surprised when it turned to stone.

"Edmund Rey's been involved in criminal activity," said Hyde in a frigid voice. "Firing him was kind."

"That makes sense but..." I thought hard, trying to ignore the sound of Anton's voice shuddering through my head. "I mean he's your uncle. Right? He was your mom's brother?" A sentiment that probably meant nothing to him, but if I could just get him to lay off Anton's dad, I could end this whole nightmare – for both our sakes.

"My uncle's done more to ruin lives than you think, Deanna."

He didn't look at me as he said it. His eyes were glued resolutely to the gates surrounding the townhouse, his hand clenching and unclenching the fabric around his knees. It didn't look as if he'd even noticed.

"Like what?" I clasped his hand in mine, but the moment I touched his skin, he shot to his feet. My heart leapt into my throat. For a second, we stared at each other, both of us too disoriented to speak.

Finally, Hyde cleared his throat. "Well. This isn't exactly how I like to end my dates," he said, rubbing the back of his neck. "I guess I'm a little jumpy tonight. You won't hold it against me, will you?"

"No." From throat to stomach. Watching Hyde struggle to keep a smile on his face even while his hands were trembling sent my heart plummeting. He reminded me so much of myself sometimes. It made it harder to hurt him to know he was already hurting.

"Hey," I said, standing. "Look, I know it's been a few years. But we're still friends." With as gentle a touch as I could manage, I placed my hands on his arms. "If there's anything wrong with you... I mean, if you've got anything on your mind, I really hope you'll be able to trust me enough to tell me–"

The next words caught in my throat. Pursing my lips I lowered my head. Asking Hyde to trust me. How much of that was genuine and how much of it was the mission that fear had hardwired into me?

"Thanks," Hyde whispered. The sound of it made my breath hitch; fragility carried it like the baseline of a melody. He squeezed my hand. Anton would've been proud. I hated myself. "So, I'm not going to have much free time next week," he said after clearing his throat. "But I was wondering if you'd like to come with me to a party Beatrice's hosting this Saturday?"

"Party?"

"Yep. Just one of my many newfound duties now that I'm back in the world of strategic schmoozing. It's going to be boring as hell, of course – the social equivalent of water boarding really – which means I'll need someone to help keep me sober."

"A lot of people from the company will probably be there too, right? Like… board members and whatnot?" I'd asked it very quietly. I couldn't even look him in the eyes as I spoke.

"Yep." He laughed. "*Bella Magazine*'s still a part of Hedley Publications. A lot of people from the company'll probably be there. But it won't be a total waste of time if we keep each other company, right? You can bring your sisters too, if you want. Well, Ericka'll probably be there anyway if her jittery husband's on the list. I'll text you the address later."

"OK," I shifted on my feet. "Thanks, Hyde."

We both fell silent. Hyde's gaze lingered on my lips a little while longer. "Deanna… would you…?" He pressed a hand against my waist, drawing me in. "If you don't have anywhere else to go, why don't you–?" When I saw his eyes flicker past me to the townhouse, I knew right away what he was trying to ask. But I couldn't do that. Not now, not under these circumstances. It would be wrong on every level.

"I'm sorry, I actually should get going. It's late. Plus it's garbage day tomorrow and I'm sure Dad and Ade forgot to take the trash out. Again."

I was rambling, but I waved awkwardly anyway, pretending nothing was wrong, and let his driver take me back over the bridge. Sighing, I lay my head against the glass window. A party this Saturday. It was the perfect opportunity to publically destroy someone. If I was going to carry out Anton's plan, then that was probably the time to do it.

Apparently, Anton thought so too. I saw my phone buzz just as I climbed into bed: *Lucien Restaurant. Noon tomorrow. Things to discuss. Wear something nice.*

I buried my face in my pillow.

13

Mission

"I said I'm here to meet someone. What, you don't believe me?"

The door guy at Lucien looked me up and down before curling up his pointed nose in a "polite" half-sneer – the kind of "polite" one used to poorly conceal one's disdain. That was fine with me; if I really did have to be at Anton's beck and call, then I sure as hell wasn't going to "wear something nice" whenever he ordered me to, the bastard.

So there I stood staring down the maître d' in a pair of beaten up jeans and stained T-shirt, half hoping he'd have security escort me out so I could have a valid excuse not to meet with Anton.

When I saw the man's sneer deepen, I shrugged. Oh well. *Can't say I didn't try, Anton.* "Well, if you really don't want me here, I guess I'll–"

"It's all right," came a voice from the dining room.

I shuddered. Anton. Like a vampire, he materialized

out of nowhere. My eyes flickered away from him almost immediately as he walked up to us, and I hated myself for it. Squeezing my hands into fists, I sucked in a deep breath and glared at him while he calmly told the maître d' that I was his "guest". My fists twitched, my knuckles eager for blood.

"Follow me, Deanna." And then he winked at me.

I sincerely hoped he could see the murderous dreams playing and replaying in my eyes. I followed him with plodding steps to his table in the corner of the dining room where three expensive-looking blondes in short, slinky dresses awaited us. They couldn't have been over seventeen.

"Deanna, please, sit." He took his seat in between the three women, who grinned at me vacantly. Maybe they were swans too. Or maybe money was their aphrodisiac. Compliance could be bought just as easily as it could be forcibly taken.

As much as I bristled at being given another command, people were staring. So I sat, making damn sure my eyes stayed glued to his. I wanted him to see it; my hatred. I wanted to make sure he couldn't ignore it.

"If looks could kill," Anton said while stroking Girl Number One's blonde locks. Giggling, she leaned over and, in a low voice, said something in Russian to Girl Number Two.

I watched her hair slip off his fingers and grimaced as if something had died in the pit of my stomach. "Then there'd be one less asshole in the world, now wouldn't there?"

The grin dropped from Anton's face and in that moment, my heart seized. Goading him probably wasn't the best idea. Still, I couldn't let him see me cower.

I eased back into my chair, cool, but not *too* cool lest he notice all the effort I was putting into it. "What do you want, Anton?"

He placed a card on the table. An invitation.

I frowned. "A party?" Probably the one Hyde had told me about yesterday. I feigned innocence.

"A masquerade party," he said. "As far as opportunities go, it's more than a little perfect, wouldn't you say?"

A masquerade party. Though I'd never been to one, I'd seen enough on TV to know that the masks involved were perfect for evil schemes.

"It's Beatrice's idea." When Anton spoke his stepmother's name, he looked somehow human. It was unnerving. "It was originally going to be a cocktail party, of course, but Beatrice's always had a flair for the dramatic."

"Sounds try-hard," I said flatly and watched his nostrils flair, though the rest of him remained perfectly still. "Sorry, I meant tired and cliché." I couldn't stop. *Deanna, stop pissing off the bad man with the gun to your head.*

Luckily for me, Anton shook it off with a readjusting tug of his suit. "It doesn't matter what you think of it. You're going."

I turned the card over in my hand. "Yeah, I figured."

"You've been doing a great job so far," he continued, giving me that sidelong creeper-gaze of his. "Wooing our boy, I mean. Coney Island? A walk in the park? Nice touch. I always knew he was a simple, honest guy at heart. I'm sure he'll be honestly heartbroken when you ruin his life."

I felt a cold shiver down my spine. Of course he'd been watching me. Part of me hadn't wanted to believe it. I folded my arms and maintained a steady glare. "OK. So party. What do you want me to do?"

"Direct and to the point. I like that about you."

"Something we obviously don't have in common. What do you want me to do?" Or was his grandmaster plan to whittle down my psychological defenses with small talk? Aren't there easier ways to get someone to do what you want? Last time I checked, blackmail sufficed.

"Only what you've been so adept at doing so far. Seducing him." He lowered his voice, which was unnecessary as we were safely tucked in a corner.

"Hyde'll be there. He'll take you. There's no way he won't ask you to come with him, if he hasn't already. Board members, *Bella* parasites, press, company employees and their drunken Botox-wives – all of them'll be there. There's no way in hell Hyde'll make a fool of himself in front of them – unless he's with you. He might let himself go if you give him the incentive."

I focused on the invitation card because it was the only way to keep my eyes from burning. "And what exactly makes you so sure Hyde's gonna fall for my feminine wiles in a situation like that?" I thought back to last night – the hunger in his eyes, the request I couldn't bring myself to grant.

"He's a man, Deanna."

I snorted. "Reductive."

"But true. And he wants you. And he'll be bored. Nothing like a little bit of danger to spice up an evening. Just make yourself impossible to resist and the rest will write itself."

"So what then?" I placed the invitation back on the table so I wouldn't crush it in my palm. "You want me to screw him on a table in the middle of a toast or something? Give everyone a show?"

I could tell Anton was stifling his laughter behind his lips. "As amazing as that sounds, no. As you can see on your invitation, the ball's being held at Arkham Hall. There's a secluded room that I'll be holding for my own private use: the Red Room. That's where I want you to take him to."

"Oh." My fingers twitched on my lap. I could feel the pressure rising in my throat. "And... what?"

With a finger, Anton pushed his glass of champagne toward me. "First offer him one of these. Set the mood."

"Giving me lessons on seducing men?" I scoffed, shaking my head. "Is this coming from personal experience?"

Anton ignored me. "Before you take him to the room, at midnight, I'll text you where to meet me."

"Why? So you can give me one final pep-talk before I give it the old college try?"

"So I can give you this." Anton reached into Girl Number Two's bag and took out a little black vial, lifting it just high enough for me to see before shoving it back out of sight.

"Is that... Are you insane?" I hissed as my nails dug into my jeans.

"I've invited reporters from five different tabloids, newspapers and gossip sites. Slip this into his glass. Make sure he drinks it. Seduce him. Wind him up to the point where he's up for anything." Anton's slimy gaze slid to his girls, still coiled dutifully around him. "They'll do the rest."

If Anton wanted to destroy the board's trust in Hyde, having a few reporters "accidentally" catch Hyde halfway through an orgy at a company event would certainly do the trick. My right hand flew to my chest, the palm pressing hard against the fabric. I couldn't help it. The pain in there was extraordinary – like my heart was going to burst through the skin and flop onto the table.

Not like I'd need that anymore anyway.

"H-how..." I straightened my back up, placing my hands back onto my lap. Controlled. Poised. Don't let him see you freak out. Don't. "So I'm just supposed to wait around for them to show up?" I flicked my head toward the models, folding my arms. "What if they don't show or... what if they're late?"

"They won't be. I'll be coming with them. My driver should get us to the hall just before midnight."

"But it's a masquerade, right? How will I know it's them and not someone else entirely?"

"You'll know." Anton slipped out his phone and after a few clicks, my own phone vibrated. I checked the text he'd sent me: a photo of a gorgeous gold mask with a cascade of lace just long enough to cover the lips. "It's what they'll all be wearing – already ordered and delivered. Jealous?" he added, when he caught me staring. "Don't worry. I'm sure whatever Hyde picks out for you will suit you just as well. Or would you like me to send you one?"

I grimaced. I already felt cheap. Having sugar daddies was the last thing I needed.

"I have to say, you're taking this all pretty well," said Anton, half-amused.

Picturing a rusty rail spike skewering your head over and over again sure helps, I wanted to say, but I wasn't about to push my luck. You could never tell with a guy like Anton just how much snark his ego could take before he snapped.

"And after this… if I do that, you'll leave me alone?"

"A deal's a deal," he answered simply. "Regardless of what you might think of me, it's not like I'm out to ruin your life." I could have laughed. "It's just business. I need something. You need something."

No, you made me need something, you asshole.

"Once we both get it," he continued, unaware of my murderous glare, "it'll be over. Just do your job and we'll both go on our merry way."

He must have noticed my lingering unease because he laughed, quietly. "Don't flatter yourself. If I were going to steal anyone's feathers it'd be someone more my type – taller, thinner, blonder." He touched Blonde Number One's cheek. The way she giggled gave me acid reflux.

I might have believed him. I wanted to believe him. But as far as virtues went, Anton had none, so I could pretty much rule trustworthiness out right off the bat. There were no guarantees. I knew it as I slipped the card off the table and tucked it into my pocket before getting up to leave. As long as Anton knew about me, there was no way I would ever be safe. Even if he let me fly free today, what about tomorrow? Next month? Year? How could I know he wouldn't hang the threat of slavery over my head the next time he needed something? Best case scenario, I'd be a pawn in his little schemes forever. Worst case...

The thought of him stroking my cheek the way he did his models forced a grunt of disgust from my lips.

If I didn't stop Anton now, I'd be in his bird cage forever.

I wasn't about to let that happen. I couldn't. I had to find a way to protect myself. And in the meantime, I had to find a way to protect Hyde this Saturday. Simply refusing would piss Anton off and send me to the nearest massage parlor bound and gagged. There had to be something... some way to keep Hyde off the chopping block without screwing myself over. I wasn't a pawn, goddamn it.

No matter what, I couldn't let that bastard have his way.

14

Preparations

Despite my determination, the evening passed without one brilliant epiphany; not even so much as a bullet point list of possible options. I spent most of the night watching reruns of *Sew or Die* on Ade's laptop while Dad watched something on some Man Network. Beatrice Hoffer-Rey's talent for crushing designers' hopes and dreams was admittedly amusing, but it failed to help me get in touch with my inner ruthlessness, and ruthlessness was what I'd need to plot my way out of this mess.

"You OK, Deanna?"

I blinked. Dad was looking at me – probably because his show had just gone to commercial.

"Yes."

But he kept staring. With a heavy sigh I paused the video. "I'm fine. Why? Do you need something?"

He shifted awkwardly in his chair, though we both

knew he wasn't exactly allowed to be surprised that I'd be suspicious of his concern. As if suddenly aware of the beer can in his hands, he set it down onto the table next to him and started flipping channels.

"Hey wait, stop," I said suddenly, when I saw the words "Hedley Publications", right below a video of people waving around signs underneath a particularly tall tower of a building.

A marching circle of bodies practically blocked the sky-high building's entrance. Obviously a protest. I managed to catch a glimpse of a tall blonde carrying a sign that read "Freedom not Fashion" before the video cut to other protesters as the Wednesday morning news reporter explained, "There's still no word on whether or not the editors of *Bella* magazine will respond to the accusations, but the question still remains: does the magazine's advertising of the clothing line equate to promoting indentured swan labor? Or have the magazine's critics directed their ire at the wrong target?"

Advertising a designer who uses slave labor to make his or her shitty clothes. That sounded just irresponsible and disgusting enough to be true.

Smelled like a scandal. Big enough to lose the Colemans? If so, it would blow Anton's plan right up; after all, Beatrice was the editor in chief. She was the one this sort of thing would reflect badly on, not Hyde. Then what, Anton?

It was a satisfying thought, Anton pulling his hair out in frustration. Anton losing.

Still, without proof, accusations were easy enough to deny. I was back at square one.

Oh my God. A familiar face popped onto the screen as the camera scanned the crowd with a few skips of jolty editing. She was a little less naked this time, and her black-rimmed hipster glasses covered about half of her face, but it was hard to forget the girl who feather-flashed a bevy of "mourning" millionaires at a funeral.

"Shannon Dalhousie," I whispered. The long red hair was the same, as was the pale skin and righteous indignation. Tough bitch.

Exactly the kind of confidence I need...

That was the spark. Those half-baked thoughts I'd been sifting through since leaving Lucien, thoughts as useless as scattered crumbs on a dirty floor, slowly started to coalesce into a legitimate idea. A half-baked, plan, but a plan nonetheless.

I had to work fast.

She wasn't hard to find. With all her blogs, each one dedicated to various social justice issues – and baking? – Shannon was easy to track down.

Sprawled out on my bed with my doors shut, I scrolled down the browser screen, trying to find her contact information. Each of her social justice blogs had the same one. Click.

I spent the next fifteen minutes crafting a passionately worded email filled with half-truths, bullshit, and a sob story I hoped would be just believable enough to get her to hit "reply".

I couldn't tell her exactly what was going on. I mean, I did ask her not to post up or mention the email on any of her blogs, but how did I know she wouldn't anyway? Even though I needed her, I didn't know her, and that meant I couldn't fully trust her. I doubted Anton used the internet for anything other than porn, but still, I had to be careful.

So instead I told her the story of a young swan whose feathers were taken by her now ex-boyfriend years ago. I threw in parts of my own life just to make it feel real – dead mother, deadbeat but well-meaning father, lazy middle sister, trophy-wife eldest sister. The part about how alone and scared I felt came from a real place too, obviously. Living in fear and paranoia, feeling other people's eyes on me, feeling used like my body was a site of transaction.

But I didn't want to get too bleeding-heart lest it all come off as fake. So I got to the point. I told her about how I wanted to do something, anything to help other people like me out there.

I want to help. After everything I've been through, I can't just stand by and watch more people be used the way I was. It's just horrifying.

Beatrice Hoffer-Rey, The editor in chief at Bella (which I'm sure you already know), is throwing a masquerade party this Saturday at Arkham Hall on Broadway (you know, that try-hard "swanky" Manhattan beehive of parasitic socialites). Can you freaking believe that? Like normal parties aren't epic enough for her. The arrogance.

I figured this might be the perfect opportunity to bring reality into their lives – force them to face it head on. Protesting outside the Hedley Building is all well and good, but after they get inside they can easily just shut you out. What about taking the protest inside?

I can't do it on my own. Honestly, I'm a little scared. That's why I was wondering if you and some of your friends wanted to help me out? I have a plan figured out. I live in East Brooklyn, so if you want maybe we could meet up somewhere and talk about it?

Please get back to me ASAP,
Dee

That was when I attached a photo I'd saved onto the desktop – the photo of me and Hyde someone took for us while we were up on the Empire State Building last Tuesday. Dalhousie would know exactly what that meant – that I had an in. I just needed the help.

With a sigh, I ran through the email once, pressed send and prayed that Shannon Dalhousie checked her inbox as obsessively as Ade did.

An hour passed. Two hours. I oscillated between stress eating, stress email-checking and then back to stress eating. Ade came home from evening shift at the telemarketing centre dismayed to find empty bags of chips strewn about the living room – not because the place was now an infestation waiting to happen, of course, but because I'd depleted her primary nutritional source and now she had to rummage through the fridge to find an apple to feast on.

I cleaned up. Three hours. False alarms in the form of junk mail from my years-old subscription to a Korean drama online streaming site. I was going crazy. Then at 3 o'clock in the morning, miraculously:

A new email from Lady Pen.

Lady Pen?

Seriously?

I was a mass of nerves. A twinge of excitement shook the breath out of my throat. Taking my laptop back into my room, I clicked.

> *Hi Dee,*
> *Hey, girl, I'm totes glad you got in touch with me, not in the least because I'm always eager to connect with and possibly even meet other survivors. I'm hella sorry to hear about what's happened to you... and I just want you to know that I can honestly SYMPATHIZE! I've been there.*
> *Some of us just don't have the luxury to ignore this kind of shit, you know? That's why I do what I do. I'm glad you kind of understand that. I'm so used to getting hate mail from clueless privileged assholes who assure me that having your autonomy stolen isn't really "that big a deal", it's become basic instinct to side-eye every email I get now and days (and I was kind of sceptical about yours too, tbh). Some of my friends and I have been trying to*

spread awareness about Bella Magazine for some time, now, but the only news coverage that we got was this morning... and I dunno, if you watched the whole thing, but the reporter kind of painted us as fanatical random hippies with nothing better to do than to hurl baseless accusations at innocent fashion conglomerates.

If what you're saying is true (that pic isn't photoshopped is it? If not you did a hella good job, but srsly, it's not is it?) This might give us the opportunity to get more exposure.

I'm cool with meeting up, but just to be careful... meet me at Grand Central Terminal tomorrow morning at nine – under the clock. I'll be around... I just want to make sure it's you first. Then I'll ~reveal~ myself lol.

Best,

SD

My hands trembled a little when I sent back a confirmation email and began trying to figure out a route to Grand Central. Not out of fear, or anything. Shannon seemed eager enough to see me, though making Central the rendezvous point seemed needlessly complicated; I guess the whole East Brooklyn thing turned her off, which wasn't surprising since her social justice blog pretty much shrieked "middle class" at the top of its lungs.

Seriously, if she wanted to meet, she could have made it less of a pain in the ass, but then maybe that was the point. Some bored dickhead wouldn't go through the hassle of getting there just to jerk her around.

It was probably the nerves that made me shake. Or maybe excitement. Once I finished writing directions, I started planning everything else, tapping the pencil against the notebook. If the meeting was at 9 o'clock, I had to make sure I got there a little early, just to make sure I wouldn't miss her. I also had to assume Anton would have me under surveillance. I'd have to disguise myself somehow. Did I still have that wig from drama club?

"Hey, Deanna?"

I shut my laptop so fast for a second I thought I might have broken the screen. Ade's eyebrow rose.

"Hmm," she said, eyeing me suspiciously as she pushed off the doorframe and strolled into my room.

"Um..." I paused to think. "Yeah, I admit that was weird."

"Porn right?" She looked absolutely touched. "I knew my little Dee Dee would hit puberty one day."

"*Not* porn," I clarified, rolling my eyes as Ade fell onto my bed with her arms spread out over the sheets. Then again... it probably would have been smarter to just let her think it *was* porn. Damn.

Ade twisted her hair around a finger, raising the lock over her head and letting it fall onto her face. "Come on now. Nothing to be ashamed about. Just think of it as an educational experience."

"It's super late, Ade."

"So?"

"Is there any reason why you're here?"

"Does there have to be?"

"Typically."

"Oh shit, now I have to quickly come up with a believable one."

Sighing, I crossed my legs. Normally, I wouldn't have minded being ambushed by Ade's shenanigans, but there was just too much to going on, too much to think about, and unfortunately the Ade shenanigans were cutting into the very important planning-fretting-time I'd scheduled for today. I was just about to ask her to leave when she snatched the scrap notebook paper I'd been writing on.

"'Take the F-train'," Ade read. "Hey, isn't that a song?"

"That's 'A-train'," I grunted while trying to grab it back from her. Ade was too fast. For a girl who lived on the couch, her reflexes were way too good.

"Huh. Why are you going to Grand Central? You meeting someone?" Her eyes sparkled with shameless mischief when she added, "You seeing Hyde off or something? Or are you gonna chase him down and beg him not to go in a big dramatic display of eternal love? Aw, how very B-romantic comedy of you."

"I'm not even sure how to respond to that." I held out my hand, waiting for Ade to give me back my train schedule. When she didn't, I groaned. "I'm meeting a friend from out of town," I lied.

"Oh, is it Susie?"

"No."

"Wait, wasn't Susie the one who went to Jesus camp in Wisconsin?"

"No, that's John." I shook my head. "Susie's Jewish. You know this. You went to her Bat Mitzvah. Why are you here?"

"Who's the friend?"

"Why do you want to know?"

"I dunno. It'd be nice to know *something* around here."

Ade had obviously been very careful to keep her tone bright, but there was no mistaking the frustration. She lifted herself off her back and faced me.

I avoided her gaze. "What do you mean by that?"

"Just that you've practically turned into a stranger ever since…" She paused, probably not eager to mention my "transformation". Admittedly, I did appreciate her perceptiveness. "It's just, you used to tell me shit, you know? And now you're all 'cloaked in secrets' or whatever and it's like… what's going on? You don't trust me anymore? You don't think I can help?"

I never thought I'd ever use the word "innocent" to describe my sister, but now, as I watched her struggle to understand what she ultimately couldn't, there really wasn't any other word to use. When I'd manifested, I'd ended up shattering the blinders we were both using to keep the world of swans far, far away from us. I knew that. But there were some things that Ade would never understand, even if I tried to explain them, which I didn't want to have to. I just… couldn't.

"There's nothing you need to help with," I said quietly, taking advantage of her distraction to pluck the scrap of paper out of her hands. "I'm dealing."

Ade rolled her eyes and fell silent for a few moments. Then, "I told Ericka."

I whipped my head around. "You told... What? You told Ericka? You told her about me?"

Ade fiddled with a loose string on my sheets, looking as if she were contemplating telling me everything. Finally, she sighed. "OK. I left out the part about you being a swan, but I admit I called Ericka to tell her there was something going on with you. Honestly, Deanna, it's like you're shutting everyone out – everyone but Hyde of course." She made a face – the first time I'd seen her do so while mentioning him. "But then, since I'm a thousand percent sure you're not telling him shit either, I'm guessing he's your boy-toy escape route out of reality."

"You're *guessing*." I let out a short, incredulous laugh. "Well, clearly you suck at it."

"What else am I supposed to think when you don't tell me anything? Ericka's worried, man. Even Dad is though he clearly doesn't have the balls to do anything about it."

"And?" I shoved the instructions into my pocket. "Look, I keep telling you guys I'm fine. It's up to you to believe me or not. But you can't force me to puke out all my problems when you want me to. This is *my* shit. Nobody can help me even if they wanted to, OK? So just get off my back and let me deal with my own *personal* issues by *myself*."

I was going to tell her to leave, but Ade was already on her feet. Quietly, she walked up to the door without so much as a glance and swung the door open.

"You know, it's funny," she said without turning, her hand still gripping the knob. "It's just like when Mom died. You shut everyone out and then angst about how alone you are. *Irony*."

Ade didn't let me respond. She slammed the door behind her.

15

I couldn't sleep. I got up at six in the morning, took a shower, dressed. I briefly entertained the thought of stealing Ade's overlarge shades. Maybe an oversized hoodie would work? Ideally, I could wear both to conceal my identity. But I needed to make sure Shannon could recognize me.

It'd be all right. Even if Anton was crazy enough to have me followed at all times of the day, all his goons would see was Deanna Davis going to Grand Central to meet up with a friend, who I was sure would be busy making sure her own identity was safely concealed.

Shannon incognito would only be convenient for me. No need to let Anton know I was meeting with the swan activist who'd flashed his uncle's funeral.

A few hours of internet-surfing later and I became too antsy to wait in my room anymore. I headed off. I took the F-train at York to Bryant Park and walked the rest of the way to Grand Central. It was a madhouse. Scores of people – some in business suits, some in flirty skirts – meandered about, lugging their suitcases behind them.

The clock wasn't hard to find. It was five minutes to nine. Shannon might already be here. She could be watching me right now. And yet there I stood, alone.

I waited. People passed me without so much as a glance. An obnoxiously loud woman chatted on her phone about possible restaurant choices. Five minutes passed. Then ten. Voices and footsteps and suitcases rolling along the floor blended into a strangely pacifying cacophony.

Shannon would be able to recognize me, I was sure of it. The picture I'd sent was clear and I made sure not to wear anything that would conceal any part of my face.

Another five minutes. A guy's suitcase rolled over my foot by accident, and I nearly cursed out loud. I shifted from foot to foot, rubbing my arms as if I were trying to warm them up despite the heat. But then another clueless soul practically mowed me down, too focused on trying to find his way to notice he'd almost ended my life. It was a miracle I'd managed to stay on my feet.

"How the hell is it that people are bumping into me when I'm literally standing out of *everyone's* way," I grumbled after he'd gone off with little more than a half-assed apology.

"To be honest you don't exactly stand out, '*Dee*'." I turned to find a tall girl leaning on the information booth next to me, her arms folded and her head cocked to the side so I could see her overlarge shades. Her dark red bangs peaked out from underneath a floppy, awkward-looking beanie. "Let me guess: you're a 'blend into the crowd' kind of gal, aren't you?"

My heart leapt into my throat. I jumped at her before I could talk myself out of it.

"Oh my god, Susie! It's been so long!" I cried, and loudly, maybe too loudly to be believable. My arms flew around her and I almost grimaced at the awkwardness of it when she let out a grunt in shock. "How was Jesus camp?"

Shannon peeled me off her, and I didn't need to see her eyes behind the shades to know how she was looking at me. "What the–?"

"I heard from John it was totally intense. They didn't brainwash you into giving up fun did they?" I gave her a simple, friendly smile, but lowered my head, gazing at her through my brow line. Thankfully, she stayed silent, though her frown told me she still didn't get it. Fair enough. "Damn there are so many people here. *Tons of people.* You know? It's crazy." I let my eyes flicker, just once, to the crowd and widened my smile. It widened still when I saw the light bulb finally blink on.

"Yeah," she said, unsure but still confident enough to add some volume to her voice. "Yeah it was good."

"Cool, you can tell me about it later. Let's get out of here first. Come on."

After one more meaningful glance that bid her to follow, I took off, making for the exit. I wanted to look around, but I couldn't let her see that I was nervous, nor could I tip off Anton's people, assuming there *were* people of Anton's around that I needed to worry about.

Once we made it outside, Shannon linked my arm and pulled me to the sidewalk, her overlarge hemp tote bag swinging behind her.

"So where are we going, *Dee*?" She'd said it so casually it almost sounded creepy. Then again, this was the same girl who'd showed an entire funeral gathering her fun-bits before taking off into the sunset. This girl could do anything. "A restaurant maybe? There are so many good ones around here."

"What? Oh no, that's way too, um, public." I definitely didn't intend for my laugh to sound so nervous. No way in hell she didn't pick up on it, but maybe that was a good thing. "I mean I want to catch up. You know, catch up and talk. Like the good old days."

Shannon burst out laughing. "Dude, honestly? I'm legit scared now," she half-whispered. Looked like she was catching on. "OK, how about this? Let's go to my place, kay?"

It was better than going back home. No way could I explain to Dad and Ade why the swan-flasher was eating waffles at the kitchen table. "Yeah, that's good."

Shaking her head, Shannon hailed a taxi. We got in.

"So what, you being followed or something? You don't strike me as the 'gets followed' type."

I eyed the taxi driver warily. "My current boyfriend and I have been having some... problems." It just came out, but since that particular half-lie seemed like it had potential, I went with it. "He thinks I'm cheating or something so I'm worried he's having me followed. I know; it's crazy right?"

Shannon shrugged and leaned against the car door. "Not really. Guys are pricks. Guys with money are bigger pricks. I'm assuming you're talking about Hy–"

"Yes!" I cut her off and flicked my head at the driver. "Though I don't necessarily like to talk about it so... openly."

"Gotcha. We'll talk about it later when we get to my place."

I was surprised to learn that Shannon Dalhousie lived in a pretty sweet apartment on 18th in Gramercy Park, a stone's throw away from NYU. For some reason, I figured she holed up in an abandoned, busted up train, or wherever hipsters lived these days. It was a small studio, filled to the brim with novelty items, everything from Foucault to Sailor Moon. The flooring was all wood, though the underwear, burger wrapping paper, magazines, plush toys and internet cables strewn about covered most of it.

"Oh, this isn't my apartment by the way." Shannon threw her tote bag onto the bed and followed after it. "It's my friend's. He's a film student at NYU. I'm just crashing until I can secure my own living arrangements, which will probably never happen since I was kicked out of my last apartment for not being able to pay the rent. And I'm sure he's aware of that so I'm kind of just making myself at home. Hey, turn on the TV or something. Way too quiet in here."

All of that in one breath.

"Uh, OK."

Nonthreatening pop music blared in the background as Shannon crossed her legs. "So, you know I'm Shannon right?" She pointed to herself with a long finger. "Lady Pen? The girl you emailed yesterday? I mean, you didn't suffer any massive head trauma on the way to the station or something, right?"

"No head trauma. Like I said, my boyfriend is jealous and has money."

"Money that gives him the financial means to act on his jealousy in surprisingly childish ways. How is it, by the way, dating a billionaire who was technically dead a month ago?"

"Not nearly as fun as it sounds." I sat on a chair next to the bed, kicking away an empty box of instant noodles. "Especially when he seems completely incapable of listening to criticism without taking it as a personal attack."

"Criticism?"

"About the magazine." I gripped my jeans. *Remember your talking points.* "I told him about how *Bella* was basically endorsing slave-labor and he didn't want to hear it. He never listens to me, to be honest. It's like he automatically filters everything I say through a 'silly woman' translator and dismisses me outright."

"Ha. Been there."

She was obviously the restless type because after sitting for about a minute, she got up again. Throwing off her beanie, she leaned against the bookcase, her shades dangling off the hook of her finger. It was the first time I'd actually seen her face in person since Hedley's funeral.

It was much more intense close up: thin with sunken eyes, high cheek bones and a strong jaw. And she was tall.

Tall enough.

This just might work.

"So, Dee. How exactly were you planning on taking action? In your email, you mentioned a masquerade party this Saturday. Sounded like you had a plan."

Right down to business. "Yes. Kind of." I crossed my legs on the chair, trying my best to sound sure of myself. "Do you have any friends that might be interested?"

"Sure. And there's tons of stuff we can do depending on the specs of the vicinity, the level of technology, the exits and so on."

Damn. She really wasn't new at this. This made me more nervous than it should have.

"But that only matters if you can get us inside," she continued. "From your email, it sounded like you had a way in. But it sounds like you and your boyfriend are on the rocks. You think he'll randomly let you add your 'friends' to the list?"

"It's a masquerade ball. We'll have to use that to our advantage; all you need is the right attire." I fished my phone out of my purse. "Hyde's cousin, Anton Rey, is gonna be there with a few models on his arm. They're all going to be wearing this mask."

I showed her Anton's text: the photo of a laced, exquisitely embroidered gold mask.

Shannon's eyes sparkled. "Ooh. Yum. So?"

"I can get you a few of these. I know where to get them." Not really. But if I asked Hyde, I was sure he'd find out where to get them and then buy a few for me. That was the plan, anyway.

I was just using people left right and center, wasn't I? I fought to suppress a shiver. It was to help him, right?

"And then?"

"And then you wear the masks and impersonate the models to get inside."

Shannon raised an eyebrow. I couldn't tell if it was an incredulous or intrigued eyebrow, but the tiniest curve of her lips told me that she was at least partly amused.

"Anton's supposed to be picking them up himself. All you have to do is be where I tell you, wearing the masks. You'll get to ride in a limo, if that's any consolation."

"You seem pretty sure Anton won't instantly know we aren't his lady-friends."

"Anton isn't exactly pro-feminist. He uses and discards girls like they're nothing. His models don't even speak English. It's risky, but I'm confident he won't know the difference as long as you keep your masks on and don't, you know, talk. Which I'm sure he'd prefer anyway."

Her smile widened. "OK, Dee, so how do we get rid of the real models? Where do we stash them?"

"I don't know. I don't want them to get hurt or anything. We just need to get them away from the party."

Shannon stroked her chin. "I guess we can figure something out."

"To make it work we'll need three girls who are skinny enough to make believable models. You'll have to be one of them."

"Sounds good. I think I can scrounge up two more girls."

"The ones I met are white and blonde... Anton said he had a type."

"Guy likes his Aryans. OK, fine. For me it's nothing a little hair dye won't fix. Though that leaves Yazmin out of the mix. Damn. She would have loved this."

"Whatever you plan on doing, you should make him one of your targets... and Hyde too. Hyde has a hand in the editorial decisions made at *Bella*," I lied. "And Anton suggests stuff to Beatrice Rey all the time since he's her stepson." Another lie. Maybe. Who knows? "Using Lamont as a designer was entirely Anton's idea, even though he knew swans were involved. And Hyde signed off. So if you're going to target anyone, they should be on the list." Lie, lie, lie.

Shannon frowned. "Well, I haven't quite figured out exactly what we're going to do once we're inside, but... OK. I'll keep that in mind I guess."

"No." I was on the edge of the bed now, back stiff. "Has to be them. Anton and Hyde. Honestly, they're horrible. Some of the stuff they do... they've done..." In my mind's eye, I saw Anton's pasty face through steel bars. "A couple of rich kids who use people however they want, whenever they want – especially swans. *Especially* swans. No matter what, we need to–"

"OK, OK, relax."

It was only after Shannon had spoken that I realized I was very nearly shrieking.

Shannon plopped back down onto the couch next to the bookcase. "This is your first rodeo, right? I'm guessing you're a little nervous. On edge?"

"Yeah." More so because I knew how severe the consequences would be if this went wrong – or more specifically, if Anton were to find out that I set this whole thing up.

"I can see this is important to you. For you to go this far… meeting me, setting this up. Takes guts. Or a lack of sanity. Or both?"

"Try desperation," I said, though I hadn't planned to. I couldn't reveal too much, couldn't let her know what this was really about or why I needed her. But I said it anyway, because it was the first truthful thing I'd said to anyone in a long time.

"Hmm." Shannon folded her legs, sheathed in deep violet tights, and gave me a sidelong glance. "Are you sure this isn't more about embarrassing your boyfriend than it is about seeking social justice?"

I pressed my lips. Targeting Hyde and Anton was critical and I needed a third party involved, a party seemingly acting based on their own agenda that couldn't be traced back to me. If Shannon did something as shocking as she did at the funeral – flashing, chanting, whatever – that could potentially make Anton's "seduce and destroy" plan completely pointless. I hadn't thought it all out yet. No, to be precise, I had no goddamn clue what I was doing. But I had to try. I had to do something.

I wasn't going to be Anton's pawn.

"No, it's not that," I told her. "If I just wanted to screw Hyde over, there are plenty of things I could do." Like drug him and try to force him into a public orgy.

"It's just that Hyde's been... the source of a lot of pain for me. And for a lot of people."

Shannon was silent for a while, chewing her frayed pink lips as she stared off into space.

"Are you OK?" I asked, but only when the silence had gone on for too long. "Did I say something?"

"You know, it happened when I was thirteen." When she talked, she looked right at me with her pale green eyes. "While I was growing up in Bakersfield. It was the short, geeky kid who sat next to me in homeroom. He'd always been nice. A little too nice, you know, the kind of 'nice' guys are when they expect ass as a reward."

I watched her sigh, but said nothing. "I didn't, of course," she continued. "I didn't want him. Eventually, he asked me out and when I said no it was like I'd broken some kind of unspoken contract. He didn't say it, but he didn't have to. I thought he'd just suck it up and move on. It was all over when he found out I was a swan." She shook her head. "Three years, Deanna. We were McGinnis High's cutest couple."

I curled over, propping myself up on my knees.

"You know, when your feathers are taken, it doesn't matter where you are. You'll be at home, at the grocery store, on your way out of town and it'll hit you. Once the sun goes down, that one thought tugging at you, screaming at you to obey: 'I have to go to him'. No matter what. Wherever he is, you have to be there.

"It's like the fairytale, Dee. The hunter steals the swan maiden's feathers. She follows him. They make a home together. But what they don't tell you is that she is his because she has to be. And no matter how far she runs, she always comes back to him, every night. As long he has her feathers, she doesn't have a choice. All the times I snuck out of my room. My parents thought I was some kind of 'problem child'. They didn't know what was really going on because I physically couldn't tell them – because of the swan's curse: that unspoken rule that forces you to be loyal to the one who's captured you. All the time. Always. As soon as he took my feathers, it was just second nature – a drive as natural as breathing. I was caged in a nightmare."

"Shannon…" I shook my head, clenching my teeth as if it would force the horrible images out. "How…" I didn't even know how to ask.

"How did I get free? He killed himself." Shannon had said it so simply that I half-expected her to ask me if I wanted to go grab breakfast next. My stomach wouldn't have been able to handle it anyway. She turned, facing the bathroom door, sinking deeper into the couch with her arms folded over her chest. "Bastard killed himself. And at the end of the day, *he* was the one they cried for, even after they found my feathers. 'Poor Matt. He'd been suffering for so long. His guilt must have sent him over the edge.' I was a footnote in someone else's tragedy."

She laughed, as if laughing were the reasonable response to something so horrifying. "So I get you. I get why this matters. It matters to me too. If I have to gatecrash a few masquerade balls and terrorize a few socialites to get the message out, so be it."

When I finally raised my head, I noticed she was looking at me. She'd just shared something personal she didn't have to. And there I was trying not to cry all over her friend's duvet.

"It's OK. This isn't tit for tat or whatever. I told you my story. You don't have to tell me yours. That's your choice. Everyone deserves a choice."

I nodded, thankful for the thousands of knots loosening in my chest.

"So. We need to talk details. You wanna get out of here? Union Square is pretty damn close. Oh, and I'll call some of my friends over too. Gotta meet the partners in crime, right?"

She stood up, throwing her bag around her shoulders, beckoning for me to follow. For one ridiculous second, I felt as if I were one of them. As if I were part of some greater movement.

"You coming?"

"No, it's OK," I said, but my smile struggled. "I've gotta get home. Let's chat online later."

I wasn't a part of anything. Just a clueless coward who'd been driven into a corner. Shannon wasn't my partner. She was my soldier and I needed her, even if I couldn't tell her exactly what her help meant to me.

And how vile I felt for using her.

16

Masked

Hyde had been so busy with his meetings, I only saw him once before Saturday night. I figured Anton would think I was slacking and dial me up, once again dangling the threat of slavery over my head like the perfect prick he was. But he didn't. He was probably banking on tonight.

"Wow. Nice," Ade said in my doorway, leaning on the frame. I was in front of my mirror, holding up the black evening dress I'd tried on yesterday morning: its tight floral bodice had just enough cleavage to make Anton think I was trying, and synched at the waist, flowing down my legs in a layered cascade of fabric.

"Yeah," I muttered and placed it on my bed.

"Looks like you're getting used to the Ericka-lifestyle. Balls and gowns. How's it taste?"

I couldn't quite look Ade in the eyes.

"I'd rather not go," I answered flatly, sitting at my

desk, pushing aside the Margaret Atwoods so I could lay my head down.

"Why not? You've got a pretty dress. Hot rich boyfriend – even these little weird glove things."

When I looked over, she was trying them on.

"Marry Hyde and you'll be Ericka: The Next Generation, except richer and only slightly less neurotic. Who needs straight As, am I right? You'll finally get to leave this dump for good."

I couldn't tell if it was jealousy or disdain lining the disgust in her tone. Could have been both.

"So what's the problem, Dee?" She paused. "Or is it Hyde? Your man giving you problems?" She chuckled. "Damn; it's always the guy who messes up the fairy tale, isn't it? Ha. Ericka 2.0 indeed."

To say Hyde was "giving me problems" was an understatement large enough to fill canyons.

"How is little Richie Rich, anyway?" she asked. "He doing OK?"

"Fine, I guess." Actually, I wasn't sure. Hyde had barely been paying attention when we'd gone out, half-nodding and half-smiling at everything I said. At first, I'd just shrugged it off as "'that thing some guys do sometimes"; that is, until I'd noticed he'd been checking his phone for messages as frequently as a text-obsessed school-girl.

"Oh sorry," he'd said when I'd asked what was up. "It's just..." He'd looked around conspiratorially. "I have my legal counsel, Roan, and some private detectives working on something for me. Something important."

"Something came in the mail for you, by the way," Ade said, snapping me back to reality. "Hyde sent it. Whatever he's doing, it's obviously not bad enough to keep him from showering you with expensive shit – or is that just a commonly accepted custom among the elite? 'Oh I treated you like crap, here's your diamond ring, see you next week when you catch me with my secretary.'"

"Go ask Ericka." I left my room and walked into the living room.

There were four thin boxes, each eggshell white, stacked on top of each other on the coffee table. I lifted the lid off one, its textured surface a little rough against my fingers. My heart gave a nervous tremor. It was the golden masks I'd asked Hyde to get me, lying that I needed a few to choose from, not really caring that it made me look like a spoiled faux-cialite. I checked my phone – yes, the mask was the same as the one in the text. Perfect.

I walked into the closet and dug out an old schoolbag of mine I hadn't used in about three years. Then I dumped all three masks inside.

Ade blinked. "Um–"

"Sorry, I'm kind of busy; can we talk later?" I rushed her out of the room and closed the door in her face – gently so I'd come off as less bitchy, if that was even possible. Then I grabbed the lid off one of the white boxes on the table. The name and number of the store was there in beautiful gold, embroidered into the lid.

"Going out," I told Ade on my way to the front door. "I'll see you in a bit."

I walked a few blocks until I found a payphone. I didn't want the call traced back to me.

Step One: get the address.

"Thank you for calling Moretta, how may I help you?" said a woman after I dialed the number on the boxes. She sounded pretty young. Hopefully she'd be easy to swindle.

"Hello, I have a problem." I forced my voice into a ditzy, breathy pitch that made me sound, somehow, like a twelve year-old from the Valley. I'd deal with the embarrassment later.

"OK, how may I help you?"

"A delivery was supposed to come for me and my friends last week. Three golden lace masks. Venetian. Paid for by Anton Rey?" This was risky. "Is there any legitimate reason why you people haven't sent it yet like you were supposed to?" I figured a pinch of entitlement would help me sell it.

"A delivery?"

"Yes, last week. *God*. Are you people completely incompetent? I have a ball to go to. What do you think is going to happen if I show up without a mask? Do you have any idea how embarrassing that'll be? Or is assisting with social suicide a part of your services?"

"I could... check for you, miss. But I'm pretty sure we delivered all our orders."

"Except I *don't have it*! And this party is *tonight*. I mean, did you even get the address right? What address did you send it to?"

"An order by Anton Rey?"

A moment of silence and the clicking of keys. "We sent the order to 315 West Broadway last Wednesday. Room number 541. Isn't that right?"

I wrote the address down in the little notebook in my jeans pocket.

"Hmm... OK, wait, let me check again." I counted to thirty in my head. "Oh wait, is it this white box thingy here? Oh my God, what? Oops!" I laughed. "Oh my God, I'm such an idiot. It was buried under the mail. I'm sorry. Forget I called."

Step Two: confirm targets are at said address.

After I hung up, I used my cell phone to call Shannon. "315 West Broadway last Wednesday. Room number 541."

"Ooh, good work."

"Remember – they're tall, blonde–"

"–Russian models, if memory serves from the last ten times you reminded me. Don't worry; I'll get back to you in a bit."

The bounce in her voice made me wonder, briefly, if she was enjoying this. Good for her. It was all *I* could do to keep from fainting onto the sidewalk.

I waited. It was all very simple, really. Shannon's friend, Mick, would "accidentally" deliver a pizza to the "wrong address". Of course, this whole plan only worked under the assumption that Anton really would be having his models picked up at their apartment.

"Good news: they're there getting ready, apparently – and not at all interested in melted cheese."

I nodded. "Good, good." I nodded again, running

a hand through my hair, my heart pounding. "This is good. Wait a second."

I dialed Hyde as I continued down the sidewalk.

Step Three: arrange for transportation.

"Deanna? Anything wrong?"

"No, nothing, it's just..." Yet again with the honest concern. My stomach squirmed at the thought of feeding Hyde more lies, but I gritted my teeth and reminded myself that it was for the greater good. "You're... sending a car, right?"

A pause. "What, you thought I'd make you bike across the bridge? I asked you to be my date, the least I can do is give you a ride."

I could hear the smile in his voice. Kind of made it harder. "Actually, about that... I kind of need a big favor."

"Favor?"

I sighed. "Well... Ade kind of did something to piss me off a while ago." Not only entirely untrue, but not entirely fair either. "So I stopped talking to her and then she stopped talking to me because I stopped talking to her first. I've been feeling pretty bad about the whole thing."

"So just apologize."

"It doesn't seem like enough, though. I really want to make it up to her. Ade acts like she doesn't care, but she really does enjoy the high life whenever she can charm her way into it. Dresses, parties–"

"You want to get her an invite to the masquerade ball?"

"No!" I said a little too quickly. "Um, no, she and her friends have this... thing at a night club in Jersey."

"Jersey?"

I bit my lip. "Well, yeah. It's this really hot, fancy party apparently."

"In *Jersey*?"

"Or something." I probably should have thought through my excuse a little bit more before trying it out on Hyde, but I had to send Anton's girls far enough away without it legally being kidnapping. I figured stranding them in Jersey would get the job done. To a high end Russian model living it up in Soho, it might as well have been Mogadishu. "Anyway, I thought she'd love nothing more than to show up and show off in style, you know, so... do you think you can get your driver to pick her and her friends up instead? She's staying at her friend's for the weekend."

It took Hyde what felt like a minute to respond.

"So...to make up with your sister, who you've been ignoring for unknown reasons, you want me to send the stretch limo meant for you to her instead so that it can take her to some sort of hoedown in New Jersey?"

A pause. "A trendy hoedown?"

Hyde couldn't stop laughing.

"I mean it! Hyde, I know it sounds stupid, but I really, really–"

"What's the address she's staying at?"

Oh, come on now. "Just like that?"

"To be honest, I'm pretty embarrassed myself. And yet: what's the address?"

So it really was possible to melt and be guilt-ridden at the same time. "Um..." I gave him both addresses: the one in Soho, as well as the one I'd written down yesterday when looking up Jersey clubs online. I'd picked the club where that one reality TV star got drunk and punched out the camera man before trying to make out with him on the floor. If Anton were planning on getting there just before midnight…

"Could you pick them up at eleven? And um, I don't know where they'll end up after said hoedown, but could you maybe have your driver drop them off at a hotel down there when they're done? I mean I don't want them to get picked up by anyone else." I shuddered at the thought. I didn't want them hurt, after all, just out of the way. Not that I assumed that they were completely incapable of taking care of themselves, but still, I had to cover all my bases.

"Yeah, yeah."

"Thanks, Hyde." With a sigh, I added, "I'm really, really sorry about this." I was. All this manipulation to prove that Anton couldn't manipulate me. *The greater good, Deanna.*

"It's all right. And since I know you're definitely not planning on biking over the bridge in a couture dress, what time can I pick you up?"

"Uh…" I fidgeted. "It's OK. You don't need to come all the way here. I'll take a taxi."

"A taxi? Why?"

Because I'm tired of taking advantage of you. "Because there's something I need to do at home first, so I won't get there until much later," I said instead. "Really, it's OK. Don't worry about me."

"How can I not?"

Stop that, I demanded, not knowing whether it was him or me I was begging. Squashing the butterflies in my chest, I smiled. "Really, don't worry. So… I guess I'll see you at the party. I'll be the one in black ruffles."

"Try and find me."

Hyde hung up.

A deep, calming breath wasn't quite enough to help me ignore the awkward-making tingling feeling rushing down my stomach. Still, I called Shannon anyway. "OK, confirmed. I'm bringing the package."

"Nice. Hey, see how fun this is?"

I rolled my eyes. She reminded me way too much of Ade.

A short trip later and I was knocking at her apartment. All the money I'd been spending on transportation the last couple of weeks was drying out my wallet. I made a mental note to sign up for extra hours of canned-food hell at the grocery store once this whole fiasco was over.

Shannon had her hair dyed a light pale blonde. She had two friends with her. They waved at me, their makeup half-done. Tall, skinny and blonde. All they'd need is the right dress and a lack of shame to fool Anton.

"This is the right shade, right?" Shannon ruffled her hair.

"Yeah, I think so. Anyway, I doubted Anton would notice or care. They're in here." I shoved the bag into her hands. "Remember, Anton's limo is probably going to be at the models' apartment a little before midnight, so you guys should get there by maybe half-past eleven."

"We know, we know."

"And whatever you do, don't say a word until you're at the party. And don't take off your masks... whatever you do has to be with the masks on. If they come off, Anton might wonder why you're wearing the same one he bought for his models."

"Well, obviously," said one friend, putting on some lipstick.

"I don't know what he'll do to me if he finds out I helped you get them." Another lie. I knew perfectly well what he'd do. "He can be really... vicious."

Shannon ran a brush through her hair. "We won't sell you out, if that's what you're worried about."

"You remember what Anton looks like, right?"

Shannon laughed. "Yes, I still have the pictures I found online. It's all *good*, Deanna, *damn*."

"She's so thorough," said the girl in the bathroom. She winked. I couldn't tell if they were making fun of me.

"OK, OK," I said. "Just make sure–"

"Yes, don't worry. We know what the plan is," Shannon said, rummaging through the backpack and pulling out a mask. She strapped the golden-laced mask over her face. "You've done more than enough. We've got this. You just worry about your end."

She was right. All the pieces were in place. The only thing left was to get dressed and call a taxi. With a shaky hand on my forehead, I exhaled and nodded.

"Right. See you there."

There was not enough makeup in the world to hide the lines under my eyes. I looked exhausted. And scared.

It meshed with the eye shadow.

Through the mirror, I stared at the black couture dress clinging to my body. I counted each of the ruffles flowing down my legs in tumbles of fabric, ruffles that for one moment reminded me of rotted feathers. I imagined my own feathers, black and rotted beneath my skin, and shook my head.

The last eggshell-white Moretta box lay open on my desk. Inside was a black-rimmed half-mask, decorated with silver macramé and studded with crystals. It was the single most beautiful thing I'd ever owned: the military badge of a society girl with few cares and endless time. I put it on, tying the ribbons at the back, pinning my black curls down. Then, once again, I peered into the mirror.

An imposter. I saw the lies fastened to my face and shuddered, truly, from the core.

Quietly, I slipped the mask off and rummaged through my drawer. *Found it.* It didn't have its own case, but there was no way I'd ever lose it. Mom's bracelet. A simple bronze chain. Ever since I'd first felt the brush of feathers against my back, I'd been trying to hold on to the girl I used to be. I clasped it around my wrist. It didn't help.

Just this one night, I told myself as I walked out of my room. Survive this one night and then you can think of a way to survive the rest. Then you'll be you again. Free.

"Wow, you look great, honey," Dad said from the couch, a beer in his hand.

"Yeah, you look great, Dee," repeated Ade from the couch, a soda in *her* hand. Both her voice and eyes had dulled at the sight of me. She set the soda can down, pushing it towards Dad with a finger and stood up.

"You think?" I asked as I watched her walk to the kitchen and open the fridge. I was pushing her. I knew I shouldn't. Maybe I just wanted to hear a bit of sincerity in her voice – or anything, really, without that frigid sting.

She glanced at me. "Yeah. Pretty as hell," she said, then took out her half-eaten slice of pie from yesterday night and set it on the table.

She wasn't looking at me. Asking why would embarrass us both. My shoulders sagged anyway, weighted by unsaid words. I repeated the mantra I'd been clinging to like a religion ever since I stumbled out of Stylo's metal cage – and maybe before:

I can't tell her what's really going on. Even if I did, she wouldn't be able to help, anyway. It's too risky. It'd only make things worse.

But even if she didn't know, I thought at the very least she'd be able to look past the couture and actually see just how thoroughly it was suffocating me.

"I kind of don't want to go," was the closest I could get to the truth.

"Then you could have said no," Ade answered flatly.

"Come on, Adrianna, don't be jealous," said Dad from the couch.

Ade nearly dropped her fork and whipped her head around to meet the back of his with a silent glare. The room shook with the intensity of it.

Jealous. But she was the sister who didn't give a shit. She was the one who'd charmed her way into Anton

Rey's party. Except we both knew Anton was a fluke. Ade had the skill to make boys, rich and poor, horny enough to fool around with her. But thus far she hadn't yet managed to make any of them care. I had always figured she didn't care either.

She was quick to recover, though. Instead of yelling, she poured herself a glass of milk. "Dad, you took care of the electricity bill, didn't you?"

An odd question. "What?" Dad frowned. "What does that have to do with anything?"

Ade knew as well I did. He was stalling – stalling because with all the insanity life had been hurling at me nonstop for the past few weeks, I hadn't been able to remind him, like I'd been doing for years. And if I didn't remind him, no one reminded him. And if no one reminded him, the bills usually didn't get paid. And yet there was Ade, looking at Dad with a cold rigidity that reminded me of someone else entirely – of the girl I couldn't find in the mirror. The old me.

That girl had never been entirely free either.

A knock on the door. I opened it to find a guy in a suit and a funny hat lowering his white-gloved hands while an exquisitely sleek black car revved behind him... the same one that had taken us over the bridge to Hedley's funeral. "I'm here to pick you up, miss. Your sister sent me."

"Ericka did?"

"Oh yeah." Dad set his beer can down and peeked over from the couch. "Ericka called a little while ago while you were in the bathroom. Said Hyde told her you'd need a ride to the party. Apparently she and Charles are already there."

An odd gesture, but then Ericka did do stuff like that once in a blue moon – when her husband let her. It was Charles who controlled the money flow, after all, Charles who sanctioned every expense. And even when it came to his in-laws, Charles wasn't exactly a giver.

"It's a nice thing they did," Dad continued. "You make sure you thank them once you get there. Hyde too."

"Look at that, little sister," said Ade with a defeated smile. "You've got a carriage and everything." She poked at the crust.

I'd have preferred the subway.

"Ade, you want to hang out tomorrow?" I blurted out suddenly. Ade looked just as shocked as I expected she would. "I mean we haven't really in a while." I hated the way Ade couldn't look at me for more than a few seconds.

She shrugged. "I can't. I'm… busy."

"Really?"

"I'm working," she said quietly. "I signed up for extra hours. You're not the only–" She stopped.

"Oh…"

"Well, I mean I might as well, right? Since…" Though she trailed off again, it was a statement she didn't need to answer for me to understand the meaning behind it. She looked at me in my couture dress. She looked at Ericka's driver, in the doorway. Then she looked at Dad, and the unpaid bills that would have to be peeled off the cheese-stained kitchen table.

"Miss," prodded the driver.

Ade grinned. "Have fun."

I nodded lifelessly. The door shut behind me with a heavy click more devastating than the whine of metal bars, or the desperate chirping of the bird trapped inside.

Twelve-feet-tall brass doors opened into a dimly lit oval ballroom underneath a high gilded ceiling. The masks freaked me out more than anything. Regardless of how exquisite the ball gowns were, or extravagant, or excessive, the masks added a grotesque quality that sent a shudder through me – half-masks and full-masks, masks of pure lace, masks of netting, masks that fanned out in all directions, masks that climbed up the wearer's forehead like black vines and stretched to the sky. Ears and beaks. Half-covered grins and beady seductive glances. They seemed to meld with the flesh, becoming part of it. The plastic faces of the wealthy elite.

I wrapped my arms around my chest, shivering partly because I'd left my cardigan in Ericka's car, but mostly because I knew I was trapped. From the stained-glass skylight to the marble floor to the Corinthian columns lining the walls. From one cage into another.

Where should I go first? Anton would text me where to meet him at midnight. He probably anticipated not being able to find me. I was masked after all. So was Hyde. Knowing that Anton couldn't have me watched or followed helped me breathe easier.

I checked my cell phone. Just about half an hour to midnight. That meant Anton, Shannon and her friends wouldn't get here for a while. What the hell was I supposed to do until then?

Try and find me.

Hyde. A wave of warmth passed through my chest, down my stomach. I squeezed my eyes shut to get rid of the lightheadedness. Perhaps I could find him. It wouldn't hurt. There was no point in me standing around on my own staring slack-jawed for two hours. Plus, I'd need to be around him when Shannon did come. I was fairly confident the plan had nothing to do with the flutter in my chest.

I pushed through the crowd, keeping my arms wrapped closely around me so I wouldn't draw attention to myself by–

"*Excuse* me!" Red wine splashed onto a finely tailored suit. Damn, I was so close.

"I'm sorry," I mumbled.

The tall man glared at me with sunken blue eyes. He might have been more intimidating if he hadn't been so scrawny and frail.

"Relax, honey, she clearly didn't mean it," said the beautiful woman next to him, her solid black macramé mask matching her strapless sequined gown perfectly. If only she hadn't sounded so emotionally exhausted and lifeless, I might have counted her among the few bright spots I could find among this socialite circus of haute couture.

"Am I supposed to care? This is a thousand-dollar

suit. If I'd known there'd be little girls stumbling around I'd have stayed in the office."

Wait. That voice.

The woman flipped back her long black hair, clearly straightened, and folded her arms in an "I'm painfully annoyed and I'm not even going to try to hide it" kind of way. Very familiar. "You'd have stayed in your cave anyway if I hadn't dragged you kicking and screaming into the outside world."

He smirked. "Yeah. Thanks for that."

"Ericka?"

The woman steeled herself, as if her closely guarded secret had been shouted from the heavens. She looked at once embarrassed and panicked, and yet still kept her head raised and her grin spread widely enough to perhaps convince me that I hadn't just glimpsed the broken marriage of a husband and wife who clearly could not stand each other. It was Ericka. The mixture of pride and shame was more solid a proof than her voice.

"It's me, Deanna," I added helpfully.

She deflated almost immediately, all the airs she would have put on dissipating before she had a chance. "Deanna, is it that really you?"

"Yes, Ericka." I laughed. "Or have you already forgotten the sound of my voice?" I slipped up my mask quickly so she could see my whole face.

"Oh." She tried a smile, but it only dissolved into more shame. Still, since she was pretending I hadn't seen it, I pretended not to notice. "Charles, it's my sister."

"Yes, I know who it is." He rolled his eyes and threw in a particularly half-assed, "Hello, Deanna."

Pfft. *Beanpole.* "Sorry about the suit."

He straightened his back. "It was very expensive."

"You're not going to cry, are you?"

"Deanna!" Ericka grabbed my wrist, playing the indignant wife quite well, even though she couldn't stop her lips from twitching upward. "She's sorry, Charles. Deanna, why don't you come with me? I'd love to talk for a bit."

It was the honesty of her grin that sold it.

"Deanna," she said, once we'd found a place near one of the columns. "Are you doing OK? Adrianna told me you were having some problems at home."

I scanned the crowd. One woman in golden chiffon teased a man's lips with a strawberry as flesh red as his horned mask. "She may have exaggerated. Thanks for sending a car, by the way. The seats were really cushy."

"She said you'd been keeping to yourself, locked in your room."

"I go out with Hyde sometimes."

At the sound of his name, Ericka rubbed her forearm with a sigh, the wineglass in her other hand wobbling a little. "OK, but other than that you're content with shunning every other aspect of life?" She shook her head. "That's not you at all."

I peered up at her, incredulous. "Not me? Who am I, Ericka?"

She blinked, startled into silence before she managed to find her voice again. "What?"

"Keeping to myself isn't me." I adjusted my mask over my eyes. "How would *you* know?"

"I didn't mean... Look, can you blame me for being worried? I don't care what you think of me, but I'm still your sister, Deanna. I care about what happens to you. I... want to know what's going on in your life."

For the first time in over a decade. If only she'd cared back when my only problems were giant-sized pimples and missing Mom.

"Nothing's going on." I turned back to the crowd. "Nothing really..."

My breath hitched. Somewhere amidst the dancing masses stood a young man in a black waistcoat. Dark hair grazed the top of his forehead, which was half-covered by a metal mask that left the right side of his face exposed. But even if his entire face had been hidden, I'd still know who it was. The way he watched me with a gentle kind of intensity that made me both nervous and excited – that was the biggest hint.

"Deanna?" Ericka held on to my gloved hand with hers. "Where are you going?"

I had to keep an eye on Hyde. I had to be around so I could make sure Shannon followed through with the plan. That was why I was floating to him. It wasn't because of that sly grin.

"Sorry, I have to go."

"Wait." Ericka squeezed my hand harder. "Come on, we just found each other – why not stick around and chat? I know I haven't been around a lot, but that's why I want us to spend some time together."

Hyde turned and slipped through the crowd.

"Sorry, I really have to go. Why don't you go find Bean... uh, Charles. Or your friends. I'm sure they're around here." I actually had never met any of Ericka's society gal pals. I always just assumed they existed. The sudden stiffness in Ericka's grip made me think otherwise. It took me another moment to realize that she was helplessly pleading me to stay with her.

"I'm really, really sorry," I repeated with all sincerity, guilt snaking through my insides. "I just have to do this one thing. I'll come find you later," I added, knowing that I probably wouldn't.

With a set jaw, I left Ericka standing there by herself. I saw glimpses of Hyde, of his waistcoat, of his hair, as he made his way through the schmoozing fashion designers and statuesque models, the socialites, the businessmen. Every once in a while he'd check back to make sure I was still following him. Then he'd disappear in a crowd, leaving me to twist around and strain my eyes for a hint of him.

Who the hell did he think he was, the Pied Piper? And yet I *was* following him, dutifully. The cat and mouse game had somehow made me even more desperate to find him. He was playing around. Maybe he thought it was hot.

It was, a little. I hated myself for admitting that.

My heart nearly leapt into my throat when I felt an arm slip around my waist. Suddenly my back was pressed against someone's chest. I would have screamed if I hadn't heard Hyde's whisper in my ear. "Meet me in the Red Room in fifteen."

The Red Room? Wasn't that the room Anton had booked? What was Hyde playing at?

By the time I'd recovered enough to turn around, he was already gone. I bit my lip. I could have gone back to find Ericka, but somehow, despite my guilt at abandoning her, I didn't quite feel the need. I wandered through the party instead, trying not to bump into anything living while wishing to God I could be at home, hanging out in Ade's room, watching movies on her laptop while we stuffed our faces with leftovers. A woman in a Victorian corset glared at me when I giggled at her mask, which looked like a lizard-cat hybrid with wide gaping eyes, crowned with a mess of fresh flowers that framed a picture of what looked like a pale seventeenth-century noblewoman. I mean, *really*.

Twenty to twelve. My phone vibrated in my purse. An incoming text from Shannon: *Limo's here. On our way, babe.*

OK. OK, OK. Shannon promised she'd text me again once they all arrived at the party. Until then, I had to relax. Five more minutes. Then I'd go find Hyde, because... why not? The Red Room, right?

After asking someone for directions, I made my way up the stairs to the mezzanine, which overlooked the ballroom. A few people were already there, kissing against the railings, sipping champagne as they stared past the columns to the candlelit chandelier. Red Room, Red Room... My heels clicked against the marble floor. Had to be around here somewhere.

I found Hyde by one of the arched windows, but he wasn't alone. A woman in a draped ice-lavender gown was stroking his face with a white-gloved finger. Though she was masked, and her figure was a long, slender figure-eight, I could tell she was at least a decade older than him. Her lips puckered as her fingers trailed down his arm. She smiled at him like she owned him. When she cocked her head to the side, I clutched my purse a little harder.

Hyde, though, was apparently not having it. He grabbed her hand and flung it away, impatiently.

"You're still not going to take me up on my offer?" I almost gasped. It was Beatrice Hoffer-Rey.

"Beatrice, don't you think your husband might get a little offended at how valiantly you've been trying to leap into the pants of the much younger man who fired him?"

"Please, dear. We both know my sex life is as much a concern of his as his is of mine." Her nasal voice, so affected, made my lips curl.

"I suppose so," said Hyde, equally disgusted. "But desperation is a real turn off. Makes you look old, Bea. All that Botox for nothing."

Beatrice only laughed as she turned, looked down the hall – and spotted me. Our eyes locked.

"I won't say this again." Hyde stepped towards her, almost menacingly. "Back off. I mean it. I'm not for sale."

"Are you sure? I've heard differently."

Hyde looked stunned. Without another word, he strode towards me, grabbed my wrist and pulled me until Beatrice's fox smile faded into the distance.

"Hyde, are you OK?" I asked, once the door to the Red Room was closed behind us. It was a small, private drawing room with birch-panel walls that matched the dark tiled floor. But the room itself was more stunning for the lit candles staged around it. A bottle of champagne waited in an ice bucket on the center table, flanked by two wineglasses. Hyde had obviously set this up. Hadn't he? In the room Anton'd chosen for us....

Frowning, Hyde sat in the leather armchair, watching the flames of a candle crackle quietly.

"Hyde... are you OK?"

It was a second before he registered my question. "What? Oh, yeah, I'm fine." He laughed. "Damn. Ruined the mood, didn't she?"

More like tore it apart and burned the pieces, but I was more worried about the lines sinking into his face. I sat next to him. "What was she going on about?"

"Her? Who knows? I think for someone who's used to coercing underwear models into sleeping with her, hearing a guy tell her no is like a slap to her face – not that she'd be able to feel it. I heard she's numb as hell up there."

I laughed. "Yeah, I know. It's a running joke on the *Sew or Die* forums over at *Angry TV Recaps*. We're supposed to take a drink every time she manages an expression."

There was something about ridiculing that woman that loosened the tension in his chest. He slipped off his mask and placed it on the table, next to the flower-vase. But when I reached for mine, he seized my hand and pulled it away from my face.

"It looks gorgeous on you." His eyes travelled down the length of my body and up again, before catching himself. "You look stunning, Deanna," he admitted with a little blush.

My face flushed with heat. "O-oh really?" I let out a strangled laugh and turned to the table, but my eyes flitted to him anyway – to his long fingers rubbing the nape of his neck. "Well, I'm glad I look good because I feel as awkward as if I'd been stuffed in a giant bear suit."

"Yeah, I figured you'd be pretty uncomfortable." Hyde adjusted his waistcoat over a particularly broad set of shoulders. "I am too, honestly. That's why I booked this room for us."

I watched him, eyes narrowed, as he stood up and popped the bottle of champagne. "I thought–" Don't mention Anton. "I heard someone else booked this room."

"Hmm? Oh yeah. Anton." He casually poured two glasses. "He was probably planning an orgy or something. I figured he can do that at home, so I re-booked it."

Of course he did, I thought dryly. Did Anton know? Being here wasn't exactly dangerous *per se* if Anton couldn't get his girls in. But if my plan ended up failing and I still had to meet him downstairs to grab the vial...

It wasn't going to come to that. Everything was going to work out. It had to.

Hyde extended his arm to me, a wine-filled glass in his hands, his arm thick and sturdy in the sleek white sleeve. Funny how once upon a time I thought *I* was the one who would end up seducing *him*.

I took the glass, but set it down. "Sorry, I don't drink."

"For religious reasons?"

"For legal reasons. I'm underage." A pause. "*You are too.*"

Hyde laughed. "And *you* are adorable." He sipped.

I had a chance to roll my eyes before they flitted to the clock. Thirteen minutes to midnight. It wouldn't be long before Shannon and Anton showed up. Discreetly, I rubbed my damp palms against my dress, pretending I was smoothening out the ruffles.

"It's quality stuff," Hyde said, and when he did I realized I'd been staring blankly at the wine in my glass. Hyde couldn't have possibly known that I was scrutinizing my own reflection instead. "I had it imported from France."

"Wow, look at you, importing things from Europe. It's like the rich boy rite of passage." I gave him a wry smile to let him know I was teasing, because sometimes even I couldn't tell anymore. "I guess you'd know all about French wine, having been there for so long, huh?"

Hyde's lips twitched right as he answered, "Yeah," very quietly. "You sure there's nothing else on your mind?"

Seconds ticked in my head. "Positive."

"You sure? I admit I'm not the best at romancing girls, but I'm pretty sure when you pour champagne and light candles, 'silent introspection' isn't the reaction you're supposed to get."

He sidled up closer to me and wrapped his arm around my waist. The spark from his arm shivered up my spine. Maybe because this was the first time in a long while that I could be certain I wasn't being watched, I let myself melt into him.

"Honestly, I thought it was strange," he continued. "How suddenly you changed that night on your front steps – when you kissed me."

Silently, I lowered my head, watching the bubbles cling to the inside of his glass.

"I didn't want to say anything. I was just happy to…" He paused. "What's been going on, Deanna? This isn't you."

I thought of the weeks of lies wrapped in fear and grimaced at how easily I drew my knees up onto his legs. I had no right to lean on him like this. "You're the second person to say that today. Except I don't even know what it means."

Hyde squeezed my shoulder. "Hmm?"

"If this isn't me, then who am I?"

I thought of the follicles in my back waiting to sprout. Hyde let out a heavy sigh and tilted his head, deep in thought, or at least managing a good impression of it.

"Well, you're unstoppable."

I blinked. "What?"

"Unstoppable. Outspoken. And a little bad ass, to be honest. Not that you're arrogant, of course. You can be sweet and cheerful, but you don't take shit from anyone. That's who you are, Deanna."

I would have laughed, but I was still stunned into silence.

"Well, that's who you were." Hyde gazed down at me, purposefully. "When we were kids. It's part of the reason why I… I don't know. Gravitated towards you. I was enthralled by you."

I ran my hand over my mask, each crystal stud rolling over my fingers. "You still are. Enthralled by her, I mean. That's why you followed me around and sent Mariachi Bands to my house. You weren't doing them for me; you were doing them for her."

"Maybe. At first." He pulled me back to him, setting his glass down on the side table. "It's not like people aren't supposed to change, Deanna. But you're a lot stronger than you think you are. That girl never really disappeared. I don't think so, anyway."

I thought of the feathers. I thought of the years I'd spent cleaning up after Dad, missing Ericka, covering for Ade.

"*You're* the one I did this for." Hyde's sweet smile made my body flush with heat. "These candles are lit for you."

I straightened up so I could look at him properly. His face was beautiful, but his words trumped even that. They nestled somewhere inside me, flickering as brightly as the candlelight.

"And what about you, Hyde?"

He furrowed his brows as he looked down at me. "What *about* me?"

"Who are you? You barely talk about yourself. It's always about the past with you."

Silence stretched between us. He kept his eyes on mine as he thought, considering, maybe, whether or not to answer me. I shouldn't have been surprised when he made his decision, tipping my chin up to him, placating me with a kiss.

"See," I whispered. "You're wearing one too, aren't you?" Lightly, I touched the left side of his face, where the mask should have been. Instead of answering, he kissed me again with a smile, this time deeper. I felt his hot breath, his tongue running along my lips. His thumb stroked a line across my cheek up to my ear. The skin sizzled beneath his touch.

My brain was screaming at me. But I just wanted this moment. Just one moment of quiet bliss.

My phone vibrated. *Oh for fuck's sake.* I broke the kiss with a breathy whimper.

"The universe might hate me," said Hyde as I reached into my purse, which had been lying at my feet, forgotten.

"Sorry, this'll only take a second." I curled a lock of hair behind my ear and grabbed my phone. It buzzed again in my hand.

Two texts had come in. One was from Anton. Quickly, I leapt away from Hyde. "Oh, uh, it's private. From Ade," was my half-assed excuse.

I'm here. Meet me at the bar. I'm at the far right. Don't be late.

The next one was from Shannon. *Here. Everything's set up. Bout to start. Where's ur bf?*

Oh crap.

"Hyde, do you want to dance with me?" I blurted. It was the best I could come up with.

Hyde raised an eyebrow. "Now?" He looked like he'd rather rip my clothes off, and honestly, a part of me wanted to let him. But a plan was a plan and this was all to save his ass. "I'm not… really big on dancing, Dee."

"I am!"

"We can dance here." He was right. Even from up here, I could still hear the music.

"Yes, but there's something romantic about dancing in a ballroom. Please? Please, please?" I batted my eyelashes for good measure. He returned the gesture with an incredulous laugh, shaking his head. I suppose that did look supremely ridiculous.

"Fine, fine. Just don't complain when I trip and land on top of you."

Something shyly seductive curled my lips. "That wouldn't be quite so bad, now would it?"

Hyde squeezed my hand in his, staring at me as if the sun were burning in him. I hoped to God this would work.

As we approached the bar, I spotted Friend Number One at the edge of the crowd, her pale red dress clinging to her thin frame, Moretta's golden mask glinting under the dim lights. I could see a sleek black rectangle peeking out of her bag: the phone she was using to record Shannon's ambush. It'd already begun. I could see the incredulousness on Anton's face from here as Shannon cornered him, as planned, about *Bella*'s promotion of indentured labor. But the pièce de résistance would come when Shannon's second friend arrived.

Wait, where the hell was she? I peered around, but only two Moretta masks crossed my line of vision. She was supposed to be here, right? Waiting? This had to be timed perfectly. Everyone had to be in place at exactly the right moment, Hyde included. He was a target too, after all. The whole point was to target them both. It was the only way that Anton would call off his plan tonight. And of course, I'd be there, standing around innocently, ready to go through with Anton's evil plan, if only those awful protesters hadn't shown up and ruined everything.

Hyde leaned into me. "Hey, isn't that Anton?"

My throat was drying up by the second. A tall girl in a mask strode towards Anton and Shannon, but it wasn't Protester Number Three.

"There you are," the girl said. "We need to talk."

She slipped between Shannon and Anton, her hands on her hips, fuming. Ex-girlfriend? Did Anton even do girlfriends?

"Um, excuse me," said Shannon, tapping her on the shoulder.

She shrugged her off. "Give me a second."

"This is actually important. Can you *move*?"

Anyone with eyes could tell; there was blood in the water. The girl looked as if she were ready to start tearing off limbs.

"You said I was in the lineup," the girl said, glaring at Anton.

Anton frowned. "What?"

"The runway show at the end of the month." She flung off her mask, crumpling it in her hand. "You said you got me in."

"...I think I said that to sleep with you?"

"*And*?"

"*Excuse* me." Shannon grabbed the model's shoulder and swiveled her around. "I believe I said *move*."

She pushed the girl aside rather violently – which, perhaps, was a mistake. Furious, Anton's model retaliated by grabbing a glass of wine off a server's tray and splashing it in Shannon's face. People were starting to pay attention.

Hyde cocked his head to the side. "Should we do something?"

I bit my lip. "Uh…" And then nothing. The nerve that connected my brain to my mouth must have snapped.

Shannon wiped the liquid off her face. "What the fuck, you crazy dumbass," she yelled and pushed her into Anton. The two tumbled to the floor with a horrible crash. That, apparently, was Hyde's cue.

"Hey. Hey!" Hyde strode into the warzone, grabbing the model's scrawny forearm and lifting her to her feet. "What the hell is going on here?"

And that was Protester Number Three's cue. She came out of nowhere; her hand rising out of her purse with a balloon that I knew was most certainly not filled with water.

"Swan labor is slave labor!" she shrieked at the top of her lungs. People gasped. "*Bella Magazine* should be held accountable for its crimes against humanity! Freedom not fashion!"

With an arm built like a pitcher's, she threw two huge balloons. One hit Hyde in the face. The last one got the model's neck, but only because by some twist of fate she was accidentally shielding Anton. Dirty gray pigeon feathers swimming in a stream of syrup dripped down their skin, down the model's chest, into Hyde's mouth – the cheaper and possibly more humane version of tar and feathering.

The model shrieked. Hyde grunted angrily, wiping the slop off his face. Anton gaped at the two of them, utterly dumbfounded, as Shannon and her friends hightailed it out of there. Anton knew as well as I did. His plan was off.

I gasped, wide-eyed, because it was what everyone else was doing. "Hyde? Hyde!" I ran up to him, positively frantic. "Oh my God, Hyde! Are you OK?"

What now, Anton?

17

Forfeit

"Let me help, Hyde." Lots of people had gathered around, either to take pictures, offer their sympathies or both. A select few actually stooped down to help. Service had been called to clean up the mess that had managed to drip onto the floor. Meanwhile, I used the napkin I'd grabbed off the bar counter to wipe Hyde's cheek. He flicked his head away.

"It's all right. That won't do much," he said, grabbing it from me. He was right – the flimsy paper was already soaked and starting to fall apart in spots. Little bits of feather and syrup dripped onto my fingers. Hyde threw it on the floor at Anton's feet. "I'm going to go find a restroom. Wait here."

Stifled anger strained his voice. He'd contained it well, but it wasn't too difficult to tell from his heavy stride or his knitted brows that he was pissed.

"I'll go with you," I called after him, partly because I

didn't want to be left alone with Anton. But Hyde had already disappeared behind the gaggle of startled patrons.

Anton grabbed my arm and pulled me close. "How did this happen?" he hissed.

"What?"

"Those weren't my models."

I kept a healthy mix of fear and disbelief slathered on my face while I met his glare. "What? How the hell–?"

His eyes narrowed. "What happened, Deanna?"

"Why the hell are you asking me? You texted me, I came." I said it loudly, pretending as though I'd forgotten there were people around. Anton let me go almost immediately, his hands flying to his jacket pocket. He was feeling for something – a vial, probably, the one that was meant to be Hyde's undoing. Judging from his panic, and the way he started to pat the other pocket frantically, it was clear he couldn't find it. Must have flown out when he and his model took that tumble. And now there were far too many people milling about. Too many feet to check the ground for illegal drugs.

I pretended not to notice, instead peering out over the crowd. "Look, I gotta go find Hyde to make sure he's OK."

Leaving Anton to fret by the bar, I made my way through the crowd towards the restroom. It was slow going. Nosy socialites and gossipy fashion personnel kept pulling me aside to ask me for the inside scoop.

For some reason, the women's restroom was in a different spot entirely from the men's restroom, so it took me way too long to find it. But when I finally did, a line of disgruntled-looking males blocked my path.

"They kicked us out," said one guy in a sleek white jacket who looked as if he were trying valiantly not to lapse into the gotta-pee-dance.

"They?"

"Beatrice, Hyde, and that guy. They've been in there way too long. I mean seriously I wish *I* were powerful enough to commandeer a bathroom for no reason."

Beatrice is in there with Hyde? Running my non-syrupy hand through my hair, I stared at the door, eyes narrowed. Swallowing, I glanced back at him. "Do you have any idea what they might be doing? And who's the other guy?"

"Honest to God, if I end up peeing my pants because they're having a threesome in there, I will scream," he said. "Not that I'd put it past Beatrice."

I stomped over to the door, only to have it burst open before I could get there. Hyde strode out.

"Hyde?" I grabbed his arm, but when our eyes met, all the air rushed out of my parted lips. Desolation. He'd never shown it so clearly, so obviously before. His arm shook in my grip, rough against my palm, as if he were crumbling from the inside. The tension between us thickened and slopped to the floor, pooling at our feet, ready to sink us both. I realized in that one moment that the game had changed. I just didn't know how.

Silently, he slipped his arm out of my hand and walked on without looking back. Beatrice Hoffer-Rey, triumphant in her open-toed pumps, slipped a brown envelope into her purse while a thickly set man with a toupee-like black mop on his head moved towards the door. At the sight of me, he merely adjusted his suit and passed by.

"What did you say to him?" I asked as Beatrice followed. She barely spared me a glance as she left.

I slept away half of Sunday. Anton hadn't called me since the party, not that I was waiting doe-eyed by the phone. Shannon finally replied to one of my thousand emails to let me know that she and her friends hadn't been caught yet. No one had even pressed charges.

Hyde wouldn't answer any of my calls. Something was going on and for the life of me, I couldn't figure out what.

"Door," Ade yelled from her room, as the doorbell rang and R&B softly hummed from her stereo into the hallway. Since I was an un-showered mess still stuffed into my pyjamas, I stayed resolutely under my sheets, screaming at Ade to go get it instead. Dad was currently engaged in yet another rousing poker night at his friend's shack in Queens, so it was between the two of us.

Another doorbell ring, then a slew of knocking. Ade turned her stereo up, the bass thumping beneath the floor boards. The old lady in the other unit was going to start shrieking soon.

With a groan, I flung my bed sheets off, threw on some sweatpants and a t-shirt and stomped downstairs, telling Ade to go screw herself as I passed her room, not that she heard me. I opened the door.

"Ericka?"

My oldest sister stood at my doorstep with her baby in one hand and a suitcase in the other. "Can I come in?"

Silently, I stepped back and let her in. I'd probably been too hasty in assuming she only had the one suitcase with her. As soon as she stepped inside the house, I finally noticed the Rolls Royce behind her, out of which the driver pulled several more. Each could have stocked its own room.

"Oh wow. This place hasn't, um, changed." She'd been here just a few weeks ago for the funeral, but apparently she'd forgotten what a dump it was. "Ivan, just set those down anywhere."

"What... are you doing here?" I asked as the driver started lining the couch with her suitcases.

"Oh, I didn't tell you? I'll be staying over for a while."

Um, what? I stepped out of the way as the driver rolled another suitcase in front of me. "Why?"

With her baby, François, sleeping in her arms, Ericka walked over to the kitchen, peering wearily at cookie crumbles and stains on the counter. "Do I need a reason to visit my family for a while?"

"Well, since it's us–"

"I left a message earlier today. Didn't you get it?"

I'd been busy hiding under my bed sheets trying to block out the horror and confusion that had almost entirely defined the past few weeks of my life, so perhaps I hadn't heard the phone ring.

"What the hell's going on here?" Ade clambered out of her room just in time to see the driver shut the door behind him. "Ericka? What are you doing here?" Staring at the suitcases, she added, "What, did they run out of room at the Hilton?"

Ericka's bottom lip curled into an indignant scowl, scrunching her nose up as she frowned. "No. Like I said, I wanted to visit my family for a few days. God, you two are acting as if hell just froze over or something."

Because it had. The room had certainly grown more frigid, at any rate. With a haughty puff, she laid her infant down gingerly on the couch and took off her ebony beret so she could run her fingers through her black, short-cut curls. "I thought François and I could use a break from Manhattan."

"So you came here?" I glanced at Ericka's baby wearily. He was an angel now that he was dreaming. But once his eyes were open it'd be nonstop screeching. Ade knew it as well as I did. "Ericka, there's not enough room for all this stuff. And where are we going to put François? Where are you even going to stay?"

"I thought of that." Ericka straightened up and patted off her sleeveless red dress. "I figured you and Ade could share a room and I could take one of yours. I already brought a portable crib – it's in one of the suitcases. Ooh, did you guys buy more of those chocolate ice cream bars?"

As she rummaged the cupboards, Ade and I exchanged weary glances. "Ericka," I started, carefully. "Did something happen between you and Charles?" It was hard to forget the utter disdain in his tone while he talked down to her at the ball.

Ericka didn't turn when she answered. "No, no, that's not it." She took out a box of Graham Crackers. Stress eating: a Davis family trait. "Though he has been pretty busy today. Apparently there's some drama over at Hedley Publications."

I frowned. "Drama?"

"Yeah. This morning, Edmund Rey was arrested for embezzlement. Charles' firm is already preparing his defence."

Embezzlement. That other day Hyde had told me he was working on "something big". So Hyde really had been trying to get some dirt on his uncle. And indeed he had.

But where did that leave me?

I'd failed. Anton's dad was going to jail. What was he going to do to me?

"That's not even all of it, apparently," Ericka went on, probably because she couldn't see my hands shaking on my lap. "Tons of drama to go around over at Hedley Publications. I tried to ask Charles, of course, but he didn't... well, he didn't quite have time to tell me what it was. And you know, when he's stressed, he... Well, that doesn't matter." Taking one of her suitcases by the handle, she dragged it up the stairs.

More drama? I thought of Hyde's broken expression last night, the silence between us as he'd passed by me without a word. The image haunted me while I moved my things into Ade's room, lingering while she helped me set up the crib. What the hell else was going on at the company? I couldn't even guess. Soon, I didn't need to.

"Uh, guys?" Ericka called us from downstairs. "You might want to see this."

As we came downstairs, we found her watching the news with the volume down low to keep François from waking up. She didn't say another word. The headline was enough:

Hyde Hedley loses the company. Beatrice Hoffer-Rey takes over Hedley Publications.

A Tale

Bring your youth and bring your maidens! Come; let them dance the Dance of Cranes!

Boys and girls – they crowd the market place. Boys and girls, their hands full of orchids. They dance together, the Dance of Cranes.

Swaying and lurching and feathers flying. Crouching and singing and bells chiming. They dance together, the Dance of Cranes, and music blesses the capital with spring.

Bring them, bring them!

The king arranges it.

They dance through the marketplace. They dance in the streets. They dance to the tunnels.

The tomb shudders shut and they are left in darkness.

18

Caught

"What in the hell is going on with these people?" I shouted, loud enough for François to jolt awake and start crying. Ade groaned from behind the couch.

"Deanna!" Ericka shot me a dirty look as she picked her baby up and started bouncing him up and down on her lap. "Do you know how hard it is just to get him to close his eyes?"

But it was all background noise. Even the reporter's blather slipped past my notice. It was Beatrice I was focused on. Lean, arrogant and surrounded by a gaggle of press at the center of the Hedley building's rotunda, she wielded her red smile like a sword as she answered questions about the sudden switch up.

"We both felt as though this was the best choice of action," she bullshitted. "As we all know, Hyde Hedley is a very smart young man, but just not ready to take on such a big responsibility. We both decided that his father's company would be better left in the hands of someone with a little more business experience and worldly wisdom."

I called Hyde's cell. No answer. "She did something," I whispered, hanging up.

Ade blinked "Huh?"

"That evil woman did something to him, I can tell!" I rushed over to the shoe mat. Anton and now Beatrice – God, was that entire family insane? "I'm going to go see Hyde!"

I slipped on some sneakers and headed out the door. I called Hyde about a dozen times throughout the trip over, and each time my rings went unanswered. The taxi dropped me off at the gate where swarms of press were already gathered outside, snapping photos, chatting into cameras. Forcing my way through would be next to impossible. I tried his cell again. No answer. I tried his house phone too. No answer. I texted. Nothing. What was he doing?

Deflated, I left the reporters to scrounge through his garbage. A day passed. Two. Finally, an entire week was dead and gone. I called, emailed, texted, begging him to talk to me. Not one of my pleas was answered.

Maybe this was a good thing. At the end of the day, Anton wanted Hyde out; he'd left and even passed Anton's stepmom the crown and sceptre. That was probably why Anton hadn't bothered contacting me at all since the party. The mission had been accomplished, after all, somehow. But it was the somehow that bothered me.

"Are you going out?" said Ericka from the kitchen, stirring the beef stew she hadn't made in years – as evidenced by the smell: a bizarre mixture of garlic and what I assumed was stale toilet water. A week had gone by and Ericka was still sleeping in my room, forcing me to contend with Ade elbowing me in the head every night.

Dad was both thrilled and ashamed when he'd found her sitting on the couch, trying to placate François. I'd figured things would fall apart pretty soon with the family dynamics shot to hell so suddenly, but the two of them had actually been getting along quite well. I would hear their long conversations at night in the living room, unable to pick out words, yet still fascinated by the eager hisses of their whispers.

"Yeah," I answered. "I'm going to try seeing Hyde again."

"Are you sure that's wise? If he wanted to talk to you, he'd have done it by now."

I shoved my hands into my jeans pockets. "He probably just needed some time to adjust or something."

Ericka sighed and shook her head. "Deanna, I know you're worried, but don't be naïve. When girls are naïve they can be easily taken advantage of. You're still young. Don't get caught up in something you don't have to." For a moment, I wondered if Ericka had forgotten who I was – or if she'd been staring at her reflection in the pot's dirty steel while lecturing me.

"I know, I know. But it won't take long."

I left. This time when the taxi pulled up to Hyde's townhouse, there wasn't a single soul outside his door.

I supposed the press had already burnt through that story and were off chasing reality TV stars outside courtrooms. The sun was sinking; soon evening would streak yellows and violets across the sky. I knocked.

"Hyde? It's me!"

No answer. I peered up at the double windows above the terrace, but the windows were tinted. I called his cell. It rang several times before someone finally picked up.

"Hello?" The voice rasped on the other end, fizzling out at the end before the last syllable could sound.

"Hyde?" I paused. "Is that you?" I had to ask because the voice could only belong to a newly excavated corpse.

"Deanna. What do you want?"

The blunt edge of his words stunned me into silence for a few moments. "I'm outside your place. Can I... Can I come in?"

Several moments of silenced passed. Suddenly, the door opened. Hyde stood with his phone in one hand while the other slipped through his dishevelled hair. "I'm busy, so this'll have to be quick."

I followed him in, too shocked to say anything about his filthy T-shirt and crumpled jeans, which looked like they'd been worn every day for exactly a week. A stale odor had infested the house, as thick and sluggish as Hyde's steps. Open bottles of whisky on the bar counter. Clothes on the stripped Persian rug and leaves of paper all over the couch.

"What's... going on?" I watched him with a frown as he poured himself another drink.

"Isn't that my question to ask? What are you doing here? Why have you been calling me?" A cold, brisk tone. This Hyde was light years away from the one who'd crushed me to him in the flickering glow of the candlelight.

"I've been worried, dumbass!" I barked, striding up to him and snatching the glass out of his hands before he could empty it down his throat. He was probably already drunk. "What is going on? Why did you give *Beatrice Rey* of all people the company? What did she do to you?"

At the sound of her name two things happened. He flinched, first. It was hard to ignore. His fingers had jolted so violently, I thought a nerve had been cut. But his eyes... his eyes softened. Not at all tenderly, of course. Having been the target of Hyde's affection, I knew all too well what tenderness looked like in his eyes. The way they softened this time... I couldn't put my finger on it, but it felt wrong. Hollow.

"She didn't do anything," Hyde answered, almost automatically. "I gave her the majority share of the company."

I gestured to the broken lamp on the ground next to the TV. "Obviously willingly as evidenced by how well you're taking things."

"Look, I don't know what you want." He strode into the living room.

"Just talk to me!" I demanded, following behind him. "I mean, what the hell! All this time, I've been telling you stuff about me – really personal stuff!" Obviously not everything, but the point still stood. "And you've told me next to nothing about you. Why am I the one who has to open up? When are you going to put a little bit of effort in?"

Hyde stopped in front of one of his pearl white ottomans. "Fine. Let's break up."

My heart thudded to a stop. "What?"

He turned to me, his face a blank canvas. It was worse than if it'd been contorted into a scowl. "Let's break up. Problem solved."

My lips parted. I grabbed his arm instead, searching his eyes, wondering why they seemed so hollow.

"It wouldn't have worked anyway. Deanna..." He paused. "I was arrogant to think I could just walk back into your life. Things are too complicated now. It wasn't fair to you. Just forget about me." Wordlessly, he stared out of the half-length tinted windows, watching the sky fade. "It's almost dark." Then an ominous silence hung over him.

My feet carried me to the couch, as if somehow they knew how badly I wanted to collapse onto it. It shouldn't have been so devastating. This whole "relationship" had begun as a lie anyway. It was only fitting it'd end on another one. Yet the tears were coming anyway. This was all so stupid. Why was I crying? It was ridiculous.

"Hyde... are you really OK with this?"

"I'm sorry," he said and gripped me by the wrist – almost violently. "I'm really sorry, but you have to go. You shouldn't have even come here. No, I shouldn't have let you in." He pulled me to the door.

"Wait! Hyde, wait a second." I grabbed the doorframe before he could push me out. "Look, I'm sorry, but can't we just talk about this? Please?"

Hyde gazed up at the sky. "I can't. It's getting late."

"What? Late? You suddenly have a curfew now?"

His face paled several shades. "I'm sorry."

He didn't look at me when he shut the door in my face. Maybe he couldn't.

"He dumped you?" Ade gave me an incredulous look as she spread butter over her toast. It was 2 o'clock in the morning when I finally told her. Ericka, Dad and François were asleep. I suppose Ade assumed something was wrong once she spotted me on the couch stuffing my face with ice cream sandwiches while watching *The Sound of Music* – or possibly when I teared up during "Do-Re-Mi."

"I suppose."

"You suppose?"

"I don't know." I pushed the chocolate stained wrappers off the couch and twisted around to face her. "It was just... it was so sudden. How do you go from lighting candles for a girl to literally throwing her out the door? He just seemed so... gone. And he'd been drinking."

For one second, I thought I smelled it again: the stale scent of alcohol curling off him.

Ade leaned against the back of the couch, her arm balanced over the ledge, sneaking in one last side glance before, turning her gaze to the stairs. "Wow. And here

I thought you two were totes 'true loves forever'," she said dryly, though she just as easily could have been telling the truth. That would explain the wisp of relief carrying her words. *Relief.* A part of me wondered if the sight of me stress eating on the couch gave her a slight tingle of satisfaction.

"I never gave that impression, Ade," I said. "You chose to interpret it that way. And I have a few guesses why."

Ade shifted uncomfortably. "I didn't mean–"

"It's not like I chased after Hyde, you know." I wiped the chocolate off the side of my mouth and glared at her. "It's not like I went rich husband-shopping in Manhattan just to one-up you."

"I know." Ade shoved her hands into her sweatshirt pocket. "I know."

Seconds passed. Neither of us said anything. Shaking my head, I leaned over and grabbed the half-empty can of soda off the table to wash the chocolate down.

Ade cleared her throat. "If Hyde seemed pretty messed up," she said, the tension unravelling in her voice, "it was probably because he just lost the company."

I squeezed the soda can in my hand. "Yeah. But he said he gave it away willingly."

"And you believe him?"

For a moment, I stared back at the fixed smiling faces of the Von Trapp family waiting for me to press play. "No. Something obviously happened. Something's seriously wrong. He just won't tell me about it. Why won't he tell me about it? Why won't he tell me *anything*?"

I dropped my head into my hands, my exasperated groan nearly drowning out the buzz of my phone vibrating on the table. Ade picked it up before I could.

"Why is *Anton* sending you a text?"

My blood froze in my veins. "Give me that!" Even she was shocked by how violently I snatched the phone from her hands – and how violently my hands were shaking. Anton. He'd finally contacted me. But why? He had everything he wanted. What else could he possibly want from me?

"Deanna?" Ade grabbed my shoulder and turned me to her. "What's wrong? Hey! He's not trying to hook up with *you* now is he? What's going on?"

I shook my head and, keeping my head lowered and hiding the screen from Ade's view, clicked the message: *My loft. Sundown tomorrow.*

His loft? I shivered, turning the phone over on my lap so that the screen remained hidden.

"Deanna, is he bothering you?" Ade shook me. "God, I can't believe I ever wasted my sexy flirting with that skeez. If he is bothering you, you gotta tell me."

But if I told her and Anton found out... "No, it's OK. I'll handle it."

"Stop being so *stupid*, Deanna, *God*!" Ade slapped me upside the head, nostrils flaring. "Why are you always like that? Just like when Mom died. You think you're a goddamn hero by keeping this shit to yourself?"

"I'm sorry," I muttered brusquely, turning off the TV before standing. "It's nothing, really. I texted Anton because I figured he might know what's up with Hyde.

I know what you're thinking," I added quickly, once her eyebrows knitted together in disbelief. "I know it's desperate, but they're still family so maybe he knows something. I have to try." It astounded me, how quickly the lies came now.

I went upstairs without looking back at Ade, because I didn't want or need confirmation that she didn't believe me. Since we shared a room now, I slipped into the bathroom and locked the door behind me. *What is this about*, I texted back. *Hyde's gone. Your stepmom has the company. You won. Why do you still need me?*

I dreaded the answer.

To find out why your boyfriend met my stepmother at Pierre Hotel tonight.

My fingers gripped the sink's ledge.

"Hyde!" I banged on his door. "Hyde, open up!" I figured if he wasn't going to answer the thousands of my calls I barraged his phone with throughout the day, I might as well ambush him at his house. It was almost sundown. I still hadn't decided whether I would go through with meeting Anton or not. I'd hoped I'd be able to hear it from Hyde instead.

Finally the door creaked open. I pushed it in. Hyde nearly toppled over.

"What's your problem?" he yelled, recoiling at the sight of me furious at his doorstep.

"What's *your* problem? Why are you meeting Beatrice Hoffer-Rey at hotels late at night? Why are you meeting Beatrice at all?"

I realized how embarrassing it was to act like the clingy jealous ex. And yet my fingers were clinging to the doorframe anyway.

Hyde frowned, maybe wondering how I had found out, but he brushed me off with a shrug. "I gave Beatrice the company, remember? There are still business arrangements I have to take care of. More importantly, this isn't your problem anymore." At least twice during his diatribe, he checked the sky.

"Oh? It's as simple as that, right? Randomly handing someone you loathe your father's company and meeting her at hotels in the dead of night is no big deal?"

His eyes were glued to the sun, half-submersed below the horizon. "Leave, Deanna."

"But–"

He pried my fingers off the doorframe and with a rough jerk, flicked my hand aside. A throbbing pain seized my chest and for a moment, I couldn't breathe. "Please," he whispered and shut the door.

With my eyes to the ground, I slowly dragged myself away, my fingernails digging into my palms. Slogging down the sidewalk, I was about to hail a cab when I noticed the stretch limo parked on the other side of the street. A tinted window rolled down.

Crap. *Anton?*

Calmly, he waved me over. I briefly entertained the idea of running off in the other direction, but I knew that if I wanted information I'd have to cross the street and get it from him. So I did.

"Get in," he ordered.

My mouth dropped. "*Excuse* me?"

"Get in, or do you want to explain to Hyde why you're still around and talking to *me*?"

I was really tired of being given orders by douchebags. "Easily solvable." With a defiant look, I simply walked around the other side of the limo.

"Really?" said Anton, once he'd rolled down the other window.

I folded my arms, grateful for the distance between us. "Sorry, I don't make it a point to get into tight spaces with guys who threaten me with rape." And after the bastard rolled his eyes, I added, shortly, "What do you want?" Though I could guess.

"I thought you'd be here," he said with a lazy drawl, flipping a newspaper over his lap in his finely tailored suit like a little business twat in training. "Even though I told you to meet me at my place. Couldn't resist getting the truth straight from the horse's mouth, could you?"

"Whatever. How did you find out about Hyde and Beatrice?"

"Coincidence, really," he said. "I was at the hotel myself, you see – a business meeting." His slimy grin suggested otherwise. "I saw him in the lobby with Beatrice."

My stomach clenched and I felt about as ready to throw up as if I'd kissed Anton. I steadied my breath.

"You talked to Hyde," he went on. "What did he tell you?"

The expectant look on his face, almost desperate, made me squirm. "He told me he was at the hotel for business."

Anton smirked, shaking his head as his arms crossed over his chest. "And just now, I told you I was at the hotel for business."

Pursing my lips, I stared at the tinted window. "Except, you're disgusting."

"All men are a little disgusting, Deanna." His lips spread even further, like a disease, across his face. "Don't you want to find out how much?"

I almost left right there, but Anton called me back with a laugh. "Get in. We'll wait here," he said. "Then, once he leaves his house, we'll follow."

We? "Why?" I folded my arms over my chest as though it'd create an extra bit of distance between us. "Why do you care about what Hyde and Beatrice do together?"

He stayed silent, throwing the newspaper onto the table next to his wineglass. The creases on his face deepened with his frown and while he crossed his legs his arms were stiff over his lap. "My father's gone to jail," he said, finally. "Though Beatrice has the company, she still won't pay his bail. She won't even help with his case. The bitch wants him to stay in prison. I want to know why. Did she strike some sort of deal with my bastard fake-cousin?"

He grabbed the glass on the table and downed an angry gulp of the wine sloshing inside. But it was all wrong. That wasn't the scowl of someone who was worried about his father, or indignant over how his faux-mom was treating him. It was something different entirely.

"And you need to follow Hyde just to find that out?" Something wasn't adding up. "Couldn't you just confront her? Why would you need me to come with you? What–?"

His glare charred the words before they could leap off my tongue. "You can leave if you want, Deanna. But are you telling me you don't want to know what's going on?"

I couldn't, because I did. And yet I blew him off anyway, beginning down the sidewalk with slow, careful steps. But then, when I'd gotten far enough away, I quickly snuck behind a parked mail truck. I wasn't lying when I said I wanted to know.

It was getting darker. Dad, Ade and Ericka were going to kill me when I got back, but this was more important than curfew. I hailed a cab and slipped inside. "Just hold on for a bit," I told the driver. I'd put the extra minutes on Ericka's tab. She was eating our food, after all.

One minute, two, ten. The sun had finally checked out for the night. Soon, I saw Hyde walk out his front door. With heavy, plodding steps, he called a cab and took off.

This wasn't happening.

With one smooth movement, the limo merged into the traffic. Anton was on the move.

"Follow that limo," I told the driver and though he gave me a "look", he went along with it anyway. I was now officially a stalker.

As I sat there, rigid, in the cab following Anton following Hyde, the spineless part of my brain prepared itself for denial, diligently gathering up every memory that could possibly disprove the conclusion the masochistic part had already jumped to. They weren't – no. Beatrice may have been that kind of person, but Hyde wasn't. Hyde could barely choke down his bile when Beatrice had tried to hit on him at the ball. It was business. Beatrice had something on him and he was negotiating. Trying to find a foothold back into the company. They did it on TV all the time. For Anton, the most disgusting assumption was always the right one, but regular people just didn't function like that. Hyde didn't.

Hyde's taxi dropped him off outside a townhouse on West 12th Street. Anton stopped a few yards away, far enough not to draw attention but still close enough to watch Hyde enter the complex. I paid the cabbie and ducked behind a tree, my breaths grating my throat.

It's business. *Stop being stupid, Deanna.*

I clung to the image of Hyde pushing Beatrice's hand away from him as the moonlight poured in from the arched windows, lighting the grimace on his face.

We waited for a long time, Anton and I. More specifically, I waited because he was waiting, though I couldn't tell what he was waiting for.

And then I couldn't take it anymore.

I strode up to the limo and pounded on the window. It rolled down. "So? Where is this?" I demanded.

A pompous mixture of amusement and satisfaction twisted Anton's greasy face. "This, Deanna, is where my father lived before your boyfriend had him hauled off in cuffs."

"I'm assuming you have keys."

"You followed me all the way here, didn't you?" He laughed, positively delighted. "Should have come with me, if for the alcohol at *least*."

Spit in his face, my instincts ordered without a beat missed. I would have. But Hyde had been in there for too long. "Look, if you're going to just sit there and jack off or something, then fine, but at least give me the damn keys."

Anton smirked. "I might like you after all."

I crossed the street and climbed the steps to the front door, shuddering as I felt Anton slide next to me. Jangling a group of keys in my face, he pinched a slick bronze key – the smallest on the chain – and stuck it in the lock.

This is insane. I shouldn't be here. I could mess up Hyde's plan.

And yet I followed Anton inside. Bathed in the foyer's blinding white, I stared past the piano and up the stairs. Beatrice was laughing. My legs seized.

"She wouldn't." Anton quietly ascended the steps.

I leaned against the railing. I have to go. This is stupid. I have to go. I'm going right now.

"I knew it, you fucking *whore*!"

Anton's growl was a punch to the gut that left me winded and grasping the railing. I climbed the stairs, crumbling with each step because I couldn't stop myself.

Last step. I could see them around the railing. Beatrice in negligee, backing away as Anton rounded on her. And Hyde, off in the corner, watching lifelessly.

He barely had his underwear on.

The sound that broke off my lips couldn't have belonged to me, but it must have, because suddenly Hyde was looking at me. In that moment, he evaporated. He was a ghost, his face pale as if all his blood had leaked out of him, pooling on the rug at his feet.

I ran back down the stairs, out the door. I couldn't remember how I got inside a taxi, but suddenly, somehow, I was there, crying in the backseat and wishing Hyde Hedley had stayed dead.

A Tale: Reprise

Somewhere, just outside a tiny village, is a lake. Eight heavenly maidens bathe there. They sit by the shore, oblivious to the world...

I woke up in a sweat and didn't know why. I lay in bed in the dead of night, my eyes tracing a trail of broken plaster on the ceiling. I breathed, slowly, clutching the sheets to my body as the dream continued to wash over me.

Water shimmers in their cupped hands, trickles through their fingers, runs down their legs.

I knew the words. I'd known them since childhood. I rose out of bed, stepping on the floor with careful steps.

Moonlight coats their white feathers.

I could see the moonlight now, streaming into my sister's bedroom. I sat at the table and looked at the moon, my elbows on the wood, my hands cupping my chin. I stared at the sky, just as Hyde had.

Just as Hyde had.

He'd checked the sky. He'd checked it twice, maybe more. He'd begged me to leave when days ago he'd have done anything for me to stay.

He'd held me by the candlelight in a room he'd booked just for us. He'd touched my cheek and heated my lips with kisses. And then he'd given his company away.

The young man sees them from behind the trees. Their beauty enchants him.

I thought of her – Beatrice. I thought of her anger as she was spurned by him – and then of her smug smile as she stood triumphant in the bathroom. Of Hyde's anguish. The envelope she handed him.

Blackmail.

A feather was all it took for Anton to put me in chains. A secret. Just one cost me my freedom, cost me nearly everything.

Quietly, he comes back and sends his dog to steal the feather robe of the youngest. The seven sisters cry out and fly off into the sky. But the youngest cannot.
Now she is his.

The last four words simmer and dissipate – and suddenly I remembered the way Hyde had looked up at the sky so desperately, and shuddered a gasp so violent I felt it throb against my chest.

Once of the heavens, she is now bound to the earth. Bound to the young man.

It couldn't be.

He builds a house and they marry. Their children sing every day.

It *couldn't* be.

My mind was racing – the secret smiles, the seductive touches, the tender feelings. Memories of Hyde. I sifted through them until I was left with just one: the one of Hyde in Beatrice's room. His hollow eyes.

And then I knew.

19

Cursed

"Hyde, pick up." My back pressed against the lock on the bathroom door. My hands shook so badly my cell almost slipped through my grip.

"Hyde, pick up, please." Each ring went unanswered. I wanted to yell and toss my phone against the wall, but it was 4 o'clock in the morning and there were three other people in the house, plus a particularly temperamental baby. Gritting my teeth, I held myself back from kicking the door and dialed Hyde's number again.

"Please, Hyde." I shut my eyes to keep them dry, but they welled up anyway. Still no answer. He wouldn't. No, he probably couldn't. Hyde was ashamed – just like I had been when my feathers first came out, and when Anton had threatened me. But I couldn't just leave it alone. I needed to hear it from him. I had to see him.

No answer. I'd have to leave a message instead. "Hyde, can you please call me back? Please. I need to talk to you. It's OK, I'm not mad. I just need to…" *Tell him*, a voice hissed in the back of my mind. *Tell him you know.* My voice wavered and without meaning to, I hung up.

Power. That was the explanation Anton had given me that night – one word, simply uttered, while his face broke into a horrifying grin on the other side of the iron bars. There were so many ways to cage someone. So many ways to take what you wanted from them. But swans were different. Each feather in your hands was a guarantee of absolute obedience, a contract they didn't make, but one they couldn't break. It was absolute power, both tantalizing and horrific. And Hyde… Hyde was…

I buried my face in my hands.

The day passed without a word from Hyde. I wouldn't give up. So, at 5 o'clock the next morning, I slipped on my shoes and walked out the door, dialing Hyde's number. "OK, this is the last time I'm going to call you. Meet me at Grand Army Plaza in front of the Bailey fountain at half-past five. If you don't come, I promise I won't bother you ever again. But you have to come, Hyde. You have to. Because I'm like you. I…" I paused, clamping my mouth shut. "I have them too." I clicked off. Was it too vague? It was too vague. I could have told him what I was – what we were. But saying the word just made it all too real.

No point in chickening out now. I sat down on the bench and waited calmly, mesmerized by the monotonous flow of the fountain's stream. Years passed. Centuries.

I wondered what it had been like, the first time they sprouted from his back. What made it happen? How much pain had he been in? How old had he been? What did he do afterwards? How did he deal? Who did he tell? The questions kept coming, louder and fiercer by the minute. I just needed to see him. All of the words he'd refused to say since seeing me for the first time in nine years. I needed to hear them now. I felt as if I'd break into pieces if I didn't.

Another year. Two more. I looked down at my watch, shocked to find that a single hour had passed. Was he with her now? Were they tangled under the sheets, nothing between them but sweat and misery?

I bit my lip.

And then I saw him approach through the rippling water. Hyde.

Hyde was here.

Holding my breath, I stood up.

"Hyde…" His eyes were sunk into the deep black circles carved into his face, bulging as if haunted by the fresh nightmares that had stolen his sleep. I didn't know where to start. For a time, I stared at him, waiting for him to speak, to utter a sound. But when he didn't I knew it was up to me. And I had to start somewhere. "Hyde–"

The moment he was within reach, he grabbed my shoulders and pulled me to him. The sheer intensity of the desperation etched into him kept my eyes locked onto his. I couldn't look anywhere else.

"Is it true?"

His voice chilled me from the inside. Low and hoarse, the weakness of it made me shake. His fingers dug into my skin.

"What?"

"Did someone hurt you? Are you...?" At once he let go, shaking his head, pacing in front of me. He paced, and paced, and paced. "Oh God." He shook his head again. "I didn't know... Did someone–" He stopped, hanging his head, though I could see his lips pursed, trembling. Before I could blink, he rounded on me again, this time shaking me by the arms. "Deanna, did someone hurt you? Did someone take them?"

"No, no!" I pushed him away, wrapping my arms around myself. His face flamed a deep red, his coarse fingers sliding through his hair as if that one action was all that kept him from falling apart. "I'm... No one's... no one's taken them. My..." I paused, letting a rush of air fill and empty my lungs before I told him. "My... f-feathers."

I'd practically mouthed the word and yet even the breath of it broke Hyde in two. He visibly drooped; his arms fell limp at his side. For a moment, all he could do was shake his head.

"I didn't want this for you," was all he said, after a lifetime. "I never, ever wanted you to have to go through this. I–" He stopped to breathe, long and deep. "When?"

"When did I find out?" I swallowed, hoping it would unclench my throat just enough to let the air through. "At Anton's birthday party." Now that I was finally, *finally* telling Hyde the truth, the words seemed to tumble off my lips. My pulse raced. "It was when I fell into the table, but my back had been hurting for days before then. Adrianna took me home, but I was still so messed up... That's why I didn't answer any of your calls."

Hyde's fingers twitched. "I didn't know."

"I didn't want you to know. I didn't want anyone to know. I was ashamed." I leaned over, searching his eyes. "But you know how that feels, don't you?"

Hyde wouldn't look at me. He stared at the fountain instead, silently considering the cascading streams, his lips pressed tight to keep the secrets in. It was the last seal to be broken. But I knew it wouldn't give easily.

"I'm not even sure how I figured it out," I said, my dry hands frigid against my bare arms. "There were just too many broken pieces, and too many holes to fill. I woke up one night and... No. I'm not even sure how I figured it out."

Hyde's head rose, slightly, but he still didn't look at me.

"I remember when we were kids," I continued. I needed to say it: "You... you were my best friend."

Hyde turned away. "Yeah. You were mine too. My only friend."

"Then *tell* me." I took his hands in mine, not sure whose were shaking, or rather whose were shaking worse. "Tell me what happened to you. Tell me the truth. Please, Hyde." Tears trickled down my cheeks. "I know you don't want to be with her. Beatrice. I know what she's doing to you."

It happened fast. At the mere mention of her name, his eyes dulled. All their passion and life and light sunk into the depths until there was nothing left but two empty holes. His jaw clamped shut. His face was still, but his lips started to quiver. I could tell they were fighting against something, some invisible force, but the spell that bound them was too strong. It was exactly as Shannon had described it while she told me about her own secret horrors: the reason she'd stayed by her rapist's side for all those years with nary a whisper as to what he was doing to her. It was the curse of silence. The curse of loyalty.

The swan's curse.

Finally, just as he looked ready to break in two, he walked past me, sitting on the park bench. Bending over, he propped himself up by his arms, head bent low so that his hair obscured his face from me. He was silent for too long.

"I didn't go to Paris," he said simply.

"I know."

"I've never been."

"I know that too."

"I wasn't a chimney sweep either."

"I figured," though I said it with a smile. It was just Hyde. No matter how many secrets he kept, how many people tried to break him. Hyde was Hyde. It was a comforting thought, among the sea of dread drowning me.

Hyde pressed a hand against his forehead. "It was because I found out about her. My mother. After she died and I found her diary. I started reading. A few weeks later, I pieced it together. It was all there in the silences. A swan can never speak out against her captor. But she can say everything else."

He paused and I wondered if he remembered every word, if he were recalling them now as he closed his eyes – the silent stories of his mother's horror etched into his thoughts.

"My mother... she never told anyone that she was a swan," he said, his gaze low. "In the world that she came from, admitting that was nothing short of social death. She'd have never been able to show her face again. But I think... in her heart, my mother wanted others to know. In her heart, she did."

What would it mean to give away your secret? Anton knew mine, and he'd almost shattered me with it. There were too many risks involved in letting others know. For a swan, giving your secrets away could mean death.

Hyde rubbed his eyes with his fingers, shaking his head. "It was Anton's father. Her own brother. He and Dad were buddies at Yale. And it was while they were at Yale that Edmund gave my mother to him in exchange for a position at the company. My dad was pathetic and obsessed and in love with her, after all, and Edmund was barely getting by on scholarships. So he told him. He told my father what my mother was and the rest just happened. It was the desperation of a scumbag."

My stomach had tumbled so horribly I nearly let a moan slip from my lips. Did Dad know? Dad had his own circle of friends during his college days. He was still friends with most of them today. Ralph Hedley was his only friend from the upper class, the only one he talked to, and while he had his own friends, Dad had never really socialized with them. He told us as much during one of his drunken reminiscences. If Dad had met Edmund, I couldn't imagine him being anything other than disgusted. And through it all, it was Clarice Hedley who had paid the price.

I wanted to scream, but I didn't. I wasn't about to interrupt Hyde, not while the words were flowing so freely.

"My father treated everyone like that. Commodities. Items for sale. He bought me out of convenience, plucked me out of an orphanage to play the happy, healthy son of a benevolent philanthropist who headed a company that promoted 'family values'. And with my help, he secured an advertiser: Colemans. It was a business transaction. If anyone was going to get rid of me, I'd figured it would be him. But Dad..." Hyde laughed. "Dad was going to come clean. Edmund was the one who sold me."

I felt oddly empty trying to grasp the word that had come out of his mouth. Sold. It slipped through my fingers like tears. Sold. What did he mean? What *could* he mean? I opened my mouth. Nothing came out.

"I would have ruined him, after all." Hyde straightened up, leaning against the back of the bench, staring blankly up at the night sky. "Once I found out what Dad had been doing to my mother, I was determined to confront him, but he'd just left on a business trip. It had to be face to face.

"I found Edmund first. I hated him. I couldn't believe what he'd done, what they'd both done. I told him that if he didn't come clean, I'd tell everyone. He pleaded with me, bribed me, threatened me, but I didn't care. He even tried to convince me, the bastard, that he was doing this all for her. For both of them. He was lifting them out of poverty. He was bettering their lives. He truly believed that. He truly didn't believe he was a monster."

Monsters never do. My lips trembled.

"But even still, I thought I knew what his limits were." Hyde laughed, once, and though it was nearly imperceptible, the sound of it shriveled my insides. "I had no idea."

I took a hesitant step towards him. "And then..." My knees nearly buckled. "And then he sold you." The words scattered across the cold ground.

"And then he sold me," Hyde repeated, eyes dead. I stood there silently, waiting for him to continue, but he'd shut his eyes, fighting against the horror of it. The blood drained from my face. I didn't even want to imagine it, but images played in my mind's eye, horrible images. Images that had haunted me since Anton locked me in a cage, except now it was Hyde's face I saw instead of mine.

I couldn't take this. I wanted to collapse onto the ground, but I couldn't. I felt as if... as if it'd be an insult to him. As if I'd be making a mockery of the courage Hyde had summoned just to lay himself bare in front of me. And so I waited for him to continue. I'd wait as long as he needed me to.

"Human trafficking is a multi-billion dollar industry, after all," Hyde said finally. I knew it, but only because Anton had told me once, his eyes leering at me from behind steel bars. "They kidnapped me. The guys Edmund had hired. They kidnapped me and I..."

Both his hands were pressed flat against his head. "I didn't go to Paris, Deanna. I never left the country. For a long time I didn't know *where* I was. They kept me in the parlor basement with all the others. Trapped like animals in tiny cages. It wasn't enough to send me away, see, not if I could come back and screw everything up. He had to make sure I stayed away, and as much as an abomination as Edmund Rey is, I suppose even he wasn't willing to cross that moral line by having me killed. But selling a swan is so appallingly simple for a bunch of assholes with money. And faking my death – he made that happen too, all while my dad was off in China. Having the right connections and shuffling a bit of paperwork was all they needed. Once the parlor owners had my feathers, I was theirs. I..."

His voice faltered. For one, fleeting moment he stayed silent, though I could hear each ragged breath. But the dam couldn't hold forever. He buried his head in his hands and started sobbing.

Biting down the strangled cry that threatened to break out of me, I ran up to him, knelt down and threw my arms around him, but he shook me off, shooting to his feet. "I'm so sorry, Deanna. I didn't want to tell you. I couldn't tell anyone. I *couldn't*. When I got back to New York... I'd have done anything to make sure nobody found out. I was–" He clenched his teeth, shaking his head so violently I thought it'd come off his neck. "You especially. I couldn't let you know. I was ashamed. If you found out, I knew you'd never want to touch me again."

"Hyde, no." I wiped my face with the back of my arms, but I didn't know what else to say. What else *could* I say? I stayed on the ground, my side twisted against the bench, fingers clinging to the wood.

"One day there was a police raid at the parlor and I escaped. I ended up in a San Diego shelter. When I found out my dad was dying I came up with a plan. I knew there were people from the company I could trust – people who hated Edmund. John Roan, for one. The sicker Dad got, the less he was able to pull his weight at the company, and the more Edmund's power grew. Eventually he fired a string of people he thought would only hold him back. That's what John told me.

"My dad's old legal counsel, thrown out into the street like trash. It was all over the news. I took a chance trusting him and it paid off. And after the DNA test, after everything..." Hyde paused. "After everything, I got to see my dad one last time before he died. I had no idea the old bastard was going to hand me the company before kicking it."

Quietly, I slid back up onto the bench and shut my eyes against the world. For Hyde to have suffered so deeply, for me to have used him, cursed him, and loved him all without knowing any of it... it killed me. My chest felt hollow, my heart scooped out and smothered.

My eyes snapped open. I turned to Hyde, watching him avoid my gaze. "She found out, didn't she?" When Hyde frowned and looked away, I stood up. "Beatrice knows. The envelope she handed you. That's what she's blackmailing you with. You just said it yourself, didn't you? You'd have done anything to make sure nobody found out. So when she did, you gave her the company in exchange for her silence. But..." I swallowed hard, the tears welling up again. "But that wasn't enough, was it? She wanted... she wanted more."

Hyde kept his back turned to me.

"Oh God. Hyde!" I jumped up and threw my arms around his waist, pressing my forehead against the back of his neck. His soft hair caressed my skin as I squeezed and squeezed and let the tears drip into his shirt. "Hyde..." My fingers dug into his stomach.

"See? That's why I didn't tell you."

Gently, he pried me off of him and turned around to face me, holding my hands in both of his. "Deanna. Just do me this one favor. Promise me you won't tell anyone."

"What?" I shook my head. "What are you talking about? We should go to the police!"

But his hand squeezed mine, a little too tightly. "Please," he whispered. "Please, I'm begging you. If it leaked to the press... if everyone knew... I just can't."

"And this is how you're going to do it? Be a slave forever?" I gazed up at him, pleadingly. "I don't understand. Please Hyde. What... what am I supposed to do?"

His smile was one of the saddest I'd ever seen. "Forget me, Deanna. You know as well as I do. I should have stayed dead."

20

Confess

About two weeks after my mother's funeral, I'd stopped writing. I was eight. The stories I used to write for fun: those sweeping epic tales about orphans in workhouses, or melodramatic teenagers, or gnomes, and sometimes all of them at once. I stopped. The pen had become too heavy in my grip.

I picked up a spatula instead, then a duster. I took my mother's place because nobody else would. Dad had been too busy drowning his tears in beer. Adrianna had used frivolity as a shield against reality – and Ericka, her boyfriends. Back then, I figured if nobody would deal, *I* would take care of things. I would handle it by myself.

So I dealt with things. I handled them all on my own. And it'd become an instinct so powerful that I didn't notice the fresh new bars caging me in. I'd locked myself in hell without even knowing it.

Hyde…

I sat on the couch in the dark and stared at the television screen, turned-off, the clock on the wall ticking away. I wanted to be loyal. I wanted to do as Hyde asked and respect his wishes. It was his life, after all. It was his choice. Who was I to take it away?

Just do what he says. The thought had become a powerful drive, an order. Be loyal. It was as if I'd been silenced by the swan's curse.

But Hyde was suffering. He was dealing with things, handling them all on his own. Like me. He'd glimpsed the bars caging him in hell and simply shrugged, defeated. Like me. And now he was asking me to forget him.

Forget him? *Can I?*

I fell onto my side, smothering my face in the arm of the couch.

"Deanna?"

I lifted myself up and peered over the couch to see Ericka coming down the stairs – she'd been so quiet, I hadn't even noticed, but she was already halfway down. I turned back around.

"What's wrong? Why are you..." A long yawn broke her sentence. "Why are you sitting here in the dark? It's one in the morning."

"It's three in the morning."

"Is it? That's even worse!" I heard the fridge doors being pried apart. "On the upside, François hasn't woken up once tonight. I think he likes it here."

Twisting around, I watched her as she rummaged through the fridge contents, passing over leftovers to pluck out a can of cheap condensed milk. "Ericka, exactly how long are you going to be staying chez Davis?"

Her head shifted in my direction before she straightened back up, and then she was off to the cupboards. "I'm going back tomorrow. As much as I love being home, we really should be returning to Manhattan. I already told Charles."

"I'm surprised he let you stay here for so long." I threw my arm over the back of the couch and leaned in.

"Oh..." Ericka pulled out a case of chocolate from the cupboards and shrugged. "No, he didn't mind... I don't think. What with all the insanity surrounding the Edmund Rey embezzlement case, he's probably been too busy to miss us."

And too busy to call. Granted, it wasn't like I'd been locked inside the house, but since the time Ericka had arrived I hadn't heard them talk once. From what I could tell, Ericka hadn't exactly been taking it upon herself to fix that.

"You... really love it here?"

Ericka smiled at me as she heated the water. "Yeah... I guess I do. Leaky faucet and all."

"Funny. When you were living here, you couldn't wait to get the hell out." Harsh, I know. It just came out.

Ericka stayed silent for a little while, but once she finished mixing her hot chocolate, she walked over and sat next to me. "You're not wrong," she said. "I did want to get out. And then I found this cute rich boy who kept showering me with pretty things." She laughed and sipped her chocolate.

I pulled my legs up onto the couch, holding my ankles with frigid hands. "The grass is always greener, I guess."

"I've been talking to Dad a lot."

I'd noticed. "About what?"

"Hmm." Ericka peered into her ceramic mug, its horrid fluorescent pink blinding in the dark. And yet that was the mug she'd been using, consistently, since she got here. "My life. His life. Past mistakes. Sometimes it feels like everything went wrong when Mom died. Like we were…" She lowered the mug onto her lap. "All looking for a way out. Freedom."

"You got yours, though. You got the whole Cinderella treatment."

At this, Ericka gave me a wry smile. "I wonder about that."

"Then why not just leave?"

Ericka brought her mug up to her lips, letting the ridge sit there. "There's François to consider, after all, but… I don't know. I guess in the end, I depend on Charles for a lot of things."

Actually, as a child, I'd always thought that there was something grotesque about *Cinderella*. The reason was there in script, written in the deep, dark lines shadowing Ericka's eyes. From one cage into another.

"Things started out well enough, though."

"Why didn't you ever tell us anything?" Better yet, why didn't *I* ever tell *them* anything? About Mom, about Anton, about anything?

Ericka twisted around, letting her side sink into the couch cushion. "Well, I guess I'm telling you now." She swirled her mug around, staring off to the side with a thoughtful smile. "Feels good, actually."

I stared at my toes. It would feel good, wouldn't it? Yeah. It probably did. It was the freedom more than anything else. I was sure of it. I was tired of cages, tired of lies. Tired of peering through the bars, desperate and lonely, while pretending I could handle it all. And Hyde. I was sure he was too. I knew his secret wasn't mine to tell, but I couldn't just sit by and let someone take advantage of it. I had to help him. He deserved freedom. But first I had to find mine.

"Ericka... go get Ade."

"What?"

I took the mug from her hands and placed it on the table. "There's... something I need to tell you."

21

Infiltrate

"I will kill him."

"I just can't..."

"His life must *end*."

"We should call the police."

"I'll gut him myself!"

"I'm calling the police."

"Guys!" I stomped on the ground to get Ade and Ericka's attention. None of this was unexpected, of course. After the initial period of silence had come the babbling, pacing and uttering of death threats, and while I especially appreciated Adrianna's bloodlust, I really didn't want to wake Dad. Telling him... still didn't feel quite right. I guess I wasn't quite ready for that. "No police."

Ericka's hand was already on the home phone's receiver. "What? Why not? That's the first thing you should have done!"

I looked down, shifting on my feet. "I didn't have any proof. I still don't. And if Anton finds out, I don't know what he'll do. He threatened me, remember?"

"So what?" Ade snarled. "We just sit on our asses? Forgive and forget? This bastard's head should be slowly decaying on a *pike*!"

I sighed. "No argument there."

Dropping the phone back onto its base, Ericka sat down, staring through the black expanse of the television screen. "You're a swan. You're... Deanna... how could you not tell me? Either of you?" She rubbed her face, which droplets of tears had already begun to stain. "Do you really think that little of me?"

"I'm sorry," was all I could say.

"Look, I know some guys." Ade folded her arms over her chest. "Over in Hell's Kitchen. If we do it right we can make it look like an accident."

Tempting. "Look, I'll figure out what to do with Anton later. Right now, I need your help."

"Ah. Hyde," said Ade. "That poor bastard."

I hadn't told them everything. It wouldn't have been right. But if I was going to save Hyde from Beatrice, I would need help.

Ericka tapped her chin with a finger. "What are you going to do? If it's true that Beatrice has Hyde's feathers, then he shouldn't be able tell anyone about it. And you don't have any proof of that either so involving the police–"

"I don't need to involve the police. Besides, Hyde doesn't want this getting out. All I have to do is get his feathers back."

"Get them back?" Ericka narrowed her eyes, incredulous. "And how do you propose to do that?"

"Easy," Ade answered instead. "Beatrice probably has his feathers stashed somewhere in her house. I mean, that's how it works, right? That's how swans know where to go every night. Oh," she added quickly, because she must have noticed the look on my face. "Uh, not that we want to think about what he does with Beatrice every night–"

"Yes, let's not," I snapped.

"But still," Ade continued quickly, "the point is that if we want to get Hyde's feathers back, we need to walk straight into the cougar's den."

"Adrianna!" Ericka clutched her nightgown collar nervously – a poor substitute for pearls. "That's trespassing. If Beatrice catches you, she could press charges. And how would you even manage to get in? The whole idea's insane."

I thought about it.

Not long.

"What the hell," I said. "I think I've got a cat-suit lying around somewhere."

"Hey, the guy gave me a year's worth of DVDs. It's the least I can do." Adrianna's smile turned wicked. "All right, then. Suit up, bitches."

Hey it's the grl from ur Uncle's funeral. Ur so h0t. Wanna meet up tmrw? Fun Timez XOXO ADE

"I can't even believe this," I said, shaking my head as Ade sent her text. "Didn't you kick him the last time you saw him?"

All the fretting had made Ericka tired, so she'd already gone to bed promising to talk some sense into us in the morning. But the operation had already begun.

"Maybe he forgot?"

"Probably didn't."

Ade thought for a second, before shrugging. "Maybe it doesn't matter to him anymore."

"Probably does."

"Maybe ass matters more."

Bingo. We waited. We stayed awake for two hours, but Ade's phone didn't buzz.

"He probably doesn't even remember you." I crossed my legs on her bed. "No offense."

Ade grimaced. "Ew, none taken."

We were about to move on to plan B when, at precisely half-past six, a text came in:

Always room 4 more. Come on down.

"Really now." Ade shuddered. "Ew."

Indeed shuddering was an appropriate response. I followed suit. "You know, he still probably doesn't even remember you."

"He will." Ade got up and, grabbing her hair straightener, started over to the bathroom.

"Wait!" I leapt up and followed her. "We're going *now*?"

"Not 'we'," Ade replied, straightening out a row of curls. "Me."

I watched as smoke curled off her hair, fogging up the bathroom windows. "What? No way, we're doing this together. We have to!"

With a sigh, Ade placed the straightener on the sink and turned to me. "Dee, there's no way I'm letting you go anywhere near the psychopath from this day forward."

"You think I want you going anywhere near him?"

Ade laughed. "Please. I can handle myself. Besides, you've been the one doing the heavy lifting all this time. It's my turn. I promise I won't actually kill him." She winked as she picked the straightener up again, raising it to the opposite side of her head. "Trust me, kay? Let me do this."

Trust Ade. It was about time I did.

An hour and a half later, Ade left the house looking gorgeous in a mauve bandage dress with her rolling charcoal hair and perfect eye-shadow. Seduce and destroy. Anton was a pig, so why not use his own logic against him?

Less than an hour later, I got the call. "Got it."

"Really?" I stood at the door, watching Ericka load her baby into her Lincoln Town Car. "That quick?"

"It wasn't too hard to manage. There were like four girls already there. Half-dressed."

The driver cursed when his finger caught in one of the suitcase's handles.

"Ew, really?"

"And I think he was slightly high. Wasn't difficult at all to get what I needed."

I heard muted traffic in the background and guessed that Ade was in a cab. "You remembered, right?" I said in a hushed voice, so Ericka wouldn't hear. "The smallest key on his key chain? Bronze?"

"Yes, yes." Ade laughed. "Like I said, mission accomplished."

The only way to break into Beatrice's house without getting caught was to have a key. But stealing Anton's would be too risky.

So we were going to replicate it instead.

"I told you this clay stuff worked," Ade said. She was probably referring to the fresh modeling clay she'd bought on the way to Anton's. "It's super easy to make an imprint. All you have to do is use your thumbs to keep the pressure even and presto, home invasion."

I probably should have been a little more worried about her knowing that. Oh well.

"Thank God I barely had to touch that skeez. He was so busy with the other girls, he didn't even notice when I left. It was a little pathetic, actually."

"So now what?" I said as the driver took his seat.

I sort of loved how the mischief slipped into Ade's voice when she answered. "Now for phase two."

Right, then. "Ericka, wait up," I called, hopping down the steps. It was time to bring her in.

"So I talked to Daisy Bennett," Ericka said over the phone.

"Who?"

"Daisy Bennett: daughter of the cosmetics mogul… Her mother knows Beatrice."

All I needed to know. "And? What did she say?"

I heard François cooing over the phone, happy, perhaps, to be back in Manhattan where the bathwater was properly prepared by maids who could probably stand to be paid a little better. "There's some gala going tomorrow afternoon."

"Another party. God, don't you people do anything else?"

"What, you mean something potentially beneficial to society and the people who live in it?" It was rare, hearing that wry spark in her voice. It was a little amazing.

"Ah to be rich and self-absorbed. So?"

"Daisy said she'd be there for a while. It'll give you some time." Ericka sighed just as Ade bustled through the door, shutting it behind her with an excited click. "I hope you're aware of how ludicrous this whole thing is." Pearl-clutching Ericka was back, right on schedule. Ade winked at me and set her tote bag down on the table next to me. "I mean don't you need a locksmith to make a new key from an imprint? But a locksmith wouldn't do it unless he had the original key to make sure you're not doing something–"

Ade plucked it out of her purse: a shiny, brand new key courtesy of her shady friend who she didn't see today, nor has she ever met, for that matter – if anyone asked. It was a perfect replica.

"Illegal?" I finished for her, grinning from ear to ear.

I could practically hear Ericka pursing her lips from here. "Promise me you guys will be careful."

"Right. And you keep an eye on Beatrice at the gala. She leaves, let us know."

The next day, I was a bundle of nerves. Excited. Anxious. A little nauseous.

"I see her," said Ericka over the phone. "B. She just walked in."

"OK."

"It's 'copy that', damn it," Ade hissed at me as she pulled her hair into a ponytail. "Look Dee, do it right or don't do it at all."

I rolled my eyes. Ade and I stood in front of Beatrice's million dollar townhouse. We'd gotten there late, but only because Ade couldn't find her sunglasses. She finally did, along with those ridiculous half-gloves I'd worn at the masquerade. At the very least I'd convinced her not to wear a black jumpsuit – though the part about not leaving any prints was probably a good idea.

Ericka was at the gala, our point man. Ade and I had worn our best outfits without being too dressy. It was the easiest way to blend in: if anyone saw us, they'd probably assume we belonged here. Besides, that girl in a cute gray corset dress couldn't possibly be illegally breaking into someone's townhouse, right?

Ade shoved the key inside the lock and with a quick twist we broke into Beatrice's townhouse.

"Damn." Ade shut the door behind her, her eyes tracing the gold rim on the French doors that separated the foyer from what I was assuming was the dining room – or living room? Dressing room? This place was definitely built to have rooms.

"I know. OK, it'll be best if we split up." I lifted the phone back up to my ear. "Ericka, text me with updates on where B is. That way Ade and I can communicate over the phone while we're searching the house."

"OK. Remember, the gala isn't that far away from where you are now, so you'd better... Oh!" And then suddenly Ericka's voice changed. The nervous tremor in her voice dissolved with a quick breathy laugh. "Frank, Nina, darling how are you?" The phone clicked off amidst the first round of cheek-kisses. It was like flicking a switch: the survival tactic a Brooklyn girl needed to learn before braving any socialite ball of the Upper East. Looked like Ericka had learned it well.

"OK." I looked from the staircase to the French doors. "If you were the Queen of Darkness and you were holding some poor boy's feathers hostage, where you would keep them?"

"God, this one banister probably costs more than our whole shitty house; there are like little designs in the wood... is that handcrafted?"

"Ade!"

"OK, OK!" Ade rubbed the back of her neck. "I don't know. It'd have to be somewhere Hyde couldn't find it easily."

Maybe. Though I wondered if the loyalty curse kept swans from even seeking them out.

"Let's just look everywhere. I'll take upstairs you take... whatever's here. Just make sure that you put everything back where you found it."

Ade nodded and we parted. I climbed the staircase. The living room looked somehow less vile without Beatrice and Hyde lying half-naked on the couch.

Beatrice and Hyde.

I shuddered at the thought, but shook it away. Hurling on the floor would leave DNA evidence. I slipped on the white tiles as I ran over to the couches; five of them, all white, of course. I checked underneath them. It was worth a shot: back home the world underneath the couch was a black hole that had sucked up every pencil I'd ever owned.

"Damn it." Nothing.

My phone rumbled with a text from Ericka. *B still in sight. Don't take your time.*

"Yeah, yeah, I know," I muttered, checking underneath the smooth ottoman by the low chestnut wood table. Posies soaked in a vase next to a bowl of fresh fruit that looked more for decoration than eating. Three magazines, all of them *Bella*, were stacked one on top of the other in order of their publication dates. None even a hair out of place. "Lord," I breathed.

"There's, like, no food in this kitchen!" Ade hissed from the other end of the receiver. "I mean seriously. I see probiotic yogurt and celery sticks in the fridge and that's it."

"I can see myself in the floor." I peered down at my reflection before heading past one of the two fireplaces. "This place is more sterile than a surgical knife."

"And we all know she's seen plenty of those in her day. Any luck?"

I checked under the table, under the chairs *at* the table – the problem was that the place was *so* sterile, so orderly and clean, that there simply wasn't any area that screamed "hiding place". I walked through the screen doors onto the terrace, looking behind the clinically-preened bushes. "What about you?"

"There's no laundry in her laundry room. Why have a laundry room if you don't plan on having the kind of laundry that usually needs to be cleaned in a *laundry room*?"

"Let's just keep looking."

Apparently, there were six floors in all. Ade took the basement while I worked my way up through the top floors. At some point I had the brilliant plan of scouring her closets, except she had several closets and several more, all of them flooded in a sea of couture.

Wait a second. Oh God, what if she'd had Hyde's feathers turned into a coat? Plucked, pinned, and dyed fuchsia... it would be the human-autonomy equivalent of skinning Dalmatians. Could people *do that*? I checked each and every item of clothes regardless and when Ade was done with her floors she came up to join me. We'd already been in the house for more than half an hour, but each of Beatrice's closets was a Cretan labyrinth and neither of us had brought any yarn.

Closet number three: the one in the main bedroom. Ade flicked a modesty tab holding together a gorgeous print caftan and shook her head. "Seriously? I might steal one of these."

"Please don't make this experience any more complicated than it already is."

"For real though, it's not like she's gonna notice. I mean, shit, if we don't find Hyde's feathers we might as well take something for our troubles."

I tossed her an ugly glare. "We *will* find Hyde's feathers if you stop eyeing your bounty and start helping."

Ade pouted. "I am helping," she muttered under her breath. And as she ran a finger down the silk of a black draped dress, she smiled. "I'm helping. Finally."

Frowning from the floor, I looked up at her. "What do you mean?"

"You finally let me help you." She flashed me a two-fingered victory sign. "I think that means I win."

I rolled my eyes even though I couldn't help but smile myself. "Technically nobody'll win, except Beatrice, if we don't find–"

"I know, I know. And we will find it. But seriously, Dee. I'm really… relieved." She turned to face me, flicking one of Beatrice's silk scarves around her neck. "I know I'm not the most responsible Davis girl in the bunch–"

"Technically, you're the least–"

"–but anyway," she continued, louder, "I can understand why you wouldn't want to come to me. I know you've been through a lot. And to be honest, there was maybe a fraction of a second or two when I was a little… jealous. Of you. A little. I mean I thought first Ericka and now you, and hey, where's my rich boyfriend to buy me a life of ball masks and glass slippers?"

I thought of Ericka and shook my head. "It's not as great as you think it is."

"I know, I know." Ade brushed her hair out of her eyes and shifted onto one foot, folding her arms over her chest. "I know. But I just want you to know that none of that crap matters. No matter what's going on in your life, I'm here for you, OK? But only if it'll eventually involve us breaking into rich people's houses."

I laughed, thinking back to the day Ade had dumped a handful of cheesy pamphlets on my bed, to the day Ade held me and cried with me, my new feathers crushed against my back, beneath her fingers. It was true. Ade was here for me. And for the life of me I couldn't remember when I'd forgotten that.

"Hey, what's that?" Ade pointed at a fancy-looking gold-embroidered case-thing at the far northeast end of the closet, just beneath the assembly line of hemmed skirts.

"Oh yeah, I already looked in it," I said as Ade walked up to it and lifted the lid. "It's got tons and tons of *Bella* magazines in it. Issues from years and years back."

Ade looked inside, rummaging through until she stopped, frowning. "Doesn't this seem... off though?" I walked up next to her and peered over her shoulder. "This case thing looks a bit bigger on the outside than it does on the inside. The base of it is here." She knocked on the surface. "But if you look outside it, it's probably not more than halfway to the bottom of the actual case."

She was right. My heart started racing. "Take out all the magazines," I said. "Carefully."

We did, leaving them in a pile behind us. The base of the chest looked completely solid.

A text from Ericka: *Beatrice just left. Get out of there!*
"Ade–"

"Wait." Ade moved her nails around the edges, tugging until something snagged. Breathlessly, I shoved my fingers into the sliver she'd made and we both tugged until we'd dragged the entire bottom to the other side. My mouth dropped, my eyes filling with tears.

"Found 'em," Ade said, because my throat was too dry to carry the words.

Hyde's feathers folded neatly in the hidden compartment, as pristine as if they'd just left his back. Slowly, gingerly, I reached down and curled my hands around them. I'd never held another swan's feathers in my hands before. It felt somehow wrong, unnatural. Hyde's free will felt like cashmere against my fingers. They fluttered against my skin when I buried my face in them, the feathers disturbed by each shaky breath. I'd done it: all I could do. And if Hyde still wanted us to part ways, still wanted us to go on living as strangers, then I would give him this as my parting gift – and an apology.

A door slammed. Ade's hands flew to her mouth. Our eyes locked as footsteps started climbing from one of the lower floors.

No way. I didn't even remember hearing someone come in. Ade's wide eyes told me she hadn't either. But Ericka's last text had come in not more than a minute ago. Was it a time-lag?

"What the hell do we do?" Ade's whisper was almost completely imperceptible. Immediately, I pulled back the trap door, threw in the magazines and shut the case. More footsteps echoed as the feet in question climbed another flight of stairs. Soon I could hear someone outside the bedroom door. Ade's face said it as clearly as I ever could have.

We are giga screwed.

The door opened and shut with a click. A loud sigh – a man's. A *young* man's.

Hyde? I shot to my feet but Ade put up a hand to stay me, shaking her head with a frown and a finger to her lips. She was right. There was no way of knowing who that was and trespassing was still an offense listed in the New York penal code. Luckily there were piles of clothes to hide behind.

We hid. The young man plopped onto the bed with another heavy sigh. I pressed my back against the corner, tucked my feet in behind the waves of fabric. Ade had wedged herself behind a rack of shoes. She was too close to the door, but it was too late to move. I expected the worst. But the young man didn't seem interested in peeking inside Beatrice Hoffer-Rey's fashion wardrobe. I barely heard him move. From what I could tell, he simply stayed on the bed, silent. Waiting.

Ten minutes passed and suddenly I heard footsteps – heels. Movement on the bed. The sound had caused the young man to stir, but he didn't move further. The door opened.

"What are *you* doing here?" Beatrice's voice dripped with venom.

"What's wrong? You were expecting your new boy toy?"

Anton's sneer was a jackhammer to the chest. My heart ricocheted into my throat. I saw Ade's jaw drop from the other side of the closet.

Beatrice laughed with arrogance. "Oh, don't tell me you're still sore about that."

"While my dad's rotting in jail, you're screwing the asshole who put him there. Yeah, I'm still sore about that."

There was something curious about the tension in his voice. It whispered beneath the bile – a breath of hesitation, or a quiver. The anger was unmistakable, but for some reason he seemed distracted.

A chair scraping the ground. Then something clattered onto the table. I knew there was a vanity mirror that took up almost half the wall opposite the bed. I'd rummaged through each of the little drawers. As I sat in the corner hugging my knees I hoped to God I hadn't left something out of place.

"Your father's in jail because he did something illegal. Can't be helped." Another clatter, light and thin – jewelry?

"Can't be helped? My father is in jail and you're going to parties?"

"Aren't you?" I could almost picture Anton's snarl. "Between the girls that leave your loft in the morning and the ones who swarm in at night, I'm surprised you have any energy to visit your father at all."

"What did you–?"

"And let's stop with the righteous indignation, shall we?" The chair dragged again. Heels clicked towards the closet. Oh God. "We both know your concern over your father's wellbeing has had more to do with securing your trust fund than familial love."

The closet doors breezed open. Ade nearly fainted behind the shoe rack, her eyes locked onto mine, wide with horror. But no sooner did Beatrice open the doors than Anton strode up to her and grabbed her wrist.

"Who the hell do you think you are saying that shit to me? You have no idea what I've done for my father. None." His face was red and he was breathing hard, but the way he was looking down at her, his hand gripping her skin hard, pulling her body close–

Oh God stop, Deanna. Stop, stop, stop. Yes, my mind had gone there. Nobody had to tell me how twisted it was. But there was just something so off about the way her grin slid up to him, how comfortable she looked in his grasp–

I said stop, Deanna. Stop, stop, stop.

Gracefully, she slipped her shoes off and threw them into the closet without looking. With a quick tug, she adjusted the fur coat over her little black dress and closed the door behind her. Ade mouthed at me from her hiding spot, and while I had no idea what she was saying I knew it was either "we have to get the hell out of here" or "have I totally lost my mind or is something else going on here that I sincerely wish was not?" I was thinking both.

Beatrice laughed. "Oh, I'm sure."

"I've done a hell of a lot more than you've even attempted."

Ade started to fiddle around with her phone, maybe texting Ericka. My fingers were too frozen to even attempt it.

"Oh yes. Like blackmailing that poor girl into ruining Hedley's son." All the warmth drained from my face as Beatrice snickered. "I'm still a little embarrassed you tried something so... juvenile."

"I had to. Hyde was going to ruin us."

"So you threatened to sell a teenage swangirl to an organized crime syndicate? Oh Anton." She was laughing full out now. Nice to know that my weeks of utter horror amused her so. "Isn't that a little over the top? Darling, there's a simple kind of beauty in subtlety."

"She was Hyde's weakness. Besides–" Anton's word clipped off as something flopped to the floor.

Sounded like fabric.

Stop, stop, stop, Deanna, stop. But even Anton's voice didn't seem quite as firm as it had before. "Besides, Beatrice, what's more juvenile? Threatening some throwaway bitch who means nothing, or blackmailing the son of a dead publishing mogul to get into his pants."

"Well, technically it was to get the company, now wasn't it?"

"Yeah, but you didn't stop there. You've got to tell me, Beatrice." His voice dipped low. "What do you have on him? If it were that easy to get him to give up the company, I wouldn't have had to waste my time on that annoying little Brooklyn slut."

I clamped my teeth shut so that I wouldn't leap up, burst out of the closet and beat them both down right then. I could see Ade's right hand squeeze into a fist from here.

"Really, Anton. Is it so hard to believe that I won him over with my beauty and charm?"

"Tell me the truth."

"Why?"

"You… owe it to my father."

But he wasn't fooling anyone. Not Beatrice, by a long shot. And not me either – as much as my stomach churned at the thought, I knew there was something more to it. "You really can't hide it, can you?" said Beatrice.

"Hide what?"

His jealousy. Everything in his words dripped with it. Oh God.

"It's been two months and you still haven't gotten over it. Twenty years old and still a child. All your manly yelling and laughable 'bravado' only make it all the more embarrassing."

She gasped, suddenly. "That. Hurts," she said. She sounded truly annoyed for the first time, but even the faintest bit terrified.

"End it with Hyde and I'll keep quiet about everything."

"No."

"Do something about my father. You have the money."

"And again, no." A playful lilt carried Beatrice's words and I didn't know whether it was infuriating Anton or turning him on. It was all I could do not to throw up into Hyde's feathers. "My two-year marriage to your father was a business transaction. I got what I needed and he got what *he* needed, and more. And yet none of this changed the fact that he was vile – about twice as much as you are."

"He could get twenty years in prison. You're really going to let him rot there?"

"Why wouldn't I when I've got everything I want right now?"

"Beatrice."

"And so do you."

"What?"

An awkward pause – awkward for me, anyway. It dripped with a tight, beating tension broken only by Anton's heavy breaths. Something else plopped to the floor.

"What... Beatrice, what the hell are you doing?"

"Do you want to know what I did to Ralph Hedley's son? I took his feathers."

"What?"

Ade and I exchanged glances, eyes wide. Anton sounded about as shocked as I felt.

"Hyde's a–?"

"Swan," Beatrice repeated. "And I took his feathers." I clutched them to my chest. "But you, Anton?"

Something else plopped to the floor. Ade's jaw dropped. The way her face contorted in horror would have made me laugh if I didn't already want to kill myself.

"I don't need feathers with you, do I? You were hooked after a few weeks. I thought you knew as well as I did that we were only playing around."

"Shut up."

"All this sudden concern for your father. Where was it when you and I were–?"

A crash. The table whined. The sounds of a struggle; and if I didn't know better I'd have assumed Anton was trying to kill her. And then I heard them: a belt buckle clinking, clothes falling to the floor one by one, gasps searing the skin in my ears. Ade's mouth was still open, her head shaking and shaking because it couldn't stop and what else was there to do?

Oh God.

Oh my actual God.

I covered my ears and buried my face in Hyde's feathers in the hope that it would stem the bile currently corroding its way to my mouth. There was no denying it. Anton was doing his stepmom. It was the last part of the Rey Trinity of Crazy, right behind threatening innocent girls with sexual slavery and planning to drug his cousin in order to force him into an orgy with masked Russian models. It was insane.

It was *insane*.

But Beatrice was no better. They were a circus sideshow, the two of them: the filthy, revolting result of having too much money and too little sanity.

And lucky us – Ade and I had front row seats.

Ade was still shaking her head.

I don't know how I got through it. Actually, I wasn't even sure if I were still alive, or if the lack of oxygen I'd deprived myself of for the past hour while holding my breath in order to keep from screaming and screaming had actually killed me dead.

I stared at Ade. She was still shaking her head, except her head was now against the wall, her neck muscles far too weak to even lift it. But it was over. It was over and we'd survived. We'd stared into the deepest bowels of hell and come out breathing.

Beatrice was taking a shower.

I flicked my head to the door. Ade grimaced, still dazed. I crawled out of my hiding spot, carefully, and stepped towards the door while the shower prattled in the background.

"Oh yeah, I almost forgot," said Anton lazily, and every word that came out of his mouth made me want to scrub myself clean with a bleach-soaked wire brush. "Dad's got some shampoo in there I've been meaning to grab."

I rolled my eyes. Just *ew*.

No matter. This was our way out. Glaring at Ade I flicked my head towards the door. She didn't need telling twice. She was on her feet in moments. We waited for the bathroom door to shut. Quietly, I pushed the closet door open a crack and peeked outside. No one. Just clothes discarded on the floor. Stepson and stepmother were in the bathroom, perhaps doing things that would give me nightmares for the rest of my life.

Which meant now was our chance. Quietly, we sneaked out of the closet, closed the door behind us and tip-toed out of the master bedroom. *Careful*, I told myself as we descended the first flight of stairs. *Careful. Don't make a sound.*

And yet, slowly but surely my feet were carrying me faster and faster. Ade wasn't far behind. We'd gotten to the third floor before we broke into a straight out run. We fled to the nearest intersection before coming to our senses and calling a cab.

A Tale

It is the children who find them, buried beneath the rice stalks. It is the children who bring them, her robe of white feathers.

It is the children who cling to her as she ascends into the sky.

What was once of heaven can never be of earth. What was taken from the skies must return there henceforth. She tells them with tears in her eyes.

The children weep beneath the shower of her feathers. They weep and weep, but know that they are blessed.

22

Surprise

The sun had gone down several minutes ago. Ade gave my shoulder a squeeze and went upstairs. I was expecting him any minute.

A soft knock on the door. Sucking in a breath, I opened it. Hyde stood on my doorstep, shock, relief, fear, everything painted in gold and red on his canvas of a face.

"Come in," I said. I suppose I didn't need to. He would have come in anyway.

There was something so wrong about this, something so wrong about the way he quietly, dutifully shut the door behind him. When he looked at me, his eyes glistened with desire and longing. But what part of that was love and what part magic? Or was it both? Could it be both?

"How?" It was all he could say. It made sense. He was here after all. He'd been summoned.

He reached out to touch my arm, but I stepped back before his fingers could brush the skin. It wouldn't have been right.

"Well, if anyone asks, Ade and I spent our afternoon quietly obeying the city's penal code." I gave him a little smile, but he just gaped at me, incredulous. "She didn't catch us, if that's what you're wondering."

"Why?"

I lowered my head for a few moments. Then, stepping aside, I gestured towards the couch. His feather robe lay draped over it, some feathers flitting out of place with each puff of our sometimes-broken air conditioner. "You deserve nothing less."

Hyde and I looked at each other for a long time. It made me uncomfortable. As long as his feathers decorated my coach, I owned him and I didn't want to.

"Hyde…"

Slowly, he walked passed me over to the couch. His fingers twitched as he lifted his arms. He hesitated, but just for a moment, before grabbing the feather robe. The feathers burst apart in his hands, each one fluttering to the floor. Just like that, the light returned to his eyes and he was whole again.

Tentatively, I crept up to him. "Hyde–"

His arms were around my waist and before I could right myself, his lips were on mine. My hands flew around his neck, pressing him to me. This was it. This was what I longed for, what I needed. I let him tilt my head back to deepen the kiss. I let him crush me to him; let his fingers trail up my cheek, through my hair. I let him lose himself completely and lost myself too, wanting to cry from the perfection of it. I let him because I could.

After a while, I slipped my hands between our chests. Though my body groaned, I gently pushed him away, just enough, so that I could gaze at him.

"Deanna?"

I trailed a path down his cheek, cupping his chin. "It's really late, and you…" I paused. He'd just been through hell. We both had. "You should go home," I said.

"I guess I can now."

He pulled me into a hug and I didn't fight it. I let my head rest on the nape of his neck, feeling his breath brush against my ear.

"There's actually something else I need to talk to you about."

With one eyebrow raised, Hyde looked down at me. "Oh?"

I shuffled my feet. The nightmare was only partially over. There was one last thing I needed to do before I could sleep again. "It's kind of a long story. I wasn't going to tell you, but I figured I owed you the truth, since you told me yours. There's something I want to do tomorrow. But I need your OK first, since it involves you too."

"Tomorrow? What's happening tomorrow?"

I let a little wicked slip into my grin when I answered. "It's a surprise. But not for you."

"So many galas." I gazed into the crowded reception hall with my arms crossed behind my back, shivering a bit in my simple blue dress.

Hyde took off his blazer and threw it over my shoulders, ever the gentleman. I gripped the sleeves and pulled it closer as the couple in front of us entered, leaving us at the front of the line. One look at Hyde's arm around me and the doorman let us in. I suppose there were perks to being acquainted with a hot young billionaire, if you considered having a free ticket into elite Manhattan social soirees to be a perk. I'd had enough of these bullshit events, personally.

But there was something I had to do today. One last gala to attend.

Hyde leaned over to read the sign by the glowing ice-sculpture. "Charity New York honors Harold and Janice Bennett."

"Ericka's friend is their daughter." I scanned the crowd of well-dressed patrons for our target.

"The cosmetics moguls." He straightened back up, adjusting the well-cut cuff over his wrist. "You know, my father was honored too, years ago. That's when he introduced his brand new son." He smirked, sweeping two champagne glasses off a tray and offering me one. I refused it. Still seventeen. "I remember the applause. I remember peering down at each of their faces from the stage and suddenly it hit me: none of them, not one, was looking at me."

"And here you are again." I flapped the sleeve of the expensive gray jacket draping me. "Is it really kosher to criticize your people?"

Hyde put his arm around my shoulder. "I've thought of that. Having a certain amount of money comes with a bit of responsibility. And now I have my freedom. There're a few things I can do with both."

"Probably best to fix this one last thing, though. Oh, good they're here. Two o'clock." Hyde's gaze followed in the direction I'd flicked my head. He grinned. Anton was seated at one table, next to Beatrice who chatted with a few balding businessmen. With Edmund Rey still in jail the two would have to show a united front in public, without, of course, clueing anyone in to just how united their front could get.

"Board members," Hyde whispered in my ear. "Has Ericka done it yet?"

"Yep." I spied her at the table next to Anton's and waved. Beaming, she motioned us over. "And Ade's text came in while we were waiting in line. They'll all be on their way over soon."

"Well then, that would be our cue, wouldn't it?" Hyde extended his arm for me to take. I grabbed it with a gleeful tug and we walked up to Ericka together. I could feel Anton's eyes following us as we slipped between tables. Once we reached Ericka's, I hugged her; we threw our arms around each other and then – a little surprisingly – she rubbed my head like she used to.

"Hey, hey! *Hair*! Come on, now." I smoothed the stray hairs back into place.

"Oh, sorry," she said a little embarrassed. I wondered if she was trying too hard to force things back to the way they used to be. I gave her a reassuring smile. She didn't have to. I gave François a kiss on the cheek and saluted Charles, who barely acknowledged me while he sat there talking to one of his lawyer friends.

"Hey Beanpole," I said, just in case he didn't see me the first time. A little crude, yes. Definitely caught his attention, though. His face went red. Indignant, he turned to Ericka for a little support. She giggled into her hand.

Hyde pulled out the seat between Ericka and me, waving to Beatrice before sitting. I had to give it to her; she was much better than Anton at feigning composure. She sat, poised, next to Anton, avoiding my eyes when I couldn't help but lean over and watch her. My lips curled into a smile even when Hyde tugged on my arm to rein me back in. She stared straight ahead of her. Very well done, Beatrice. But she was wondering, wasn't she? Why Hyde didn't come back to her last night. Where his feathers had gone. Who'd taken them – and when. All sorts of things she wouldn't dare speak of lest she implicated herself.

Anton, on the other hand, glared at Hyde with a mixture of disdain and jealousy. Must have been hard watching the boy he'd tried so hard to destroy and the girl he'd used to do it grinning so shamelessly in public when by all rights they should have been drowning in a pool of despair and angst.

It was going to get harder.

Another old guy in a suit climbed the stage with his glass of wine in hand and tapped it lightly with a spoon until everyone else in the gala was doing the same. By the time the clinking had stopped, the reception was silent.

"I'd like to thank everyone for coming this evening to honor two very outstanding members of our community," he said and prattled on about the philanthropic wonders of the Bennetts while the video screen behind him played images of Harold and Janice surrounded by puppies. I had to smother a laugh. "Now, without further ado, I would love–"

The video screen went blank. Nobody seemed to notice the glitch. Harold and Janice walked up onto the stage to dainty applause. Ericka and I exchanged sneaky glances.

Show time.

"Thank you, thank you," said Harold while Janice smiled sweetly and, of course, silently next to him. "Thank you for this wonderful honor." He cleared his throat, obviously about to lapse into whatever practiced speech he'd prepared. "As you all well know, social justice has always been a primary concern of Bennett Industries–"

"Oh yes. Like blackmailing that poor girl into ruining Hedley's son."

Harold frowned, confused. The voice had poured in from the speakers that had up until now been playing classical music.

"I'm still a little embarrassed you tried something so... juvenile."

"I had to. Hyde was going to ruin us."

I couldn't help it. I peeked over at Anton's table. Beatrice's face had paled several shades, her fingers grasping and un-grasping the pearl bracelet around her wrist. Poor Anton still hadn't quite worked out what was happening. Surely, he would have recognized the voices by now? Others were already starting to. I could see the glances sliding over to them, the mouths agape, each one wanting to hiss out whispers, except that would have made it harder to hear the next gasp-worthy line of dialogue in this little impromptu show of mine – and this one was a killer:

"So you threatened to sell a teenage swangirl to an organized crime syndicate? Oh Anton."

Gasps. Dozens of them, all on cue. As Beatrice's laughter filled the hall, Anton jumped to his feet, finally aware of what was going on. The board members stared at Beatrice in shock, who had frozen in place, all her wit and arrogance dried and dusted until there was nothing but a hollow statue draped in fashion's finest.

"What... What is going on?" said Harold while he, Janice and about half the gala turned every which way, desperate to find the source of the sound and the one controlling it; except the tech guy who had Ericka's flash drive was safely in the control room backstage.

"She was Hyde's weakness. Besides... Besides, Beatrice, what's more juvenile? Threatening some throwaway bitch who means nothing, or blackmailing the son of a dead publishing mogul to get into his pants."

"That's a lie!" screamed Anton, frantic as the gala stared at the two of them in horror.

"Well, technically it was to get the company, now wasn't it?" smarmed yesterday's Beatrice.

"Stop! This isn't... What the hell are you doing?" He was flailing his arms frantically, which perhaps was meant to be threatening, except he looked more like a parakeet in the throes of a mating dance. "Cut that off!"

But why would they? Socialites and businessmen alike were whispering. Reporters were busy scribbling down notes, some holding up their phones to capture the magic, just like Ade had captured the magic on hers while we hid in Beatrice's closet. And there I'd been thinking she was texting Ericka for help. But when we got home and Ade played the recording back – in that one moment, Ade had secured her place on the "win" column forevermore. Well deserved.

I grinned in secret gratitude, and when Anton's eyes locked onto mine, I winked and tipped my glass his way.

"Yeah, but you didn't stop there. You've got to tell me, Beatrice. What do you have on him? If it were that easy to get him to give up the company, I wouldn't have had to waste my time on that annoying little Brooklyn slut."

"What?" Ericka cried out in the loudest, most ridiculously affected voice imaginable. "Anton Rey sexually threatened a swangirl to get her to ruin Hyde Hedley? And Beatrice Hoffer-Rey blackmailed Hyde Hedley's son to get him to forfeit the company to her?"

Hyde leaned back in his chair. "Dramatic, isn't it? I was quite shocked myself."

"This is absolutely absurd." Beatrice was on her feet now, bearing down on the two of us. Somewhere in the recesses of her subconscious she must have at least partly put it together. The sudden disappearance of Hyde's feathers. A faithful recording of her unwitting confession, retouched for sound quality. I could see the gears turning like clockwork behind those panicked blue eyes. No, Beatrice, you're not wrong. Go on. Put it together. I'll wait here.

"How is it absurd?" Like Ericka, Hyde made sure his voice carried over the commotion. I wasn't worried about my little production, though; a transcription of the dialogue flashed on the video screen in huge black letters, Arial script. If people couldn't hear it, they could always read it. "When Edmund Rey found out I was a swan, he sold me into slavery. And when you found out, you bought me yourself."

I pursed my lips, ignoring the shocked whispers, focusing on Hyde alone. Last night I'd told him everything and then given him the choice. This plan, after all, would have exposed him too, and I couldn't go through with it without knowing how Hyde felt. But he'd decided on his own that he was finally ready to speak.

"I was ashamed," Hyde said. "So ashamed that I chose to be your slave, and that gave you leverage. Gave you *power*. Without that, what are you?"

"Disgusting." I stood up and walked past her until I was face to face with Anton. "Like your stepson: the one who made my life a living hell for the past few weeks all to keep his trust fund." While Anton's chest heaved, I cocked my head to the side. "What can I say? Payback's a bitch."

A table crashing, grunts, moans. The frantic sounds of stepmother and stepson ripping each other's clothes off sent the gala into a frenzy. It was the perfect musical backdrop for Dad and Ade's entrance into the reception hall, flanked by the police who she'd given another copy of the flash drive to, as per the plan.

Cameras snapping, lights flashing, phones in the air. Beatrice and Anton's sexcapades roared out in full volume for all to hear: in a matter of minutes, Ade's and my private hell would be only as private as the internet allowed.

Anton lunged at me. Right when I was distracted by the sheer wonder of it all. He grabbed me by the shoulders, but tripped over the leg of a chair before he could hit me. We both crashed to the ground. His fingers scraped against my throat, squeezing my windpipe. People were screaming. My back was burning, feathers sprouting in my flesh, poking at the skin from inside me.

I kicked my right leg up hard, my shin finding the soft part between his legs. Direct hit. With a strained whimper, he faded to the side, cowering against the chair while his legs squeezed into a single line. Two cops hooked his arms and dragged him to his feet, slapping cuffs on him while a frantic Beatrice was already being led away.

"Like in the movies!" Ade said, helping me up. "You OK?"

She, Ericka and Hyde crowded around me. Dad squeezed my arms, looking like he'd aged about twenty years since last night, when I finally woke him up to what was happening around him. "Honey, are you OK?" He started to swivel me around, checking for bruises, but I put up a hand to stop him.

"Yeah I am, just one last thing." Running, I caught up with Anton and his escorts, yelling for them to stop. Anton glared at me with his hands behind his back and his disheveled blonde hair tumbling every which way over his face. The ugliness in his scowl could have sliced a butterfly in midair. "What do you want now, bitch?"

I thought of that face peering at me from other side of Stylo's steel bars. "Just this." I punched him in the face. Just once. I didn't want to be charged with assault. Still, it landed and landed well. The blood dripping down his nose sent wonderful tingles through me.

"OK. Take him away boys," I said, ruining a perfectly good moment. One of the cops rolled her eyes and hauled Anton off. I turned to the congregation, peering at the baffled faces and for the first time in what felt like forever, my breaths turned slow and easy. I shut my eyes and let a calm sigh pass through my half parted lips, only to break out into a stream of giggles. Finally.

Finally.

"Well, it's been fun everyone!" Ade waved before skipping to my side. Dad and Ericka followed, François bouncing around in Ericka's arms while Charles looked on, pale-faced and baffled. Hyde stood at the center of a swarm of reporters, but he winked at me, telling me it was OK to leave him with a flick of his smile. I nodded.

"All right, all." Ade was positively giddy. "Move out."

She just couldn't help herself.

Epilogue

Ade and Ericka sat on the couch, François fast asleep in the portable crib upstairs. I sat on the floor, my back to the TV because I'd already heard the news a thousand times: the Hoffer-Rey scandal – blackmail and extortion and sex crimes oh my. Edmund's embezzlement case wasn't going so well for the defense. And while Edmund had already made sure to cover his own ass ten years ago, the rumors of his dealings with shady criminal organizations and sex trafficking were enough to ruin his life forever. Like father, like son.

But the Davis family had chosen not to worry about that for the time being. Though we'd had our fair share of reporters digging through our trash, in the four weeks that had gone by, the press had become less and less interested in the Brooklyn family who lived in their narrow yellow house, a couple of narrow yellow houses down from a Chinese restaurant.

Dad dropped a newspaper down on the table, pointing at the news that'd been shoved into a corner of the page, all buried in the scandal.

"'Hyde Hedley, son of Ralph Hedley and reinstated senior executive of Hedley Publications starts an International Counseling Program for Survivors of Swan Slavery'," Ericka read, leaning over carefully so as not to spill her hot chocolate.

Crossing her legs, Ade plucked the mug out of Ericka's hands and sipped the chocolate generously. "Well, he did say he was going to do something substantial with all that cash."

"It was my idea," I clarified.

Tilting her head, Ade gave me a sidelong, teasing glance. "Pretty great, though, eh Dee?"

I touched the words on the page and smiled.

Really, it was just the beginning.

ACKNOWLEDGMENTS

There're a lot of people I want to thank for helping me bring my debut book out into the world. I guess I have to start at the beginning, because before a girl can publish a book, she has to love to write.

Thank you to my brothers, Chris and David, whose unabashed geekery, in too many ways, nourished my love of storytelling.

Thank you to my fourth grade teacher, Mrs. Spratt, who, after reading my short story about gargoyles (inspired by the awesome cartoon), told me I had a gift for writing. I still have the comment slip.

Thank you to my fifth grade teacher, Ms. Braun, who let me stay in and finish my first book when I should have been outside for recess (I never liked physical activity anyway).

To Tracey Martin, who beta-read the first draft of this book, and the pit crew who were there when the world of writing caused many a headache. Thank you for listening to me whine.

To my wonderfully supportive agent, Natalie Lakosil,

as well as my editor Amanda Rutter and the rest of the fabulous Strange Chemistry team. All of you helped make my dream a reality.

To my loved ones across the oceans. But especially, to my mother, Margaret, who never stopped encouraging me. And to my father, Patrick, who I wish were here to share this joy with me. Thank you all, endlessly, for your love and support.